A

I found Shirley Angowski, attired in a pink nylon peignoir edged with a profusion of pink boa feathers at the hem and cuffs. She was shaking with hysteria and clawing her cheeks with her *Baby Flamingo* fingernails. "He's dead. Look at him. He's dead. He's dead."

"Who's dead?" I asked as more doors were flung open.

She pointed toward the spill of light in the room next to mine. I followed her gaze.

Supine on the floor lay Andrew Simon, his mouth contorted into a hideous rictus, his skin pasty even beneath his tube tan, eyes wide and bulging, hair disheveled, dressed in a handsome black satin smoking jacket with matching ascot that was pulled dreadfully askew. I thought the ascot was a bit over the top, especially since it looked as though Andy hadn't a clue how to knot the thing. Now he'd never know.

Shirley Angowski was right. Andrew Simon was dead.

Not a good way to begin your Golden Swiss Triangle Tour.

maddy
HUNTER

A *Passport to Peril* Mystery

Alpine for You

POCKET BOOKS
New York   London   Toronto   Sydney

This book is a work of fiction. Names, characters, places and incidents are products of the author's imagination or are used fictitiously. Any resemblance to actual events or locales or persons, living or dead, is entirely coincidental.

An *Original* Publication of POCKET BOOKS

POCKET BOOKS, a division of Simon & Schuster, Inc.
1230 Avenue of the Americas, New York, NY 10020

Copyright © 2003 by Mary Mayer Holmes

ISBN: 0-7434-5811-7

First Pocket Books printing February 2003

10 9 8 7 6 5 4 3 2

POCKET and colophon are registered trademarks of Simon & Schuster, Inc.

For information regarding special discounts for bulk purchases, please contact Simon & Schuster Special Sales at 1-800-456-6798 or business@simonandschuster.com

Interior design by Davina Mock
Front cover illustration by Jeff Fitz-Maurice

Printed in the U.S.A.

DEDICATION

To my dear friend and traveling companion, Elaine Snyder, who suggested the adventure.

To Brian, who gave us his blessing.

To Jack and Lavonne Frandsen, whose unexpected friendship made the trip so special.

To all of you with love ~
mmh

Alpine for You

CHAPTER 1

"I am NOT sleeping with Andrew Simon for the next nine days!" My voice hovered at a pitch that could cause spontaneous insanity in dogs. I was squeezing the tour guide's forearm so tightly, his fingers had turned purple. "Major mix-up in the room assignments. MAJOR mix-up." I might have added that had I wanted to sleep with Andy Simon, I wouldn't have had to fly all the way to Switzerland to do it. I would have done it back in Iowa, like everyone else. But why ruin a man's reputation when he was doing such a good job of it himself?

The tour guide, who'd introduced himself at the Zurich airport as Wally, slid his attention from the hand I'd manacled around his arm, to my chest. A stunned look appeared in his eye. And why not? Thanks to the genius of Victoria's Secret, those of us who were modestly endowed could now flaunt awe-inspiring bosom beneath our turtlenecks. I had to watch myself though. My Click Miracle bra was set on maximum cleavage, so if I stood any closer, I'd poke his eye out.

"Have you misplaced your name tag already?" Wally

chided. "It's supposed to hang right there, in the middle of your chest."

Wally was your typical boy next door with a few pounds on his bones and lines on his face. Beaver Cleaver at thirty-five. Brown hair. Receding hairline. Hazel eyes with no apparent eyelashes. Chipmunk cheeks. Pudgy around the middle. But he was half a head taller than I am, wore a suit that smacked of custom-made rather than off-the-rack, and he wasn't wearing a wedding ring. He had serious potential. However, if the only thing he noticed about my chest was the absence of a name tag, I figured we didn't have much of a future together. I consoled myself with the fact that he probably wasn't my type.

Of course, I had no idea what my type was anymore. The issue had gotten confused when I'd met Jack Potter seven years ago. I'd graduated from college with a degree in theater and was trying to peddle my talents as an actress in New York City. To pay the rent, I took a job as a ticket seller at Radio City Music Hall, where I worked beside Jack. We had so much in common, I suspected we were soul mates. He was an aspiring actor. So was I. He loved to shop. So did I. He was compulsively neat. I picked up after myself occasionally. And since both of us were having trouble choosing between eating or paying the rent each month, we decided to pool our resources and share an apartment.

The roommate thing might have worked if Jack hadn't had the body of a dancer and the face of a Roman god, or if I hadn't been consumed by raging hormones and lust. Within a year we became husband and wife. More good fortune struck when we were both offered parts in *Joseph and the Amazing Technicolor Dreamcoat*. Me, in the chorus. Jack as one of the brothers. But things deteriorated when he started borrowing my lingerie and makeup, not just for shows, but on a daily basis. Six months later he pulled a disappearing act and ran off with the actor who played Joseph's understudy. I moved back to Iowa after that, a little older and wiser, but my romantic life has been muddled ever since.

I squeezed Wally's arm a little harder. "My name is Emily Andrew. I don't wear name tags. And I don't sleep with married men."

Wally wrenched his arm from my grasp. "Do you mind? I have no feeling in my hand anymore. And look, you crushed the press on my sleeve." He gave his arm a vigorous rub and me an exasperated look. "We encourage all our Golden Swiss Triangle Tour members to wear their name tags, but of course, we can't force you." He looked me up and down, eyeing me like meat on the hoof.

I exercised regularly to keep cellulite from attaching itself to my five-foot-five-inch, 112-pound frame, so I knew I looked pretty decent in my favorite black leather skirt with the little slit up the side. But my hair was problematic. Not the color, which was a deep mahogany, but the texture. The minute a hint of humidity crept into the air, my coarse, wavy, shoulder-length hair acquired the kind of frizz that straight-haired people only achieved by sticking their fingers into electrical outlets. Since it was raining in Lucerne today, it was only a matter of time before I morphed into Little Orphan Annie, only with green eyes instead of the empty sockets.

"Aren't you a little young to be on a Golden Tour?" Wally finally asked.

"Traveling companion," I said. "I'm with my grandmother."

Nana belonged to a seniors' travel club run by the bank in Windsor City. The bank scheduled tours through a national company called Triangle Tours that arranged transportation, lodging, and a professional tour guide in the country of destination. Since many of the seniors were novices at foreign travel, the bank also provided a local escort to cater to the individual needs of the group. Nana invited me to accompany her on the trip because she said I'd be less bossy than my mother and a lot more fun than the other seventy-eight-year-olds in her retirement village. So being a sucker for flattery, I turned my back on the lure of Club Med for the opportunity to spend nine days in Switzerland with thirty white-haired seniors who made twenty-nine look young.

"Now," continued Wally, "who did you say you don't want to sleep with?"

"Look, Wally, someone made a mistake. I'm supposed to room with my grandmother, not Andrew Simon. In case you didn't know, Mr. Simon is our escort from the Windsor City Bank. He's being paid to accompany the group, not sleep with the guests."

Someone sneezed loudly behind me. I felt a hand caress the back of my neck. "Emily, honey, I just heard the good news. How do you suppose an old coot like me got lucky enough to room with the prettiest little trick on the tour?"

Andrew Simon was short, stocky, and stuck on himself. His year-round tan was out of a tube. His hair color was out of a bottle—Surfer Blonde, which was something of an anomaly considering the only surfing you can do in Iowa is on the Internet. He'd married his sixth wife, Louise, three years earlier, and since then had whiled away his time swinging golf clubs by day and rehearsing lines for the local community theater by night. Louise was sister to the Windsor City Bank president, which explained how Simon had landed himself the cushy job of escort on the Golden Swiss Triangle Tour. He'd left Louise back in Windsor City, however, since the thought of flying gave her hives and caused her windpipe to swell shut. Not a good way to begin your Golden Swiss holiday.

I snatched his hand from my neck and stood toe-to-toe with him, our noses separated by bare inches, my chest every bit as inflated as his ego. "There's been a mistake. Your first name, my last name. Some out-of-touch administrator must have thought we were family and stuck us in the same room together. What's wrong with your eyes?" They were painfully bloodshot and weepy. "Are you contagious?" I took a giant step backward. He'd probably contracted a fatal disease on the plane and was infecting everyone within a six-mile radius. Bad idea for a holiday. Arrive in Switzerland. Die.

"It's that damned air on the plane. I shouldn't have worn my contact lenses. The pharmacist warned me, but I didn't listen. My eyes are so itchy, I feel like I have the worst case of hay fever in medical history."

He looked as if he had the worst case of bubonic plague in medical history. I inched back another step. I didn't want to be within hearing range when he peeled off his lenses. They'd probably dried out so badly, they were superglued to his eyeballs by now.

"About the room assignments, Emily, I don't know how that could have happened. The bank made all those arrangements. Frieda saw to it personally, and Frieda never makes a mistake."

Frieda Olson had been a fixture at the bank since the first ice age. At eighty-five she was still sharp as a tack and drove into work daily, but her glasses were thick as pond ice, which cast serious doubt on her ability to process paperwork. "I suspect you filled your travel form out incorrectly," I accused. He'd probably written ANDREW in the space for LAST NAME and SIMON in the space for FIRST NAME, which would conveniently give us the same surname and room assignment.

"Emily, honey, why would I do that?"

"Because I'm female and conscious?"

"Emily Andrew, are you hinting that I planned this mix-up?" His gaze drifted to my chest. It made me wish Victoria's Secret had come out with a padded underwire that lifted, separated, and launched rocket grenades. I seized Wally's arm again.

"Wally here is going to fix the problem. Aren't you, Wally?"

"Emily, dear! Don't bother our tour guide. I've worked everything out myself." Nana, who dutifully wore a name tag identifying her as Marion Sippel, was four-foot-ten, built like a bullet, and still wore her hair in tight finger waves that had been fashionable in the sixties. "I been talkin' to that nice Mr. Nunzio over there. I couldn't understand everything he was sayin' 'cause he don't speak real good English, but I think he said he'd share the room with me if you'd found another roommate. Italians are so hospitable."

I'd scanned the roster of travelers on the flight over, but I didn't remember seeing a Nunzio. Nunzio I would have remembered. "Where is this Mr. Nunzio?"

Nana pointed to a marble pillar in the middle of the hotel lobby. "He's the gentleman wearin' the black trench coat. Standin' beside Bernice Zwerg."

I stood on tiptoe. But for the absence of a print cloth draped about his head, Mr. Nunzio was a Yasser Arafat look-alike—hair like a cactus, face like a ferret, knees like old potatoes. Knees? "He's not wearing trousers." Leave it to Nana. Three hours in Switzerland, and she'd managed to find what was possibly the only Italian pervert in the entire country.

"I did notice about the trousers, dear, but this is Europe. I thought he was makin' a fashion statement."

"Mr. Nunzio isn't on our tour, Nana. He'll have to room

with someone else." I said this with more calm than I felt because if I let anything happen to Nana, my mother would kill me.

Nana looked disappointed. She was the most accommodating person I'd ever known. She'd hauled wood before the days of electricity, hauled water before the days of indoor plumbing, and hauled tail out of Minnesota after the roof of Grampa's ice shanty collapsed, killing him and the thirty-pound muskie he'd been struggling to pull in for the better part of the afternoon. She had them both laid out at the wake—Grampa Sippel in a cherry casket and the muskie on a bed of crushed ice. The whole town of Brainerd, Minnesota, turned out for the viewing, and everyone in attendance had the same thing to say about Grampa: he'd caught the plug-ugliest fish ever to swim the waters of Gull Lake.

Nana moved to Iowa afterward to be closer to my parents, my married brother and his family, and me. She arrived a wealthy widow, not because Grampa was a piker who'd squirreled away every penny he ever earned, but because she won the lottery jackpot on the day Grampa's ice shanty collapsed. Seven million and change. People said it was tragic Grampa hadn't lived long enough to see the size of the check. Nana said he would have been more impressed by the size of the muskie.

Nana glanced back at Mr. Nunzio. "It's too cold to be runnin' around without pants. Cold air blowin' up a man's privates can cause real bad prostate problems. You think I should tell him?"

Simon burst out in laughter. "Go ahead, Marion. I bet he's dying to have you tell him what he should do with his prostate."

Nana's eyes turned steely. "A man should never laugh at prostate problems. Don't think I didn't see you lined up to go potty a whole lot on the trip over, Andrew Simon. Bernice was havin' to get up all the time to let you by."

Other people went to the rest room. Minnesotans went 'potty' all their lives. Obviously, toilet-training in Minnesota was as life-altering an experience as marriage and visiting the Mall of America.

"Anyone tell you there's drugs you can take for potty problems these days?" Nana continued. "They even advertise 'em on the TV. I forget the names, but one of them ads shows a bunch a men about your age drivin' convertibles with little outhouses on the back. If we could find that nice pharmacist lady, I bet she'd know what the stuff is called. She might even give you some free samples."

All the color drained from Simon's face. With his suddenly white complexion and pink eyes, he was looking more and more like the Easter bunny. "And what's wrong with your eyes?" Nana added for good measure. "You're not contagious are you?" She took a step backward.

"My contact lenses." He spat the words out like BBs. "They're irritating my eyes. There seem to be quite a few irritants in the vicinity at the moment."

Wally took that instant to jump onto a nearby table and let fly a shrill whistle. Heads turned. The lobby of the Grand Palais Hotel grew quiet. "Okay, people. One word of caution about the elevator. The door doesn't open automatically, so when it stops, wait a couple of seconds, then open the door yourself. We're not in the States anymore. Everything doesn't run on automatic pilot. Your luggage will be delivered to your rooms within the hour. Get some rest and we'll meet here in the lobby again at six o'clock sharp and proceed into the dining room for supper. Any questions?"

I didn't have a question for Wally. I had a comment. I raised my hand. "Nana and I are going to wait for you on those comfy chairs near the front desk. When you have our room assignment figured out, let us know."

The Grand Palais, a century-old hotel overlooking Lake Lucerne, had the look of a Hollywood soundstage disguised as a European chateau. Pillars of polished pink marble encircled the lobby and rose twenty feet to a ceiling that reflected the sparkling brilliance of a half dozen crystal chandeliers. Gilt-framed mirrors the size of Beautyrest mattresses lined the walls. Oriental carpets spanned the floor. Furniture upholstered in rich cut velvet and standing tiptoe on delicate scrolled feet huddled in intimate groupings around the room. And then there were the finishing touches. The vases of fresh-cut flowers. The antique gold cabinets. The dozens of cut-crystal ashtrays accompanied by silver baskets brimming with tiny matchboxes. The Swiss had obviously failed to read the Surgeon General's report on the hazards of smoking. I ranked the Grand Palais a ten on the "old world elegance" scale, but for all its opulence, the hotel had one elevator to accommodate its multitude of guests. The shaft was located near the front desk, across the room from the burgundy velvet chairs where Nana and I sat waiting for our room key. If there was a silver lining to our room mix-up, it was that by the time we received our key, the line waiting to use the elevator might be shorter. Though we'd been sitting for ten minutes, and the line hadn't moved at all.

"What's the holdup?" Lars Bakke asked every time the elevator arrived at the lobby and went up again without releasing its passengers. Lars was a tall stringbean of a man who owned and operated a grain elevator just outside Windsor City, so he knew the skinny on elevators.

"You gotta open the door yourself!" Bernice Zwerg yelled at the shaft. "It's not automatic." Decades earlier Bernice had worked as a photographic model for *Iowa*

Living magazine, but age and hard times had taken their toll. Her hourglass figure had disappeared, leaving her with a body like a rubber chicken and a dowager's hump that ruined the hang of her clothes. She had hair like a wire whisk, a voice like fingernails scratching a chalkboard, and a bank account that was running on empty. The only highlight in her life these days was that she was the undefeated champion of the five-yard dash in the annual Senior Olympics at the mall, a title the other contestants argued was undeserved due to the fact that she removed her hearing aid for the event and couldn't hear the starting gun go off, so she always got a head start.

"This place needs a bigger elevator," Solvay Bakke complained to her husband. "How many people does that one hold?"

"Three," I said, having seen the trio who'd squeezed in earlier.

Solvay shook her head in disgust. "Who's in there now?"

I knew that too. "Dick Teig, Dick Stolee, and Dick Rassmuson." The three men had attended grammar school together, lived in the same subdivision in Windsor City, and always vacationed together with their wives, though if they had their druthers, they might have opted to leave the wives at home. They enjoyed being referred to as the three amigos. I referred to them as the three Dicks.

Lars Bakke took control of the situation. "Those guys have been joyriding long enough. When that elevator gets down here again, someone yank the damn door open and get those Dicks outta there!"

I guess Lars wasn't fond of calling them the three amigos either.

Forty-five minutes later, Nana and I stood before our room in a high-ceilinged corridor whose only illumination was an occasional motion light. Our key looked like a brass

Sugar Daddy attached to a square of leather that was stamped in gold with the number 3310. Nana measured its weight in her palm before handing it to me. "Your grampa coulda used this as a sinker. Don't drop it. You'll break your foot."

I inserted the brass part into a slot in the front face of the doorknob, then turned the knob to the left. "Wally said to keep turnin' until we hear a click," Nana advised. So I turned, and turned, and turned.

"Did you hear a click?" I asked.

"Nope. But my hearin's not so good anymore. You hear anything?"

"No." So I turned, and turned. I was glad Nana had asked me to accompany her on the tour. How did management expect old people to get into their rooms when young people couldn't even figure it out? This was worse than wrestling with the childproof cap on the toilet bowl cleaner. Two weeks from now I envisioned thirty elderly people from Iowa walking around with wrist braces and full-blown cases of carpal tunnel syndrome. The litigation alone would be enough to close the hotel down.

I glanced up and down the corridor and wondered why none of the other people on the tour were outside their doors, rotating their knobs. Obviously, Nana and I were the only guests from the tour in this wing.

"Shall I try, dear?"

I stepped aside and made a sweeping gesture toward the knob. "Be my guest. But don't fuss with it too long. You're seventy-eight years old. Your bones are fragile. I'll see if I can find a maid to—"

CLICK.

All right. So there would be one frizzy-haired twenty-nine-year-old from Iowa in a wrist brace. "How did you do that?" I asked as she pushed the door open.

"It's like a one-armed bandit. I'm pretty good with slot machines. My bone density's improved since I been hittin' the casino circuit."

I tried not to knock her down in my haste to see what a deluxe room in a four-star Swiss hotel looked like. Recalling the elegance of the front lobby, I envisioned a four-poster bed, flowered settee, marble fireplace, panoramic view of Lake Lucerne. Maybe a chocolate mint on my pillow.

Nana stopped dead in her tracks and looked left and right. "Well, would you look at that. It's just like your college dormitory room, Emily."

With one exception. My dorm room had been bigger. "No, this can't be right." I noted the twin beds nestled lengthwise against the wall, the exposed pipe and hangers that served as a closet, the narrow desk and chair that sat below the shelf where the television perched. Bare walls. Brown carpet. White drapes. No chocolate mints. "We're paying three thousand dollars apiece for this room?"

"I've stayed in worse," Nana commiserated. "I've lived in worse. At least we got a bathroom with runnin' water ... or was that only with the super deluxe rooms?" We exchanged horrified looks. Nana headed for the bathroom. I headed for the window. A spectacular view of Lake Lucerne and Mount Pilatus would go a long way to help me feel that our six thousand dollars hadn't been completely wasted. I threw open the drapes.

Yellow brick straight ahead and to either side. A service area and waste disposal unit below. Tiers of windows all around. I peered at the window across the way to find the drapery open and a man standing in the window recess. He was buck naked and had flattened against the window-pane the most hideously wrinkled body part I'd ever seen. Mr. Nunzio, no doubt. I winced at the sight. Just my luck. I was being mooned by an eighty-year-old.

"Good water pressure," Nana announced from the bathroom, "but I'm not sure about the shower. There's no safety strips in the tub, and the showerhead is in a strange place. And it has a weird dingus on it."

"Don't touch the dingus!" I snapped the drapes shut. Nana would go into cardiac arrest if she looked out the window. "We'll figure it out later."

She rejoined me in the bedroom. "I'm relieved the bathroom's so nice. But there's no washcloths. How do Europeans wash themselves without washcloths?"

"I guess they use their hands." I stood guard by the drapes, ready to concoct the mother of all excuses should Nana want to see the view.

"By the way," Nana said, "there's an elderly gentleman moonin' us from across the way so we'd best keep the drapes drawn for a while."

"How did you know that?"

"There's a window in the bathroom, dear. I got a clear shot of him. I don't know about men these days. Your grampa never woulda stuck his naked bum in a window for all the world to see. But let me tell you, he *coulda.* He had a fine bum, as hard and round as a rump roast, though gravity got to it in later years and it got pretty dimpled." She heaved a nostalgic sigh. "He photocopied it for me once. I wish I could remember what I done with it so's I could show it to you."

I winced again. This was much more than I ever needed to know about Grampa Sippel. "So do you want to keep the room, or should we request a new one?"

"Whatever you want to do, dear. But we're Midwesterners, and Midwesterners usually don't complain."

Right. But I'd lived in New York City for four years, which explained my occasional willingness to bellyache. I picked up the phone and punched a button.

"Front desk," said a curt male voice.

"This is Emily Andrew in thirty-three-ten. There's been a terrible mistake. We're in the wrong place. We paid for a deluxe room and you've given us a standard. When would it be convenient for you to move us to the right room?"

A pause. A clatter of computer keys. "Room thirty-three-ten *is* a deluxe room."

I eyed the narrow beds, the bare walls, the eleven-inch television screen. "You've got to be kidding."

"I'm Swiss, Madame. I never kid. Is there anything else?"

"How much would it cost us to upgrade to a super deluxe room?"

"There are no super deluxe rooms available at this time."

"Then place my name on a waiting list, and when one comes available, call me." I hung up the phone and shook my head. "I don't know, Nana. It doesn't sound too promising. We could be stuck here for a while."

"That'd be fine with me, dear. The room's not so bad once the shock wears off. It has a cozy feel to it. Kinda puts me in mind of your grampa's little ice shanty." She looked left and right. "Only your grampa had room for a La-Z-Boy recliner . . . and his TV was bigger."

CHAPTER 2

In the midst of a dead sleep, I felt a light tap on my shoulder and heard Nana's voice close to my ear. "Emily, dear, it's a quarter to five. Can you be dressed for dinner in fifteen minutes? Remember, Wally said to meet in the lobby at six o'clock sharp."

I opened one eye. I felt as if I'd been hit with a sledgehammer. "How long have I been asleep?" I mumbled.

"Five hours."

"FIVE HOURS?! But . . . but how could I sleep that long? I wasn't tired. I slept on the plane. I was only taking a catnap."

"Must be jet lag. I seen on *Dateline NBC* that crossin' the Atlantic by plane can really disrupt your circadian rhythm. Throws your sleep pattern way outta whack. You sleep when you should be awake and you're awake when you should be asleep. They done a study."

I scrubbed my face with my hands and eyed Nana through my fingers. "Have you been asleep, too?"

"I slept for twenty minutes, 'til the bags arrived. Then I

unpacked, and showered, and set up my laptop, and sent an E-mail to your parents to tell 'em we got here okay. I checked Hometown temperature and would you believe it's warmer in Iowa today than it is in Lucerne? Back home it's seventy-five degrees. It's only fifty in Lucerne. I'm headin' down to supper now so's I won't be late. You come when you can."

"But supper isn't until six. It's only quarter of five. You have an hour and fifteen minutes."

"So I'll be right on time. I'll leave the key on the desk for you, dear. Don't forget to bring it."

Iowans were always punctual. Insanely punctual. If they were an hour early, they thought themselves "on time." If they arrived at the appointed time, they considered themselves late. Even though Nana wasn't a native Iowan, she still had the compulsion. I guess it came from growing up in a bordering state. After my stint in New York, I'd schooled myself to become less compulsive about time. These days, I could remain calm and in control even if I was a few minutes late.

I stumbled out of bed and headed for the bathroom. I stared at the bathtub, wondering why the shower apparatus was attached to the wall directly in front of me rather than the end wall. Nana said she'd taken a shower, but the showerhead looked too complicated for a person suffering from a disruption in her circadian rhythm to figure out. Besides, I didn't want to get my hair wet, so I'd be better off taking a bath. I turned on the faucet.

"YEEEOOOOOOOWWWW!" Cold water blasted me in the face. It needled into my eyes. Shot up my nose. I leaped out of the way. Cold water pounded onto the tiled floor and formed rivers in the grouting. I stared in amazement. Nana had been right. The water pressure was great.

I grappled with the faucet to turn it off then stood for a

moment in abject shock, assessing the damage. The floor had become a tidal pool. My feet were soaked, my hair was drenched, my dry-clean only silk turtleneck was plastered to my Click Miracle bra. I glared at the showerhead knowing exactly what had caused the disaster.

Nana had touched the dingus.

I stepped out of my wet leather skirt and mopped up the floor on my hands and knees, then realizing I'd used our entire supply of clean towels in the endeavor, I unpacked my blow-dryer and blew myself and my turtleneck dry. My turtleneck ended up stretched to my thighs, with a splotch like a six-headed amoeba tattooed on the front. And it had been my favorite! Berry. To match my nails. I'd bought it in a little boutique in Ames because it had spoken to me. I love clothes. They speak to me a lot. But considering the size of my bank account, I wish they would speak to me in a language I didn't understand, like Latin or Croatian.

I checked the time. The crystal on my wristwatch was fogged up and I could see tiny droplets of water clinging to the inside. "Aaaarghhhh!" I whipped off my watch and punched on the power to the television. Local time was 17:59. Terrific. It was 5:59 and I was going to be late. REALLY late.

I hopped into a pair of champagne-and-black python print slacks and a glazed-linen blouse, pulled my hair back into a ponytail, jammed my feet into my funky new black platforms, grabbed the key, locked the door, then raced down the corridor to the elevator. I heard movement inside the shaft. A light appeared through the glass above the floor indicator. The car stopped. I heard male voices inside. I waited for the door to open. I waited some more.

The car started to descend. "Wait!" I yelled at the door.

"You need to open the door from the inside! It's not automatic!" I let out a silent scream. Okay. Time to execute alternate plan B. The stairs. There were a lot of them, and they were really close together. Just the kind of stairs you want to walk down on platform heels when you're in a hurry. Good thing I'd begun wearing heels at age twelve. I'd had lots of years to practice.

I clung steadfastly to the railing and clunked down all three flights with slow, guarded steps. I was glad my wristwatch was waterlogged. I didn't want to know what time it was.

I arrived at the entrance of the chandeliered dining room and skulked into the room, looking for Nana's face among the tables of diners. People looked up at me as I passed, set their silverware down, and regarded watches that were still working. They obviously hadn't tried out their showers yet. Eyebrows lifted. Brows furrowed. I could hear damning whispers above the clink of china. "My watch," I explained to Bernice Zwerg as I squeezed behind her chair. "It stopped." But that wasn't going to cut it. I'd committed the Eighth Deadly Sin. The one they'd accidentally omitted from my grade-school catechism. The sin that was worse than gluttony or sloth to any Iowan.

I'd committed tardiness.

"Being on holiday is no excuse for being late," Lars Bakke grumbled when I passed.

"Are we going to have to wait for her if she's late for the bus in the morning?" Solvay Bakke asked.

I found Nana seated at a table for four with three other ladies. She glanced at her watch. "You're late, dear."

"How late?" My heart was pounding. I was breathing hard. I guessed I was hyperventilating. Okay, I'd work on the calm and in control thing.

"It's 6:04." She shook her head. "You've very nearly missed dinner, Emily."

I looked around at the empty place settings. "But they haven't even served yet!"

"Excuse me, Madame." A waiter with slicked-back hair and a five o'clock shadow circled around me. He set a plateful of food in front of Nana and one of her companions.

"You better find a place to sit," Nana said. "There's an empty chair over at that table with the Dicks." She gestured toward the wall.

I located the table and rolled my eyes. The table was set for eight. Seated around it were Dick Teig and his wife, Dick Rassmuson and his wife, but no Dick Stolee and Grace. I wondered what the scoop was there. The Dicks *always* sat together. Hmm. Filling out the rest of the table were our local pharamacist at the Pills Etcetera store in Windsor City, a blonde lady I'd never seen before, and Andrew Simon. And wouldn't you know. The only empty chair was beside Mr. Casanova himself. I gritted my teeth. I'd eat fast.

"Is anyone sitting here?" I stood behind the empty chair that separated Andrew Simon from Jane Hanson, the pharmacist. Helen Teig flipped open the cover of her pendant watch.

"It's 6:05. Didn't you hear Wally say dinner was at six?" Helen was a squat, roly-poly woman with no sense of humor and no eyebrows. She'd lost them when a gas grill blew up in her face on her fiftieth birthday, but she remedied the situation by drawing them on with a black grease pencil. Today, one eyebrow slashed over her eye like a hyphen while the other shot upward in an arch. It made her look as if one side of her face was permanently surprised.

"Sit down, Emily," Dick Teig invited. Poor Dick was half a foot shorter than his wife, with a head like a helium balloon. The upside of this was, his head was so big, no one ever noticed he was shorter than Helen. Earlier in the year he'd addressed his problem of male pattern baldness by having hair plugs implanted from his crown to his forehead. He bragged that the new growth made him look like Gregory Peck. No one had the heart to tell him it made him look more like a Chia Pet. "Hell, I don't see food on the table yet," Dick reasoned. "Late is when you come to dinner after the food is served."

That was nice of him to say. Maybe I needed to rethink the Dicks. By Iowa standards, they were far too brash and boisterous when they were together, but maybe this vacation would bring out their kinder, gentler selves.

"I like your slacks, Emily." Jane Hanson helped slide the chair back for me. "We have scarves at the drugstore in that same reptile print. You should have a look at them when you're back home. They're in aisle four, next to the exotic pet food."

Jane Hanson was five years away from retirement and devoted to her job at the pharmacy. She'd worn her limp salt-and-pepper hair in the same Dutch boy cut for the last twenty years, always wore sensible shoes, and never wore lipstick. I chalked it up to defective shoe and makeup genes. But I liked Jane. She always included a free sample of Oil of Olay Refreshing Eye Makeup Remover when I filled a prescription.

I smiled at her as I sat down. "I hardly recognize you without your lab coat."

She primped the lace collar of her sweatshirt with barely restrained excitement. "To be honest, I'm feeling a little naked without it. But we're actually in Switzerland. Can you believe it?"

"Did I hear the word 'naked'?" Andy Simon interrupted. "My favorite word. Is someone offering?" He cupped his hands over his mouth to cover a deep, bronchial cough. He wore glasses this evening—gold wire rims to blend in with his mane of surfer hair. Normally, he was too vain to wear glasses, so I figured his eyes must really be bothering him. Maybe the glasses had bifocals so that when he looked in a mirror next time, he could see his fake tan was all streaky at his hairline. He could definitely use a touch-up. When he coughed again, I leaned away from him and closer to Jane.

"What's wrong with your eyes?" Dick Rassmuson barked at him in a voice that was sandpaper harsh from too many years of booze and cigars. Dick was another of the "sixtysomething" crowd. He'd produced pesticide for most of his life and had recently turned the company over to his son. "Did you catch a bug on the way over? A bug. Get it?" Dick's company motto had been, *We get rid of what's bugging you,* so vermin had always played a big part in his life.

"Where are you hiding the Stolees?" I asked, when Andy stopped coughing.

"Over there." Helen Teig pointed to a table somewhere behind me. "We were saving seats for them"—she leveled accusing eyes at the blonde interloper sitting beside Andy "—but it didn't work out."

Okay. I was getting the picture. No one had bothered to tell the woman that two places were being saved. That would have been rude. So they'd let one seat go but were quietly stewing about it. And not making the woman feel very welcome. Shame on them.

I made eye contact with the blonde and flashed her a smile. "Hi. I'm Emily."

"I'm Shirley Angowski. From Rhode Island. I'm part of the East Coast contingent on the tour."

East Coast contingent? We were sharing our Golden Swiss Triangle Tour with a group of Easterners? No one had said anything about that.

"What do you mean East Coast contingent?" Lucille Rassmuson asked. Lucille had a flawless ivory complexion, short permed hair that was the color of the froth on a frozen peach Margarita, and no lips. Her mother had no lips either. The condition was probably a genetic thing that had to do with her being Irish and had nothing to do with the fact that Lucille had attended Helen Teig's fiftieth birthday party and was standing near the gas grill when it exploded.

"Since there were so few of you people, the Triangle tour agents recruited twenty-five of us from the New England area to fill up the rest of the bus. You all seem to know each other. Are you from the same place?"

"Iowa," said Lucille, tucking in her lips with displeasure at the idea of sharing her bus with strangers. Bad move. Now she had no mouth.

"Iowa." Shirley Angowski looked pensive. "I know where Iowa is. It's west of Rhode Island, isn't it?"

"You bet," Dick Teig said with a wink. He smoothed back his Chiahair. "Right between East Dakota and West Dakota."

Shirley nodded. "I think I might have relatives in East Dakota."

I studied Shirley Angowski for a moment. She was probably just shy of sixty, and sported big hair, big eye-glasses, and big breasts. I envied the breasts. She looked as if she could put the Click Miracle bra people out of business.

"Are you working or retired?" Helen Teig asked Shirley in a smug tone. She was probably hoping Shirley would claim to have a degree in geography from Stanford so she could jump up and say, "Liar, liar, pants on fire." Helen wasn't a native Iowan, which explained her penchant for liking to confront people.

Shirley held up her hands and wiggled her fingers for us. Her fingernails were like stilettos and were painted a color that looked like Pepto-Bismol. "You see this color? It's called *Baby Flamingo* and I named it. I make up all the names for the nail and lip products at Revlon."

I used Revlon products. I glanced at my fingernails. "I'm wearing *Crystal Berry*. Did you make that one up?"

"I sure did. That was part of the Summer Berry collection, along with *Raspberry Soufflé* and *Boysenberry Sherbet*."

"We carry Revlon products," Jane added helpfully. "Aisle one. Along the wall. Just like Walgreen's."

My impression of Shirley Angowski skyrocketed. So what if she didn't know the exact location of Iowa? Her value to womankind was unimpeachable. How else could we distinguish between subtle shades of nail polish if the Shirley Angowskis of the world didn't provide really cool names for them?

"What about you?" Shirley inquired politely of Helen. "Working or retired?"

"We're retired now, but Dick owned a professional dry-cleaning and dye business."

Shirley looked exuberant. "You dyed things? That's SO exciting. Were you able to create a lot of exotic colors?"

"You bet," Dick Teig replied. "Red. Green. Black."

I could see where this conversation was leading. Shirley was going to ask all of us what we did for a living, and I'd have to admit I was currently unemployed. I'd lost my job in phone solicitations two weeks ago when the president of Playgrounds for Tots, for whom I'd done fund-raising since returning from New York, had been hauled off to jail for fraud. Apparently, the only playgrounds he'd built had been for himself—million-dollar mansions in Palm Beach, Palm Springs, and Tahiti. The police said I'd been one damned fine fund-raiser and asked if I'd like to raise money for their Policeman's Ball. Nana pointed out later that it had been a trick question because only firemen have balls.

Andy Simon coughed again and started to wheeze.

"How about those rooms!" I said in a quick change of subject. "Anyone try the shower yet?"

Dick Rassmuson gave me a surly look. "You have a shower?"

Unh-oh. Dick and Lucille must have opted for a super-saver room with a bathroom down the hall that was shared by six other people.

"We don't have a shower," Dick grumbled in his smoker's voice. "We have a damned Jacuzzi."

"And that bed is so high off the floor, I had to stand on my suitcase to climb onto it," Lucille added. "The bed-spread and canopy are pretty though. And the view of the lake will be really nice once the fog lifts."

"I didn't much care for the chocolate wafer," Helen complained. She scratched her eyebrow, accidentally smearing it across her forehead. "Too much rum in it. But I hope the weather warms up so we can use the balcony."

"You got a wafer?" I asked in a strangulated voice. Not to mention a balcony and a view. "What kind of rooms do you have? Presidential suites?"

"Standard rooms," the two Dicks said in unison, to which Dick Rassmuson added, "No sense paying deluxe rates for a room we'll be occupying only a few hours a night."

The Swiss obviously structured their hotel room rating system in the same way they structured their banking system: Don't tell 'em nothin'. But I was on to them.

Andy Simon's wheezing grew worse. If he'd paid extra for the luxury of a deluxe room, I could understand his reaction. I felt like wheezing myself. He reached into his jacket pocket and pulled out an inhaler.

"What's wrong with him?" Shirley asked, as he shoved the apparatus into his mouth.

"Asthma," said Lucille. "He's had it for years. But it hasn't killed him yet, has it, Andrew?"

He gasped, then wheezed, then after several moments, seemed to breathe more easily. He held the inhaler up for all to see. "Pirbuterol Acetate. The best concoction in the world. And if you ever need any, I recommend you buy it from Janie Hanson at the Pills Etcetera nearest you."

Jane dismissed his comment with a wave of her hand. "He's such a flatterer. What he didn't tell you is we're equipped to handle all types of insurance now, including Medicare, HMOs and PPOs."

"Do you take the Discover card?" Lucille asked. "As many times as I've filled prescriptions, and I still can't remember."

Jane nodded. "Discover. VISA. MasterCard and American Express. Sorry, no personal checks."

"And," Andy continued, "Pills Etcetera is now on-line, so if you want to order anything from Viagra to contact lenses, e-mail Janie at pillsetcetera dot com, and she'll see that it's mailed to you. And she always includes free samples. Rewetting solution with your contact lenses. Toothpaste with new toothbrushes."

I wondered what she included with the Viagra. An inflatable woman?

"I love free samples," said Shirley. "Do you ship to Rhode Island?"

"She ships anywhere." Andy responded for her. "She can even put you on her mailing list so you'll know about upcoming sales and specials. Why don't you give me your E-mail address, honey, and I'll forward it to her when we get back to Iowa."

A waiter plopped a plate in front of my face at that moment, so no one heard the gagging sound I made. The E-mail thing was Andy's favorite line. I figured it was his personal brand of foreplay. When we'd appeared together in *Sweeney Todd* last spring and *A Christmas Carol* last year, he'd chatted up several of the actresses electronically, which led to his having extramarital affairs with a couple of them. But he was easily bored, so when a theatrical production ended, he'd dump the old lover and search for a new one at the next production. The man was a slimeball. I was surprised more women couldn't see through him, but I guess when a man bombards you with daily E-mails that claim you're the most important person in his life, you prefer to believe him rather than think he says that to anyone with a uterus.

When he'd asked for my E-mail address, I'd told him it was getlost@screwu.com. I guess he must have copied the address down wrong because I never received a message from him.

"This is such fun," Shirley cooed as she patted Andy's hand. "My E-mail address is all in capital letters. LOVESLAVE at HERA dot COM."

I cringed. All in caps. Of course. You might miss it otherwise.

"And mine is simonsays at spirit dot net. Just in case you ever want to drop me a line."

I wondered if Shirley realized it was Andy who'd just dropped the line. I stared at the plate of food in front of me. Mashed potatoes. Cauliflower smothered in cream sauce. White meat smothered in white sauce. The brochure had said the hotel cuisine was superb. It didn't necessarily say it would be colorful. I poked at the meat with my fork. "What is this?" I whispered to Jane.

She scraped away some of the sauce. "*Uff da*. I think it's whitefish." *Uff da* is a common expression among Norwegians in Iowa. From what I can figure, it means, 'Holy crap!'"

"What's this under all the white sauce?" boomed Dick Rassmuson.

"It's chicken," said his wife.

Dick Teig shook his head. "Tastes like pork to me. But it's not as good as Iowa pork."

"Well, it looks like *Seashells and Snow* to me," said Shirley. "That shade was a really big seller last Christmas. Part of the Pearlized collection."

"I think it looks more like shit on a shingle," Andy offered, sending the Dicks into gales of loud, hysterical laughter and table pounding.

I shook my head. Nana had a point about being punctual. If you were on time, you had a choice about whom you wanted to eat with. Tomorrow night, I planned on being *really* early and sitting as far away from these guys as possible.

"What did you think of the food?" I asked Nana, when we returned to the room after dinner.

"There's probably children starvin' in China who would've loved that meal, but frankly, I found the white sauce on the veal a little lumpy."

"You had veal? We had chicken. Or pork. Or maybe whitefish."

"You had veal, dear. The entire dinin' room was served veal."

"How do you know that? You must have asked. I tried to ask, but our waiter didn't speak English."

"I read the menu. It was in a plastic holder in the middle of the table. And since you were so late, you missed the announcement Wally made before dinner."

I didn't want to hear. He'd probably warned us not to eat any food we couldn't identify.

"He said to remember the faces of the people you were eatin' with tonight because you're supposed to eat at the same table with the same people for the rest a the trip. I guess that works out better with the waiters and tippin'."

"The same people? No. NO!" I flopped onto the bed and buried my face in the crook of my elbow. I considered my options. I supposed I could give up eating in the dining room and subsist on Swiss chocolate for the next nine days. This would require my having to walk back to Iowa to get rid of all the fat calories, but I didn't have a job to rush back to, so I had the time. And chocolate releases serotonin into the brain, so I'd be happy.

"Did you see our waiter, Emily? We all agreed he looks like a young Sean Connery. He wears a little gold hoop in his right ear, though. Does that mean somethin'?"

"Yes," I groaned. "It means he's cool. Does he speak English?"

"He has buns of steel, dear. Who cares what language he speaks?"

"Oh, I finally figured out the rating system on the rooms here and I need to call downstairs and ask to be taken off the super deluxe room list and placed on the standard room list. The standards are the good rooms."

"If it's all the same to you, dear, I'm gettin' more fond a this room all the time."

"You don't want to move?"

"Not really."

"Aw, that's so sweet." I gave her a little hug. "It's because the room reminds you of Grampa's ice shanty, isn't it? I bet when you look around, you can just feel his presence. Can you hear him saying anything to you?"

"You bet. He's sayin', 'You just got all your clothes hung up and put away, Marion. It'd be a pain in the ass to have to do it again.'"

Yup. That sounded just like Grampa.

We were in bed by nine. I fell asleep immediately and remained asleep until sometime in the middle of the night, when I came wide-awake. I grabbed my miniflashlight and shined it on my wristwatch, which I'd set out to dry on the built-in shelf above the headboard. The crystal was still fogged up. Nuts. I considered tiptoeing over to Nana's bed and checking the travel alarm, but since she was snoring like a trumpeter swan, I didn't want to chance waking her up. One of us deserved a decent night's sleep.

I began counting sheep. I hummed the theme songs from old TV Westerns. I made up naughty verses for the Oscar Mayer Weiner Song. An hour passed. I suspected this was a glaring example of my sleep pattern being thrown out of whack. I heard noises from the room next door. Groans. Loud groans.

Always respectful of other people's privacy, I pressed my ear to the wall.

Thrashing. Pounding. Moaning. Thumping. A couple of high-pitched cries of ecstacy. A gazillion rooms in this place and I get stuck next to the one where there's an ongoing reenactment of *Debbie Does Dallas*. Great. I flopped back onto my pillow, covered my ears, and went back to the Weiner Song.

That's the last thing I remember until I heard the scream.

It was a woman's scream. Loud. Shrill. Blood-chilling. I recognized it immediately because I'd let out the same scream my freshman year of college when I'd stepped onto the scale and discovered I'd gained ten pounds in two months.

"Good Lord!" Nana was up like a shot. "What's wrong? Emily? Are you all right? Who's screamin'?"

"Someone in the hall." I was across the room and fumbling with the doorknob in the dark. "You stay here." I flung the door open, expecting to find another guest who'd misinterpreted the room rating system.

Instead, I found Shirley Angowski, attired in a pink nylon peignoir edged with a profusion of pink boa feathers at the hem and cuffs. She was shaking with hysteria and clawing her cheeks with her *Baby Flamingo* fingernails. "He's dead. Look at him. He's dead. He's dead."

"Who's dead?" I asked, as more doors were flung open.

She pointed toward the spill of light in the room next to mine. I followed her gaze.

Supine on the floor lay Andrew Simon, his mouth contorted into a hideous rictus, his skin pasty even beneath his tube tan, eyes wide and bulging, hair disheveled, dressed in a handsome black satin smoking jacket with matching ascot that was pulled dreadfully askew. I thought the ascot was a bit over the top, especially since it looked as if Andy hadn't had a clue how to knot the thing. Now he'd never know.

Shirley Angowski was right. Andrew Simon was dead.

Not a good way to begin your Golden Swiss Triangle Tour.

CHAPTER 3

The hotel management allowed Nana and me to change into street clothes before they escorted us to a private office on the first floor. Street clothes for me consisted of a pair of London jeans and a warm Green Bay Packers sweatshirt. For Nana, it meant her Minnesota Vikings warm-up suit, but since we were going to be interviewed by the Swiss police, she decided to put on the dog, so she opted for the panty hose with the tummy control rather than the ones that were sheer to the waist.

I paced the office and peered through the window miniblinds into the darkness beyond. "What time is it?"

"A quarter to eight."

"But it's still dark outside. Why is it dark?"

"My guess is that the sun hasn't come up yet."

"Well, they should have said something in the brochure about Switzerland only having three minutes of sunlight per day in the month of October. We might have decided to visit the Congo instead."

"I'm not sure the Congo's still a country, dear."

Too bad Shirley Angowski wasn't here. She'd probably know.

"Why do the police need to interview us?" Nana wanted to know when I returned to my seat. "All the action happened while we were asleep."

"The police are interviewing everyone in the rooms adjoining Andy's. According to the night manager, they usually conduct the interviews one individual at a time, but they think you might be more comfortable with a relative in the room, so they're letting me stay."

"That's very considerate. They must suspect that my bein' grilled in isolation by the police might give me a coronary. I suppose that's a concern when you cater to the senior set. You were real nice to that Angowski woman, Emily. Too bad about her peignoir moltin' all over the place though. They'll never get all those boa feathers off the hall carpet."

Management had whisked Shirley off to calm her down before the police arrived. I didn't know where she was now, but her feather trail had terminated at the third-floor freight elevator. I'd felt a twinge of indignation as I'd passed by the shaft, and a twinge of guilt for my reaction, but it seemed the only way to get prompt elevator service in this building was to find a dead body in one of the rooms.

"What do you s'pose this policeman is gonna look like?" Nana asked. "I hope he looks like Columbo. I know I won't have a coronary if he's wearin' an old trench coat and has a glass eye. Or he could look like Kojak. I like bald men. Did you know bald men have more testosterone than men who have full heads a hair? I seen it on Tom Brokaw. They done a study." She paused thoughtfully. "I wonder what would happen if a bald fella started wearin' a toupee? You think the fake hair would make his testosterone level drop? Maybe they should do a study on the testosterone levels of bald guys who wear rugs."

The door opened behind us and I peeked over my shoulder to see the most gorgeous man I'd ever set eyes on enter the room. No trench coat. No glass eye. No bald head. More like Italian suit. Piercing blue eyes. Hair like liquid coal. "Ladies." He strode across the floor and sat down at the desk, referring to a small notepad before looking up. I knew his type immediately. One percent body fat. Reflexes like a panther. Testosterone level off the chart. I wanted to have his children.

"I'm Inspector Etienne Miceli." His voice was deep and resonant and started at his knees. He had the most beautiful French accent I'd ever heard. Or German. Or maybe Italian. "I'm told you ladies are visiting from America."

"Windsor City, Iowa," I said, reeling my tongue back into my mouth.

"Iowa," he repeated. "That's close to Chicago, isn't it?"

I was impressed with his geographical acuity. He could probably even point to Rhode Island on a map and be fairly close. "It's west of Chicago."

"I visited Chicago only last year. My sister is married to a man who works at the Art Institute there. I assume you've been to the Art Institute?"

"I've-uh, I've been to the Marshall Field's flagship store. That's within ten to twenty blocks of the Institute."

"You must be Emily. Emily what?" His mouth curved into a soft, dazzling smile that revealed teeth too perfect not to be capped and dimples in both his cheeks. Unh.

"Emily Andrew. How did you know my first name?" Was it possible we were so mentally connected that he could simply look at me and know my name?

"The night clerk told me that Emily and Marion were waiting for me. Since I'm reading 'Marion Sippel' on this lady's name tag, that makes you Emily."

Deductive reasoning. I hated deductive reasoning.

"I assume from the family likeness that you ladies are related?"

That was kind of scary. Nana had two chins, a bulbous nose, and ears like Alfred E. Newman. If he was seeing a likeness, I was in big trouble. "Emily's my granddaughter," Nana piped up. "And she's not married. She used to be, but it didn't work out."

"Ah, yes," the inspector commiserated. "In Switzerland first marriages often don't work out either."

"She got an annulment though," Nana continued. "The Church will do that anytime when a couple has serious issues involvin' closets."

Nana was a whiz with E-Trade over the Internet, but she'd never been able to understand the gay thing about coming out of the closet. I blamed it on underexposure. In all of recorded history, only two gays had ever lived in Minnesota. Then she moved to Iowa, where there were none.

"In my day we didn't even have closets," said Nana. "We had wardrobes."

Inspector Miceli leaned back in his chair, trying unsuccessfully not to grin. "Please allow me a few questions, Mrs. Sippel, then you'll be free to go."

"It was the asthma what killed Andy, wasn't it?"

"We don't know what killed him. We'll know more after the autopsy is performed. Can you tell me anything unusual you remember about last night, Mrs. Sippel?"

Nana shrugged. "I ate dinner. Went to bed. Fell asleep. Dreamed about the Ponderosa."

"The steakhouse in America?"

"No. Ben Cartwright's spread in Nevada."

Miceli made a quick notation. "Ben Cartwright?"

"He's a make-believe cowboy," Nana explained. "He was head of the Cartwright clan in *Bonanza*. You ever see *Bonanza*? It was on for fourteen seasons back in the sixties. I wonder what you'd have to do to get Westerns here in Switzerland?"

"Razing the Alps would be a good first step," said Miceli, scribbling out what he'd written, "but it would kill the tourist industry. Go on with your dream, Mrs. Sippel."

"Ben was havin' a reunion at the Ponderosa for a bunch of gunslingers I recognized from the old Westerns."

Miceli leaned forward and narrowed his eyes as if he were definitely on to something. "Sometimes, external stimuli can incorporate itself quite seamlessly into a person's dream. For instance, gunfire in an adjacent room could become gunfire in your dream. Were the gunslingers in your dream having a shoot-out, Mrs. Sippel?"

"They were at a buffet table eatin' Oscar Mayer weiners."

I slunk down several inches in my chair.

"And then I woke up and heard that Angowski woman screamin'."

Miceli nodded and penciled something onto his notepad again. "Is there anything else you can think to tell me that might be of significance?"

"Are you sure Andy's really dead?" Nana asked. "He fancied himself an actor, so's he might be fakin' it to get attention."

"I assure you, Mrs. Sippel, Mr. Simon would have to be an extraordinary actor to fake death this well."

"He must be dead then because he wasn't a very good actor. Just ask Emily. He chewed his words and spoke too fast. The only reason he got to play Ebenezer Scrooge in *Christmas Carol* was because his wife donated five thousand dollars to finance the production. He'd a made a better Tiny Tim, but I'm not sure he was tall enough."

Miceli made another notation, then stood up and escorted Nana to the door. "Thank you for your time, Mrs. Sippel. They'll be serving breakfast in the dining room about now. I'll send your granddaughter in to join you when I'm through with her." He returned to the desk and riveted his eyes on me. "I apologize for interrupting your holiday, Miss Andrew, but I promise to be as quick as possible with my questions. These interviews often end up being a waste of everyone's time, but it's procedure."

"Nana must have said something important. You were taking notes."

He held up the notepad for me to see. At the top of the page was written a word in a foreign language. Beneath it appeared two more equally mysterious words. "I don't know what those words mean," I said.

"My grocery list." He shrugged. "Power of suggestion. I just remembered that my refrigerator's empty."

My refrigerator was empty most of the time, too. We already had something in common.

In the next instant he was back in detective mode. "How well did you know the deceased, Miss Andrew?"

"We were in a couple of community theater plays together in Windsor City. But we didn't hang out together. I spent my time memorizing lines. He spent his charming all the bosomy blondes."

"Was he successful?"

"Unfortunately, yes. He'd scope out the prospects at rehearsal, target one of them, then woo her with attention, phone calls, dates to rehearse lines, intimate E-mails. He was big into romancing over the Internet. He'd tell her they were soul mates, that they shared a bond that transcended space and time. He'd make a woman feel so special, she'd fall into bed with him before the end of rehearsal for scene one."

"Ah, yes. We have a saying in Switzerland. 'Men fall in love through their eyes. Women fall in love through their ears.' You were a witness to all this?"

"When you're in a community theater production, the cast becomes your family. And the ladies talked. About everything. Including Andy."

"How often did Mr. Simon exhibit this kind of behavior?"

"He had a short attention span, so when auditions would begin for the next play, he'd pick out a new victim, end the affair with his current lover, and start the pattern all over again. It was really insidious because he always hooked up with women who had no self-esteem—the ones he could brainwash into believing their lives were worthless without him. Poor things would be completely devastated when he dumped them. Last spring, one of them overdosed on sleeping pills afterward and had to be rushed to the hospital to have her stomach pumped. But Andy didn't care. As long as he was getting his ego stroked, it didn't matter who suffered."

"He never tried to woo you?"

"I'm not suffering from low self-esteem." I grabbed a hunk of my hair and held it out. "And I'm not blonde."

Miceli scribbled something furiously onto his pad.

"What are you writing?"

"I'm reminding myself to invite you to dinner while you're here. I happen to be enchanted by women from your Midwest. I find your accents quite charming."

Men usually asked me out because they said I was friendly, or had a great smile, or a good personality. My brother told me that was a guy's way of saying he liked my breasts and was hoping I'd take my blouse off. No one had ever asked me out because he liked the way I pronounced my vowels. I didn't know whether to be flattered or disappointed. "You're not married, are you?"

"Widowed."

"Gay?"

"Straight."

I thought about my ex-husband. "Do you dress in ladies' lingerie?"

"That would be my cousin, Jean-Claude. But you've no cause to worry. He's adopted."

"I'm in room thirty-three-ten."

He smiled one of those bedroom smiles that caused every organ below my neck to tingle. My Golden Swiss holiday was definitely looking up.

"If you would be so kind, Miss Andrew, I have only a few more questions."

In response to his queries, I told him about Andy's red, watery eyes the day before, the mix-up in our room assignments, and his minor asthma attack at dinner.

"His asthma undoubtedly worsened as the night progressed," Miceli commented. "We found his inhaler on the floor beside him."

I told him about Andy's request for Shirley Angowski's E-mail address and the disturbing noises I'd heard in his room during the wee hours of the morning.

"What time did you hear the noises?"

"My watch was drying out, so I don't know what time it was."

"You must have touched the diverter on the shower. Can you describe the noises for me?"

"They were like World Wrestling Alliance noises. Thumps. Grunts. Groans. Maybe a flying dropkick."

"Could you tell if he was alone?"

"It sounded more like a tag team."

"So he might have been entertaining a paramour and they woke you with their spirited . . . lovemaking." He paused. "Given Mr. Simon's sexual appetites, would you be surprised if he'd arranged assignations with two different women on the same night?"

"Not at all. But if Shirley Angowski was assignation number two, who was assignation number one?"

"Something to ponder, Ms. Andrew. Perhaps he was having a secret liaison with someone else on your tour."

This last thought stuck with me as I located Nana in the dining room. Had Andy been boffing women other than aspiring actresses? Women with husbands, and grandchildren, and varicose veins? I sat down opposite Nana and eyed her speculatively.

"Is Andy Simon the kind of man you'd want to have an affair with, Nana?"

"He's dead, dear. I never have sex with dead men, though after your grampa started havin' those erectile dysfunction problems, I had a pretty good idea what it would be like."

I shook my head in bewilderment. "Why would any self-respecting female want to have an affair with that self-centered, self-important, undersized gnome?"

Nana shielded her mouth and spoke in a stage whisper. "He wasn't so undersized, *down there,* if you catch my drift."

My heart stopped beating. How could she know that? Oh, no! Not my own grandmother! "You didn't! You couldn't! I can't listen to this."

"Margi Swanson accidentally walked in on him when he was doin' his business into a cup at the clinic—Margi works part-time for Andy's doctor—and she told me at the Legion a Mary meetin' that his hoho reminded her of a big old eel she'd seen washed up on a beach on the coast a Maine. Can you hear me with your hands over your ears like that, Emily?"

Fortunately, I'd left enough space between my fingers to catch the important words. "Yuck," I said, thankful that Iowa is landlocked.

"Margi said he was pretty proud of that hoho a his. Called it his 'Pile Driver.' " She slipped into a moment of nostalgia. "We called your grampa's 'Mr. Handsome.' It had lots a personality. Before the prostate problem, he could even make it do tricks."

I'd named my husband's, too. "Rover." But after he'd started stepping out on me, the only trick it could perform with any regularity was the one where it rolled over and played dead.

"I don't mean to rush you, dear, but you better grab some breakfast before the food's all gone."

A diversion. I could use a diversion. Considering my tension level at the moment, food was a good choice, especially food at the breakfast buffet in a four-star hotel.

I started salivating as I squeezed around chairs enroute to the buffet table. I thought I'd start with hot buttered toast and a sweet roll, then move on to scrambled eggs, pancakes with maple syrup, bacon, sausage, and smoked salmon if they had any. A twinge of conscience made me rethink my choices. Okay, maybe out of respect for the dead, I'd forgo the sausage. But only for one morning.

I grabbed a plate and lifted the cover of a huge silver serving tray. Empty. I lifted the cover of the next tray. Empty as well. I caught the eye of the waiter with the buns of steel. "Where are the bacon and eggs?"

"No no." He made a sweeping gesture toward the rest of the table.

"Are they all gone?"

"Gone? Yes, gone." And before I could ask another question, so was he.

I proceeded down the table. I passed a bread basket that was empty save for a pair of tongs. A glass bowl that was half-full of Elmer's Glue. A bowl that was full of Elmer's Glue with raisins. A platter with one slice of cheese that was curling at the edges and two slices of luncheon meat with large chunks of lard embedded in them. A bowl with a single wedge of canned grapefruit floating in liquid. And three bowls that held the scant remains of what looked like dried cereal. I peered into each bowl and noted the choices. Cornflakes. Cornflakes. And cornflakes. We should have stayed in a five-star hotel. Their dried cereal selections probably included Cocoa Puffs.

I threw some food together and returned to the table with Nana. "What did you end up eating?" I asked her as I motioned the waiter for coffee.

"I had the plain glue. It wasn't bad actually. Tasted a little like Cream of Wheat without the wheat." She regarded my meal. "We'll have to come down earlier tomorrow, Emily. I don't see how you're gonna survive the mornin' on six cornflakes and a cup a coffee."

The waiter appeared at my shoulder, sloshed coffee into my cup, and rushed off again. I peeked into my cup. Correction. Six cornflakes and a half cup of coffee. I took a sip. A half cup of cold coffee. I refused to be upset, however. My anticipated dinner date with Etienne Miceli made even cold coffee seem palatable.

"While you was with that nice policeman, Wally announced to the dinin' room that we're gonna have a group meetin' in the lobby after breakfast," Nana said. "He probably wants to tell us about Andy."

I wondered how the Windsor City group would react to the news of Andy's death. I was particularly curious to see if anyone would respond with more than casual sorrow. I was no detective, but if one of the ladies in the group burst into uncontrollable fits of weeping when she heard the news, she'd win my vote as the person most likely to be Andy's secret lover.

The lobby was buzzing with conversation when we arrived. Thinking I might be able to shed new light on the case within the next few minutes, I sat down on one of the velvet sofas, butterflies in my stomach. Or maybe it was hunger pangs. Nana joined me after exchanging a few words with Bernice Zwerg.

"Poor Bernice says she didn't sleep a wink after two o'clock. She's still operatin' on Iowa time. You should see the bags under her eyes."

"I have concealer." I rummaged in my shoulder bag.

"Concealer won't cut it. She's gonna need a face-lift."

Wally hurried into the lobby, then stood for a moment with a stunned expression on his face. The room grew quiet. He looked very patriotic this morning, dressed in his khaki pants, navy blazer, and perfectly knotted red necktie. "You're all so prompt, I can hardly believe it. This doesn't usually happen until day four. Is everyone here?"

"Andy Simon's not here," yelled Dick Rassmuson. "Maybe you oughta phone his room."

The expression on Wally's face became grim. "Mr. Simon is the reason I've called this meeting. I'm afraid I have some tragic news, people. Sometime last night Mr. Simon passed away in his room. He's no longer with us."

A moment of shocked silence ensued before a terrible wailing sound filled the room. "Nooo!" cried Dick Rassmuson. "Not Andy!"

My eyeballs froze wide-open. Dick Rassmuson and Andy? But Dick wasn't Andy's type. Not only wasn't he blond, he didn't have hair at all. And Dick didn't have an

E-mail address. As far as I knew, he didn't even own a home computer.

"I bought him a frozen custard in the airport yesterday," Dick whined. "He never paid me back!"

Lucille elbowed him in the ribs to shut him up, but he continued to grumble. I breathed a sigh of relief. If anyone else had made that wailing sound, I'd accuse them of being the secret lover. But since Dick Rassmuson was reputed to be Windsor City's biggest tightwad, I concluded he truly was more upset about the loss of his money than the loss of Andy. I erased the picture of Dick and Andy locked in a lovers' embrace. Whew. I wouldn't have wanted the job of explaining the term "bisexual" to Lucille.

"Has anyone told Andy's wife yet?" Jane Hanson asked.

"I talked to Mr. Erickson, the Windsor City Bank president this morning, and since he's Mrs. Simon's brother, he said he thought it would be more appropriate if he broke the news in person."

"Is this going to affect our schedule?" Solvay Bakke called out. "We're supposed to meet the bus this morning at nine o'clock. It's eight-forty now. We're already running late."

All eyes in the room darted to their collective wrists. "I have eight-forty-two," said Bernice Zwerg. "I bet the bus has left without us."

Everyone in the lobby rose en masse and gathered up their belongings.

"People. People. The bus isn't going anywhere without us. Sit down. Please. Just for another minute."

Dick Stolee whipped out his stopwatch and clicked the crown with his thumb. Dick Stolee was blessed with the kind of all-American good looks that don't fade with age. He was athletically built, pink-cheeked and blue-eyed, with a mop of steel gray hair that never blew out of place.

Could be he used a lot of hair spray, but for hold like that, I suspected spray starch. He was addicted to techno toys and gadgets and probably spent most of his monthly pension buying batteries to keep the things running.

His wife, Grace, sat primly beside him, her back straight as a steeple. She was Dick's height, trim but thick-waisted, wore her hair stylishly short and wavy, and had the best posture of anyone I'd ever known. I attributed that to the many years she'd spent teaching ballroom dancing at the Arthur Murray Dance Studio in Windsor City. She was a pretty woman, lithe, dignified, and could move as quickly and quietly as the wind. If she ever decided to compete in the Senior Olympics, she'd be a cinch to unseat Bernice in the dash.

Wally continued. "The authorities may need to interview some of you about Mr. Simon, so please be cooperative."

"What did he die of?" Helen Teig inquired.

Wally shrugged. "We won't know for a few days. They have to perform an autopsy. But chances are, it was probably from natural causes. Mr. Simon's death shouldn't affect our schedule, so you needn't worry that your holiday is going to be interrupted. Triangle Tours promised you nine days of breathless sights, and it's nine days of breathless sights you'll get."

"Your brochure also promised us temperatures in the seventies," groused Lars Bakke. "I been out this morning already. It's forty-five degrees, tops."

I turned my head in the direction of the huge picture windows that supposedly afforded a panoramic view of Lake Lucerne. Well, would you look at that. While I'd been scarfing down my six cornflakes, the sun had come up. Kinda. You couldn't actually see it for all the fog and drizzle, but it was definitely lighter out there.

"The temperature *was* in the seventies," said Wally. "Last week. Today's weather is an unfortunate blip. It'll warm up tomorrow. You'll see."

Dick Stolee clicked his stopwatch, and yelled out, "Time." Everyone stood up.

"Sit DOWN," Wally snapped. He wrenched his necktie loose and unbuttoned the top button of his shirt. "I have one more item to discuss with you. It'll only take another minute."

Dick Stolee hit the reset button.

"With Mr. Simon having departed the world, you don't have a bank-appointed escort anymore. When I spoke to Mr. Erickson this morning, he suggested that someone from your group might want to volunteer to take over Mr. Simon's duties."

"What kind of duties?" George Farkas ventured. George had lost a leg in World War II, but he'd been fitted with a prosthesis that seemed to work better than the original. He ran marathons in Windsor City, skied in Aspen, mountain climbed in Yosemite, and at Christmas, he'd unstrap the thing and let the grandkids crack nuts with it. It was pretty much an all-utility limb.

"The duties are pretty light," said Wally. "You'd have to keep track of the medical forms everyone filled out for the trip. Dispense any over-the-counter medications people might need if they get sick. Help people make phone calls back home if they can't figure out the phone system. Give assistance to anyone in the Windsor City group who's having a problem. Things like that."

I'd worked with the public before, so I knew what a can of worms this job could turn out to be for the misguided soul who volunteered. Phone calls at all hours of the night. Complaints about the food, the service, the weather. Whining about the locals not speaking English. Griping about not being able to figure out the conversion rate from Swiss francs to American dollars. The volunteer would be chugging antianxiety drugs by the fistful within twenty-four hours of accepting the position.

"Mr. Erickson authorized me to tell you that the volunteer will be reimbursed all expenses for the trip once he or she is back in Windsor City."

"I'll do it!" I stood up. "I volunteer!" Okay, so I was misguided, but I was practical. I'd lost my job. I needed the money. I had bills to pay.

"Emily's a good choice," agreed Dick Teig. "Chances are, she won't kick off before the end of the trip. All in favor say, 'Aye.'" A chorus of "Ayes" echoed through the room. "The ayes have it. Emily is our new escort."

"Time!" shouted Dick Stolee.

The entire room stood up and hurried in an orderly clump toward the side door, where the bus was scheduled to be waiting.

"Don't forget to leave your keys in the box at the front desk!" Wally reminded everyone.

I was too shocked by my impulsiveness to move immediately, but Nana elbowed George Farkas out of the way and set off in a footrace to get to the door first. From somewhere in the middle of the crowd, I could hear her yelling that she'd save me a seat on the bus.

Wally found me in my stupor and shook my hand. "Welcome aboard."

"Sure," I said. I'm not usually one to second-guess my own decisions, but I was having a weird feeling about this one. Did I know what I was doing? Could I handle the responsibility of thirty old people? Had anything in my lifetime prepared me for such a mammoth undertaking?

I'd played the Pied Piper of Hamlin in a grammar-school play once. It was kind of the same thing, wasn't it?

"And by the way," Wally confided, "I hate to tell you this, but the police are going to cordon off the whole area around Andy's room on the third floor. You and your grandmother are going to have to pack up your things and change rooms."

CHAPTER 4

"Change rooms? But we just finished unpacking!"

"The hotel says they'll have another room available for you around noon."

"My grandmother is happy where she is."

"We should be back from our tour of the city around twelve-thirty. That'll give you a half hour to get situated in your new digs before we head out to the Lion Monument for group pictures at one."

"No can do. She doesn't want to move. This room speaks to her."

Wally pinched the bridge of his nose as if he were warding off a migraine. "They don't pay me enough to do this job. All right, Miss Andrew, I'm not above bribery. What do I have to do to get you out of that room?"

Hmm. This was handy. "I want another room."

"The hotel is *offering* you another room!"

"I want a good room. A really good room." I poked my finger into his sternum. "A standard room."

"A standard room. You want a standard room? I'll get

you a standard room. Now, do you promise to be out by one?" I nodded agreement. He looked me up and down. "Is that what you're planning to wear today?"

Okay. So I hadn't had time to dress like Audrey Hepburn this morning. Middle of the night wake-ups tended to skew my fashion sense. But I allowed no one to insult my Green Bay Packers sweatshirt. The Packers were former world champions. "I was planning to wear my beaded Vera Wang, but wouldn't you know, the zipper broke."

"Look, Miss Andrew, Triangle Tours has an image to maintain, so if you could manage something more professional, you'd make my life a whole lot easier."

"Make *your* life easier? Hey, I've been mooned by somebody's grandfather, pummeled by a killer shower, grossed out by a dead man, and treated to famine conditions at breakfast. And the kicker is, I paid three thousand dollars for the privilege!"

"Memories, Miss Andrew. Think of the stories you'll have to tell the grandchildren."

"I don't *have* grandchildren. I have goldfish."

Wally tapped the crystal of his watch. "I may be running a little fast. What time do you have?"

"My watch died."

"Couldn't have happened in a better place. Bucherer is right down the street from here."

"What's Bucherer?"

"Only the premiere shop for watches in Europe. The bus is going to leave us off right in front of it this morning. You're on the payroll now. Live a little."

Normally, when my day started out this poorly, I'd pop a couple of Hershey Kisses® to lift my spirits. But since I was fresh out of chocolate, maybe I'd have to settle for a new watch and hope it had the same effect. Wally was right. I was on the payroll now, and this *was* Switzerland.

I'd be crazy to pass up a chance to buy a really good cheap Swiss watch.

"We're due to leave in twelve minutes," Wally said. "If you're going to change your clothes, you'd better get moving."

With the prospects of a shopping spree making the day appear a little brighter, I took the stairs two at a time and sprinted down the corridor toward room 3310. A couple of uniformed policemen outside Andy's room did their best to ignore me as I plugged the key into the doorknob and turned the knob . . . again, and again, and again. I made a growling sound.

"Do you need help with that, Madame?" one of the policemen inquired.

"Please. I only have ten minutes before my bus leaves."

He reinserted the key and turned the knob. CLICK.

"There's a trick to this, isn't there?" I accused.

"I don't think so, Madame." He nodded politely and returned to his colleague. I flew into the room, throwing off my sweatshirt on the run. I shrugged into an aubergine cashmere sweater set, then ripped off my jeans and hopped into slim black cigarette pants and chunky heeled shoes. Wally wanted professional? I'd show him professional. I ran into the bathroom to brush my teeth, applied lipstick and blush, threw on my raincoat, grabbed Nana's raincoat and our umbrellas, then raced back out the door. On the first floor I dropped the room key into the box at the front desk, then dashed out into the cold October mist and drizzle.

Wally stood beneath the protection of his umbrella outside the open door of the bus. When he saw me, he made a hurry-up gesture. "You're the last one. All the Rhode Islanders are even here. Let's go."

I gave him my version of the evil eye and jogged past

him up the stairs of the bus. Scattered applause as I appeared. A few grumbles. "I told you we were going to have to wait for her," Solvay Bakke groused, as I maneuvered down the aisle toward where Nana was sitting. I slid in beside her, winded and sweating, and handed her her raincoat and umbrella.

"That was sweet a you to go back to the room for my things, Emily."

"Maybe our new room will be closer to the lobby," I said, gasping.

"New room? What happened to the old one?"

"Police orders. We have to pack up and move when we get back from our tour of the city. But Wally promised we'll have a much nicer room this time, so the move will be worth it. And I'll help you pack your things so it won't be such a hassle for you."

The bus driver revved the engine. The doors closed. We nosed out into traffic. Wally stood at the front of the bus, talking into the loud speaker.

"The bus will leave us off at the *Schwanenplatz,* also known as Swan Square. You'll have a half hour to browse through some of the shops before we meet in front of the Bucherer store for our walking tour. Our local guide's name is Sonya, and she knows everything there is to know about Lucerne, so don't be afraid to ask her."

We passed lampposts hung with baskets of pink and purple flowers, old stone hotels swathed in mist, shrubs clipped with military neatness, and a steady stream of morning traffic. It was obvious we weren't in Iowa anymore. There were no combines toodling down the road at ten miles per hour. No field cultivators hogging both sides of the highway. No sport utility vehicles spinning off into the ditch as they gunned past the farm vehicles.

"Lake Lucerne is on your left," Wally announced. "There's

a promenade along the lake that'll take you right into the center of town. Mount Pilatus is across the lake. It's seven thousand feet high and is a pretty spectacular sight. The entire lake is surrounded by mountains."

At the moment, the entire lake was surrounded by fog. Not exactly a Kodak moment, but that didn't stop Dick Stolee from whipping out his camcorder in the seat in front of us and pointing it out the window. "Mount Pilatus and Lake Lucerne," he narrated into the microphone. I guess he wanted to make sure he didn't confuse this fog with the fog he'd shot from the window of the plane when we'd left Chicago.

We passed a building called the Hotel Montana, which seemed geographically misplaced here in Switzerland, but since it put me in mind of Shirley Angowski, I looked toward the back of the bus to see if I could spy her.

"Pssst." Nana elbowed me. When I turned to her, she nodded toward Dick Stolee's head. "When I first moved to Windsor City, he had a bald spot at his crown," she whispered. "I know 'cause him and Grace always used to sit in front a me in church at the eleven o'clock Mass. Then I switched to the five o'clock service on Saturday. Now the bald spot's gone. He's wearin' a rug, and a pretty good one, too. Musta bought it new for the trip."

My big purchase for the trip had been a new Kevlar umbrella with an unbreakable exoskeleton. If it didn't rain, I could use it to fend off bullets. Red, to match my raincoat. And best of all, it was automatic.

"I wonder how he keeps the thing on?" Nana puzzled. "I saw somethin' on one of them news magazines once where a man had metal snaps sewn into his scalp so's he could snap his hairpiece on. You suppose Dick went that route?"

I didn't remember him setting off the alarm at the security checkpoints in Des Moines or Chicago, so it didn't seem likely. I studied his hair with a critical eye. "It looks pretty authentic to me, Nana. Are you sure it's fake?"

"When a man Dick Stolee's age sprouts a whole new crop a hair, it's not real. It's synthetic. Maybe he had Velcro strips implanted in his head. Velcro would keep a hairpiece on real good."

As we drove past an elegant pale yellow building that was the size of a city block, Wally spoke into the loudspeaker. "The structure on our left is the Casino. Some of you might want to try your luck at the gaming tables some night, but you'll need to dress. Sport coats for the men. Sunday dresses for the ladies. The twin spires on your right are part of the Collegiate Church and date from the thirteenth century. The cathedral itself was completed in 1633. The other church of note in the area is the Jesuit Church which was built between 1666 and 1673. Sonya will be taking you there this morning."

My eyes started to glaze over with the onslaught of historic dates. I hoped he didn't intend to test us on the information later.

The bus made a right-hand turn into an area reserved for tour buses. "Our bus is number 222," Wally reminded us, as we popped out of our seats. "We'll board from this spot at twelve-fifteen. And remember, at nine-forty we'll gather in front of Bucherer to begin our walking tour."

As we left the bus, the wind picked up, blowing rain into our faces and chill air down our necks. "Wind's a good sign," said Dick Stolee, whose hair remained unruffled in the gale. "Maybe it'll blow the fog away. What time are we supposed to board the bus again?"

"Two-twenty-two," said Grace.

Dick Rassmuson snugged on his seed-corn hat and pulled a cigar out of his pocket. "I heard him say nine-forty."

"I thought nine-forty was the year they built that church back there," said Dick Teig, who would like to have donned a seed-corn hat, but the only thing big enough to fit over his head was an airplane hangar.

I rolled my eyes. The Dicks had better hope we weren't going to be tested either. As the newly appointed escort to the Windsor City group, I thought it my duty to intervene. "Our bus number is 222. We leave on our walking tour at nine-forty. We board the bus again at twelve-fifteen."

"We only have a half hour until the walking tour begins," fretted Helen Teig. Her eyebrows formed such perfect arches today, they almost looked real.

Lucille Rassmuson gnawed her bottom lip with worry. "We'd better wait in front of that store Wally talked about so we'll be on time."

"But you have a whole thirty minutes!" I reasoned. "You could get out of the rain. Browse. Buy a cup of coffee."

"Too risky," said Dick Rassmuson, who angled his umbrella over Lucille's head, lit up his cigar, and herded the other two Dicks and their wives through the rain toward the meeting place.

"Well, I'm not gonna stand out here in the rain," Nana informed me. "Bernice and me are gonna find us a chocolate shop. This is good weather for chocolate. You don't have to worry about it meltin'. You wanna come with us?"

I shook my head. "I need to see a man about a watch."

Bucherer dazzled. Opulence. Glitter. Crystal chandeliers. Gleaming display cases. Precious gems set in eighteen-karat gold and platinum. Mont Blanc pens. Reuge music boxes. After receiving directions from a clerk on the ground floor, I climbed the stairs to the watch department on the first floor. Clerks abounded behind a maze of glass counters—tall, slender, unsmiling clerks with no-nonsense faces. I inched my way toward one of the nearest counters and scanned the multitude of watches displayed on blue velvet trays.

"May I help you, Madame?" The woman looked anorexic. She was dressed in a body-hugging black dress, had a thin red slash of a mouth, and wore her hair pulled back so severely from her face, her eyes slanted halfway to her ears. Blinking was probably a major undertaking.

"I'd like to buy a watch," I said.

"Of course." With cool disdain and an elegance of movement, she unlocked the case in front of her and withdrew a tray of ladies' watches. "This is a very nice timepiece. An eighteen-karat gold Piaget. You'll note the diamonds encrusted in the bracelet and around the case frame. This sells for 36,110 Swiss francs."

I didn't have to do the conversion to American dollars to figure out I could buy a small house for the same price. I nodded. "There's no second hand. I need a watch with a second hand." A whopping lie, but it allowed me to maintain my dignity.

One of her eyebrows arched imperceptibly, no small feat considering the rest of her face hadn't moved at all. "Very well." Into the case went the Piaget tray. Out came another. "This is a popular model called the Lady Datejust. The bezel is diamond-set. The dial is mother-of-pearl with rubies. It's an eighteen-karat gold Rolex and sells for 29,400 Swiss francs."

I wrestled with the possibility that I could be in the wrong place. "Did you say gold? I can't wear gold. It turns my skin green. Do you have something a little less fancy?"

"How much less fancy?"

"Say, something that straps to your wrist and tells time?"

She shoved the tray into the case and yanked out

another. "This is called Paradiso and is made by Bucherer. It has a sapphire crystal, three interchangeable leather bracelets, and sells for 580 Swiss francs."

We were getting closer. "How much is that in American dollars?"

She punched a few numbers on a nearby calculator. "Three hundred fifty-three dollars and eighty cents."

Three months' worth of groceries. Hmm. "Do you carry Timex?"

I caught up with Nana and Bernice just as the group was departing the area for the city tour. I buttoned the top button of my tomato red raincoat and pulled my hood over my head for warmth, but there was no hiding from the wind. I was already starting to shiver.

"Did you find a watch?" Nana asked.

"I sure did," I said proudly. "And it's a beauty."

Bernice didn't find my enthusiasm contagious. "Did they forget to set the time for you? You almost missed the tour. Then what would you have done?"

Right. Like there was a chance I could lose thirty name-tagged, white-haired, camera-toting seniors wearing Pioneer Seed Corn hats and schlepping canvas bags with TRIANGLE TOURS stamped eighteen thousand times on the front and back. But I couldn't be upset with Bernice. If I'd woken up this morning with bags the size of craters under my eyes, I'd be grumpy, too.

"What do you think?" I asked Nana as I flashed my wrist in front of her face.

She made a little whistling sound through her dentures. "Gucci. Looks expensive."

"The clerk said the magic word."

"Half price?"

"Water-resistant." So what if it was going to set me back

three months rent? At least I could walk past the shower in the hotel now without breaking out in a cold sweat. Besides, the clerk hadn't believed I could spring for one of her watches, so I needed to prove that I could sink into debt just as well as the next guy. Boy, did I show her!

We snaked our way down a cobblestoned alley whose storefront windows sported the latest fall fashions on mannequins who looked more anorexic than the salesclerk in Bucherer. I had a sneaking suspicion Lane Bryant didn't do much business in Lucerne. We stopped in an open courtyard and vied for position around a woman I couldn't see for the sea of umbrellas in front of me. "Good morning!" she called out to us. "My name is Sonya." She spoke with a heavy accent that sounded kind of Russian to me. Or maybe Swedish. Somewhere close by I heard a high-pitched humming like a smoke alarm going off.

"What's that noise?" I whispered to Nana.

"Bernice's hearin' aid. Her battery must be gettin' low. Always sounds like her head's gonna blow up when that happens."

"Is anyone having trouble hearing me?" Sonya shouted.

Not now, but I would if Bernice's head decided to explode. Time to move to a better spot. I circled around the back of the crowd and stopped in front of a stone fountain that stood in the middle of the square.

"We're standing on the site of . . ." SPLAT SPLAT SPLAT! The rain pelting the cobblestones drowned out her voice. I cupped my ear to hear better.

" . . . built in 1178 . . ." SPISHHHHHHHHHHH! The fountain behind me geysered into life like an open hydrant, spewing cataracts of water in eight different directions. I hurried closer to the crowd.

" . . . it's the oldest . . ." WORRRRRRRRRSH! A man with a garden hose started power blasting the cobblestones beside me. WORRRRRRRRRSH! I leaped out of the way to avoid the spray. Good time to be washing down the pavement. I guess he figured a driving rain wouldn't do the job well enough for him. WORRRRRRRRRSH! This was nice. Not only couldn't I *see* our local guide, I couldn't *hear* her anymore either.

"Can you hear anything?" Jane Hanson appeared beside me, hunched beneath her umbrella and shivering in the cold.

"What I've gotten so far is that this place is old."

"If Andy were here, he'd know." Jane was dressed for the weather in a fatigue green belted raincoat that looked as if she'd picked it up at the Salvation Army Thrift Shop, a plastic rain bonnet, white bucks on her feet, and a camera bag over her shoulder. All she was missing was a sign around her neck that said, TOURIST. She raised her voice to be heard above the background noise. "Andy came into the drugstore last week and told me he'd done a lot of reading about the area. The Rassmusons and Teigs teased him about his cushy job, but he was very serious about his escort duties. I can't believe he's gone. He was one of our best customers. We issued him a Preferred Customer card only last year. The platinum version."

She looked genuinely sad as she continued. "I hope they don't discover that drugs played any part in his death. It's every druggist's nightmare, you know. Thinking that the prescriptions they fill might be used to cause someone's death. Poor Andy. He was always so nice to me when he'd come in to pick up a prescription. He even gave me a free ticket to that Christmas play the two of you were in. I gave him a little bouquet of flowers backstage after the play was over. He was so appreciative. He said no one had ever given him flowers before."

The crowd started to break up and move down another

alleyway in groups of two and three abreast. Jane and I followed at the back.

"That was thoughtful of you to give him flowers," I said. The only thing I'd received during the production was a ticket for parking too long in a loading zone.

"Just my way of saying thank you. He surprised me though. *Uff da.* He was so stiff and unemotional onstage. Not a very good actor, was he?"

Maybe not onstage, but in real life, Andy was a great actor. How else could he trick all these women into thinking he was a nice guy? "He had a knack for playing certain parts."

"I overheard someone say you're the one who discovered his body."

"Actually, Shirley Angowski discovered his body. I discovered Shirley."

"Shirley Angowski?"

"The blonde lady who ate dinner with us last night. Remember? The geography expert from Rhode Island."

Jane nodded recognition. "Andy was going to send me her E-mail address so I could include her name on our mailing list. I guess she'll have to give it to me herself now. We'll be running a two-for-one special on hair care products when I get back. She looks like she uses a lot of hair care products."

She had my interest now. "Two-for-one? Even on specialty items like strawberry volumizer and kiwi mousse?" The volumizer smelled so real, I counted it as a fruit exchange on my list of daily nutritional requirements.

"Andy never should have come on this trip," Jane said, as we crossed a promenade leading to the waterfront. "He put himself under too much stress wanting to be the perfect escort. All that planning, and reading, and packing. The pressure must have killed him."

He'd probably read a couple of guidebooks and thrown his underwear into a suitcase. She was right. Way too much stress for a guy to handle.

"Do you suppose his wife will fly over here to accompany the body on the trip home?"

I shook my head. "Louise is phobic about flying. Maybe one of his five ex-wives will get the urge to volunteer."

"Poor Louise is going to be grief-stricken when she hears the news," Jane brooded. "I should find a sympathy card and send it to her. You wouldn't happen to know where the nearest Hallmark card shop is, would you?"

"Nope, but I can tell you where you can find a nice watch."

We stopped along the promenade at the base of a really long covered bridge that spanned the water at a lazy forty-five-degree angle. It was constructed of weathered brown wood, and in flower boxes across its expanse was a profusion of red geraniums that brightened the pewter grayness of sky and water. From the front of the crowd I heard Sonya's voice. "This is called Chapel Bridge. It was constructed in the year 1300. As we cross over it, please note . . ."

The wind caught her words and scattered them in the opposite direction from where I was standing. It was chillier standing by the water, the wind more gusty. Cold glazed my cheeks. Cold numbed my mouth and fingertips. I turned my back to the wind.

"Whoa!" My arm nearly wrenched out of its socket as an updraft swooshed under my umbrella and snapped it inside out. The wind ripped my hood off my head. Rain spat in my face. In my eyes. Down my neck. A sudden strong gust tore at the unbreakable metal spokes and bowed them into the impossible shapes of a broken Erector Set. "My umbrella!" I fussed with the spokes, not knowing whether they should be straightened or bent. I scrunched the Kevlar panels together and tried to slide the runner back down the rod, but the damage was irreversible. The mechanism was shot. "It was brand-new," I grieved in a small voice. "It was unbreakable. It matched my raincoat." But worst of all, "It was automatic."

The group surged forward, carrying me with it. I pouted for a few seconds over the loss of my umbrella, then pitched it into a nearby trash receptacle before we maneuvered up the stairs to the bridge.

"The triangular paintings under the gables were painted in the seventeenth century by Heinrich Wagmann," Sonya began. I hugged my hood more closely around my face and shifted my feet from side to side. I couldn't hear what Sonya was saying anymore. I checked my watch to see how much more time we were scheduled to walk around. Two hours and twenty minutes. Great. In two hours and twenty minutes I'd be suffering frostbite and would need to have my fingers and toes amputated, which would be a real waste considering how much nail polish I'd bought recently. I sneaked up behind Dick Teig, hoping his head would give me some protection from the wind.

"Say, Sonya," Dick Rassmuson called out in a cloud of cigar smoke, "how much would it cost me to buy a house around here?"

"We discuss paintings this morning! In two days you may ask me about real estate."

"Then how about cars?" Dick persisted. "What's your average car sell for?"

"You may ask about automobiles when I arrive at that part of my talk on day four."

"What did you say is the name of this river we're crossing?" George Farkas wanted to know.

"I didn't say! You don't need to know that now!"

Wally had been right. Sonya knew everything there was to know about Lucerne. If you asked her on the right day, she might even be willing to share the information with you.

The wind chased us along the bridge. An octagonal stone tower rose from the depths of the river and abutted the bridge near the opposite shore. It had a witch's cap of a roof and looked like part of a castle. "This is the Water Tower," Sonya told us. "It was erected in the fourteenth century and measures 140 feet from top to bottom. The people of Lucerne have used it as a watchtower, a corner pillar of the city's fortifications, a prison, and a torture chamber."

I wondered what kind of torture the Swiss had used on their prisoners. Probably forced them to take the walking tour, with a test afterward.

By the time we left the bridge and struck out along the promenade toward a two-towered stone church, the rain had diminished to sprinkles, but the wind was still howling off the water and cutting through every layer of clothing on my body. Sonya led us to a plaza that fronted the church and positioned herself in front of an old-fashioned black wrought iron lamppost. "Behind you is the Jesuit Church . . ."

I stood on tiptoe to see her. Black coat. Black slacks. Black hair with neon yellow highlights streaked across the front. Lily Munster meets Dennis Rodman. Off to my right, Dick Teig and Dick Stolee wandered toward an area where granite steps led down into the river. I suspected that, in the summer, this would be an ideal place to sit and dangle your feet in the water, but today, I was more interested in getting inside the church to get out of the wind.

"We can proceed into the church now," Sonya instructed. "Please use the door on the left and remember, this is a church, so . . ."

"Balls!"

I turned to my right to see an object that resembled a clump of parched sod swirling in the air above Dick Stolee's head. I heard Nana whistle through her dentures behind me. "Boy, when his hair decided to fall out, it went really fast. Lookit him. Bald as a Q-Tip. Poor fella. Someone shoulda warned him about the wind here. He mighta opted for the Velcro strips."

He leaped into the air after the toupee, but it sommersaulted higher, floated for a moment, then dive-bombed straight into the river. "BALLS!" He shoved his camcorder at Dick Teig and ran to stand at the top of the stone steps, gesticulating wildly. "It's starting to sink. Son of a bitch!"

I jogged over to where he was standing as the rest of the tour group filed in a hurried line into the church. He grabbed my arm. "I paid three thousand dollars for that hairpiece, Emily!"

We stood for a moment watching it tread water. "I hope it's insured for water damage."

Dick Teig palmed the camcorder and started filming. "The river." He panned left and right then held steady. "Dick's hairpiece in the river."

Dick Stolee bent down to unlace his shoes. I eyed him curiously. "What are you doing?"

"If I lose that rug, Grace will never let me buy another. I've gotta jump in there and fish it out!"

I looked at Dick. I looked at the river. I looked at the hairpiece. "ARE YOU NUTS?"

"There's time. It's still floating." Off came one shoe.

"Can you swim?"

"Of course I can't swim. No one in Iowa can swim." Off came the other shoe.

"I bet Sonya can swim," shouted Dick Teig. "I think Sonya should do it."

I could see Dick Teig capturing the whole event on tape:

Dick Stolee diving into the river. Dick Stolee sinking to the bottom of the river. If he ran off half-cocked and killed himself, *I'd* be accused of allowing someone to drown my first day on the job. This would not be a big selling point on my résumé. Nuts.

I looked at Dick. I looked at the hairpiece. I sighed with resignation. "Put your shoes back on, Dick. I'll do it."

"You can swim?"

"'Fraid so."

"Why didn't you say something sooner? Hurry up." He jammed his feet back into his shoes and urged me down the steps. "It's getting away."

It was four feet from shore and doing a slow backstroke toward the middle of the river. I shrugged out of my raincoat and kicked off my shoes. I pulled off my cardigan. I looked up to find Dick Teig focusing the camcorder on me. "This is the plaza in front of the Jesuit Church. This is Emily getting naked on the plaza in front of the Jesuit Church."

I rushed down to stand on the last step above water level. I reached out as far as I could. It was about five feet away now and completely out of reach.

"If you wait long enough, maybe the tide will carry it to shore," Dick Teig called out. I rolled my eyes. Being a native Iowan, the only tide Dick Teig knew about was the laundry detergent, and if Helen was in charge of the wash, he wouldn't even know that much.

"Be careful when you grab it," Dick Stolee advised. "Try not to damage the part."

"How deep is this water?" All I could see were steps disappearing into liquid murk.

"Don't sweat the water. Just dive in and get it."

"I'm wearing cashmere, all right? Diving is not an option!" I was sorry already for taking this job. With mindless courage, I stepped onto the first submerged riser. "YEOOOOOOW!" My ankles and toes numbed instantaneously. I could hear Dick Teig filming behind me.

"This is Emily freezing her ass off."

I lunged for the toupee. It bobbed away on a little wave. I descended another step, and another. The water was up to my knees. I hopped to the end of the riser and stretched as far as I could. Almost. It was just beyond my fingertips. Just a little farther . . .

KERPLUNK!

I thrashed to the surface in a frenzy of sodden clothing and frozen limbs. I opened my eyes. The hairpiece was just beyond my nose. I'd taken Red Cross lifesaving. I knew how to save a drowning body, but I wasn't sure if the same technique would work on a hairpiece.

I swiped at the toupee and crushed it in my fist, then swam the four feet to shore. Dick Stolee helped me out of the water and up the stairs. He snatched his hairpiece from me. After wringing a gallon of river water out of it, he smacked it against his thigh in what I figured was the male version of the blow-dry method. "Looks like it'll be good as new. Thanks, Emily. You're all right."

"D-don't mention it." I was shivering so badly, I thought my jaw would crack. My teeth chattered. My knees knocked together.

"It's damn cold out here, Emily. You'd better get into some dry clothes." Dick looked at his watch. "And you'd better hurry. We only have a couple of hours until we head back to the bus."

I stared at his watch in horror. Unh-oh. Everything had happened so fast. Had I remembered to remove my watch before I'd done my Little Mermaid routine? I lifted my arm and reluctantly coaxed the sleeve of my sweater past my wrist. No. NOOOO!

"Something wrong with your watch?" Dick inquired.

I waved it in front of his face. "It's f-full of water. How can it be f-full of water? It's brand-new! It's w-water-resistant!"

"I think what you wanted was water*proof.* Remember that next time. Gotta run. Have to see what the big deal about the church is. Thanks again." He held his toupee up like a prized fish and posed in front of his camcorder for a final shot.

"Dick's hair," narrated Dick Teig. "Reunited with Dick's head."

"*Sacre bleu,*" I muttered as I peered down at the ruined watch that was costing me the equivalent of ten years' worth of curly fries. *Sacre bleu* is a common expression among non-Norwegians in Iowa. From what I can figure, it means, *Uff da.*

This was great. This was JUST great. How could I have let this happen? I was the student who'd been voted "Most Clever" in my high school graduating class. How could a supposedly clever person be so oblivious?

With a grunt of disgust, I squeegeed water out of my pant legs and shoehorned my feet back into my shoes. "Miss Andrew?" That voice. I knew that voice. I spun around to face Inspector Miceli. I felt liquid heat arrow downward from my navel.

"Inspector. Wh-what a surprise."

His blue eyes assumed a sooty, grayish cast in the daylight. "Someone from across the river pointed out a commotion over here."

"I saved a man's hairpiece from drowning."

He smiled that beautiful smile of his. "You must have done a thorough job. You're incredibly wet. Though I must admit, it's a look that rather becomes you." He slung off his leather trench coat and wrapped it around my shoulders.

This was getting serious. We were already at the part of the relationship where we were sharing each other's clothing. "What happened to the rest of your group?"

"Inside the church."

"You shouldn't stay out here, Emily. I'll take you back to the hotel so you can change into dry clothes."

"But I c-can't go. I need to stay with the group. I'm their new escort."

"You need to go back to the hotel," he said matter-of-factly. "With me."

"Okay." Could I play hard to get, or what? "But I'll need to stop inside the church and tell my grandmother where I'm going."

"You go on to my car. I'll tell your grandmother."

I gathered up my cardigan and raincoat. We'd only walked a half dozen steps when Etienne's trench coat started making a sound. I looked down at the coat, startled. "Is it my ears, or is your coat chirping?"

"My cell phone. Excuse me, please."

He dug the phone out of his pocket, then walked a short distance away to converse. When he returned, he wasn't smiling.

"Bad news?" I asked.

"Your Mr. Simon. It appears he might have died from something other than a severe asthma attack."

I remembered what Jane Hanson had said. "You mean, the stress of wanting to be the perfect escort really did kill him?" I felt a trill of alarm. I was only twenty-nine. I had a lot more living to do. Maybe I should rethink this escort thing.

"Something more deliberate than stress killed him, Miss Andrew. There are indications that your Mr. Simon may have been murdered."

CHAPTER 5

"Murdered?" Sure, Andy had been a lowlife. He'd thought of no one but himself, hurt countless women, and ruined a lot of lives. But if every man who acted like that was murdered, we'd be a planet of Amazon women. "How could he be murdered? He's from Iowa. Iowans aren't murdered. Iowans die from overdosing on bacon, or from being crushed in customer stampedes when Fareway runs a special on Iowa chops."

"I can't give you details, but I will tell you that his death appears more suspicious now than it did at five o'clock this morning."

"You think someone on the tour killed him?"

"In a majority of homicides, the victim and his killer are usually acquainted. We have one possible lead to follow, but should that turn out to be a dead end, do you know anyone on the tour who would have a motive to kill him?"

He had me there. I was acquainted with many of the seniors in the group, but if one of them despised Andy enough to kill him, I didn't know who it would be. I shook my head.

"When we have the results back from serology, we'll know more. Until then I can only caution you to watch yourself, Miss Andrew."

"Watch myself?" I felt my stomach drop to my knees. "Am I in danger?"

"What you assumed to be the sounds of sexual acrobatics last night in Mr. Simon's room may well have been the sounds of Mr. Simon being murdered. If the perpetrator thinks you heard something that could implicate him . . ."

He left the sentence unfinished, but his expression spoke volumes. Unh-oh. This wasn't good.

"I'd appreciate your keeping this information to yourself until our findings are more conclusive, Miss Andrew. There's no sense causing panic among the people in your tour group."

What about causing panic in me? I was going to be constantly looking over my shoulder now, expecting some friendly acquaintance to stick a knitting needle through my ear. "You think the killer might strike again?"

"Until we discover the motive for the murder, we've no way of knowing that. But as the group's escort, you should be alerted to the possibility that someone on your tour could be capable of murder."

I felt honored to be taken into his confidence, but the honor did nothing to calm my frazzled nerves. How could I keep this to myself? "Can I tell my grandmother about this? I promise she won't tell anyone. Telling a secret to Nana is the same as stashing gold in Fort Knox and throwing away the key. I think she should know. After all, if the killer suspects I heard something, he might think Nana heard something, too."

Inspector Miceli nodded. "If that will allow you to sleep

better, by all means, share the information with your grandmother. I urge both of you to be aware of your surroundings at all times and to report anything that looks suspicious." He handed me a card with his name and office phone number on it. "I can be reached here anytime, day or night. If the need arises, call me."

He dropped me off at the side entrance to the hotel. Leaving his trench coat behind, I ran through the drizzle into the welcoming warmth of the lobby. "Room thirty-three-ten," I said to the clerk at the front desk.

He checked the grid of slots behind him. "Did you leave your key in the box this morning?"

"Yes, I did."

"It's not here." He checked the box on the front desk to find it empty. "It's not here either."

"Well, I put it in the box before I left. Where else could it be?" Then it occurred to me. What if the killer had been watching my movements? What if he'd snatched my key from the box after I'd deposited it there this morning? What if he was waiting in my room, intent on killing me, too? Oh. My. God.

I could see the nattily attired clerk studying my tangled nest of wet hair and sodden top. He arched an eyebrow at me. "It must be raining outside. We sell items for such occasions in Lucerne. I believe you call them umbrellas."

I would have gritted my teeth if they hadn't been chattering so hard. "How about you send someone up with a master key to open the door for me?" And to check out the room for maniacal killers before I set foot in it.

"Your name, Madame?"

"Emily Andrew."

"If you'll kindly have a seat in the lobby, I'll see what I can do about locating your key."

In my present state, I didn't dare sit on the room's velvet

sofas, so I threw on my cardigan and raincoat for warmth and stood in front of the lobby window, watching the mist and fog cloak the daylight. I regretted having trashed my umbrella. With a killer on the loose, I might need a weapon. And even though a broken umbrella wasn't in the same league as a hand grenade, I bet I could poke someone's eye out with it, which would be eerily prophetic since my mother had been warning me about the likelihood of that happening from the time I'd turned six.

I supposed I could use my new watch as a weapon, but giving the killer the incorrect time didn't seem threatening enough. I needed something with more punch.

"Emily?"

I turned to find Shirley Angowski heading across the Oriental carpet toward me, and she wasn't looking so hot. Her hair was flat, her eyes were puffy, and she was wearing a navy blouse with black pants, which was as big a fashion faux pas as wearing blue-green with olive green. I figured she must be really rattled about Andy to have her color sense thrown so far off kilter.

"What happened to you?" she asked, staring at my hair.

"Midmorning dip in the river. I don't recommend it as a scheduled activity."

"I'm so glad you're here," she said, taking my hand for comfort. "Everyone is out on that tour this morning, so I'm all alone. I don't know what to do with myself."

I noticed she'd done something with herself. Her fingernails were no longer the color of Pepto-Bismol. They were black as licorice Jelly Bellies. "Nice color," I said. "I sometimes do black on Halloween."

She held out one hand so we could both admire it. "It's called *Galactica*. It's part of the Millennium collection. I did it out of respect for Andy."

"Did you name this one?"

Shirley shook her head. "Revlon assigned someone else to do the Millennium collection. I don't know much about outer space. I don't even know where the Milky Way is."

No surprise there.

She sighed. "What am I supposed to tell people about last night, Emily? I'm so embarrassed. Andy invited me to the hotel lounge after dinner, and while he was at the bar ordering our drinks, some old geezer who looked like Yasser Arafat hit on me."

Unh-oh. The Italian pervert strikes again.

"I was very polite and told the guy I was with someone else; but his English was pretty minimal, so I don't know if he understood me. He just stood there jabbering at me, refusing to leave. Then Andy came back with our drinks and told the guy to leave, but he still refused, so they had words, Andy motioned for the bartender, and the old guy got kicked out on his ear. And he wasn't happy about it, Emily. You should have seen the evil look he gave us on his way out. It gave me the willies. I was so nervous after that, Andy suggested we retire to someplace more private, so we went up to his room and I helped him practice lines for a play he's going to audition for."

"Did you tell the police about the man in the lounge?"

"I sure did. And I gave them a really good description, right down to his trench coat and knobby knees."

Was this the lead Inspector Miceli had mentioned? "His name is Nunzio."

Shirley gasped. "How do you know that? Did he hit on you, too?"

"He hit on my grandmother."

Shirley nodded as if this behavior were perfectly normal. "He must have a thing for older women. I better call the police and give them his name. Anyway, Emily, Andy was very gentlemanly when we were in his room. Nothing happened. Honest. He didn't do a thing wrong except flub a few of his lines."

"How was his delivery?"

"Pretty stiff, but I didn't want to hurt his ego, so I didn't tell him. When I was about to leave, he told me if I felt like coming back anytime during the night, he'd leave his door unlocked as an open invitation. All I'd have to do is walk in."

That made sense. If he'd given her his key, she could have been standing in the hall all night trying to unlock the door.

"He said he hoped I did come back, because he sensed we were soul mates. That we shared a bond that transcended space and time."

I tried not to roll my eyes, but they flew up into my head despite all my efforts to the contrary. I had to hand it to ole Andy. What he lacked in originality, he made up for in consistency.

"Why did you roll your eyes?" Shirley asked.

"If there was a chance Andy could get a woman into bed, he'd always claim she was his soul mate."

"You mean, I'm not the only one he said that to?"

"I don't want to seem insensitive, but no, you weren't."

Shirley removed her glasses to dab at the tears that had sprung into her eyes. "But, he seemed so sincere. He said he was trapped in a bad marriage with a woman who refused to have sex with him. He said he knew that making love to me would erase all the hurt he'd suffered through the years. He seemed so wounded, so forlorn. I . . . I . . ."

"Couldn't refuse?"

She nodded. "He made me feel so special. Ordinarily, I'd never sleep with a married man, but he told me he planned on filing divorce papers when he got back home, so I thought, what the heck. I'm fifty-nine years old. What am I saving it for? If we hit it off, I was even going to give him a pedicure later in the week. I feel like such a fool. But I suppose I'd feel like a bigger fool if he'd kicked off while we were doing it. I've heard stories about how a man's thing can get stuck inside you if he dies all of a sudden. Then someone has to call the fire department and they use a special instrument to pry the two of you apart. I think it's the Jaws of Life or something. Do you think they have the Jaws of Life in Switzerland?"

"They seem to have everything in Switzerland. Except sunshine and edible food. Look, Shirley, Andy's death wasn't your fault, so at the risk of sounding trite, I'd advise you not to dwell on what happened last night. You were simply in the wrong place at the wrong time. Bad karma. It happens to lots of people."

She apparently liked that answer because she stuffed her tissue back into her pocket and straightened her shoulders. "You're right. I'm going to get on with my vacation and not feel guilty or embarrassed about what happened last night. I probably did Andy a favor by finding him like I did. He might have been putrefying in there for a long time otherwise." She squeezed my hand. "Thanks for talking to me, Emily. I was going to skip the group picture at one o'clock, but you've made me feel so much better, I think I'll go after all. See you there."

Okay. So being the quintessential escort had its rewards. It felt nice to brighten someone's day, and I especially liked it that people felt inclined to spill their guts to me. Of course, I didn't believe for a minute that Andy intended to serve divorce papers on Louise. She was his cash cow. No way would he cut her loose. He'd lied to Shirley about his intended divorce and ended up dead. I could hear my mother now. "See what happens when you break one of the Ten Commandments?" Of course, in Andy's case, he'd broken more than one, so maybe it was the cumulative effect that got him.

One thing was for sure. He never should have left his door unlocked, especially after he'd just humiliated a man in public. Another clear-cut case of a man discarding common sense and thinking with his Mr. Peppy. It *had* to have been Mr. Nunzio who killed him. Granted, killing a man because he'd gotten you thrown out of a lounge was pretty extreme, but Nunzio was Italian, and Italians were notorious for their explosive tempers. He had a motive, and Andy's leaving his room unlocked had given him the opportunity. I just hoped the police dragged Nunzio in for questioning quickly. I didn't like the idea of having to watch my back with everyone in the group, but until the police were certain and charged the guy, that's exactly what I'd be forced to do.

With a possible suspect identified, I was beginning to feel a little calmer, until I remembered that my key was missing. Oh. My. God. Was it Nunzio who'd stolen my key out of the box this morning? Could he be in my room this very moment waiting to—

"Miss Andrew?" An unfamiliar female clerk motioned to me from the front desk. "I believe we have everything in order now. You should have mentioned you were in the room the police cordoned off. We put your key in a special place to remind us that you can't go up there."

"So no one stole it?" My knees wobbled with relief. I felt a hundred pounds lighter . . . for a millisecond. "What do you mean I can't go up there? Look at me! I need to change my clothes!"

"Hotel policy."

"I could come down with pneumonia and die!"

"There's a hand dryer in the ladies' toilet by the dining room."

If I still had my umbrella, her eye would be history. "All my stuff is in that room." I lowered my voice and skewered her with an icy glare. "I need my stuff."

"Sorry."

This wasn't going well. I decided I'd have to appeal to her feminine nature, provided she had one. "Are you telling me I'm going to have to go around looking like this all week?" I opened my raincoat to reveal the grossly distorted shape of my cashmere sweater.

Her lips did a little quirky thing, like a silent, "Euwww." She looked over her shoulder to the main office, then slid the key to room 3310 across the desk toward me. "I'll give you a half hour. Pack up your belongings and leave your suitcases outside your door. I'll have a bellman transfer them to your new room when we decide where we're going to put you."

Now we were getting somewhere. The only problem nagging me as I rushed up the stairs was, how could I unlock my door in a half hour's time?

Luck was with me. The policemen who had been in the corridor this morning were still there. "Excuse me. Could you possibly help me with my door again?"

The officer who had helped me earlier shook his head. "I'm sorry, Madame. You can't go in there."

Oh yeah? "I've been given permission to pack my belongings."

"By whom?"

"Inspector Miceli." Okay. So he hadn't exactly given me permission. But he *had* suggested I change my clothes. Close enough.

He exchanged a look with his fellow officer, shrugged, then opened my door for me. I checked Nana's travel alarm. Eleven-twenty-nine. I ran into the bathroom to take a hot shower but had to scrap the idea when I realized the only towels we had were the ones I'd used to mop up the floor yesterday. Yuck. I stripped down to my skin, fired up my blow-dryer, and for the next ten minutes blew hot air all over my body. When I was done on both sides, I threw on the warmest clothes I could find—tights, heavy cotton socks, wool slacks, a cropped Berber pullover sweater, and thick-soled Nubuck walking shoes, then opened both our suitcases and started pitching things inside. I passed the mirror and glanced at my reflection. "EHH!" My hair was frizzed straight out like the bride of Frankenstein, but I had no time to fuss with it now.

When I had all our things packed, I gave the room the once-over, locked the suitcases, and wheeled them out into the hall. Before I closed the door, I flipped on the television and checked the time again. Eleven-fifty-eight. I had a whole minute to spare. God, I was good.

I gave my key back to the front desk clerk, who informed me that I should have my new room assignment within the hour. "If you'll kindly wait in the lobby, Madame."

It was noontime, and now that I'd caught my breath and was dry again, I realized I was hungry. "Does the dining room have any luncheon specials?"

"The dining room isn't open for lunch."

Of course. That would be too convenient. "Is there any-place nearby where I can pick up a burger and fries?"

"You mean, like a McDonald's Happy Meal?"

"Exactly."

"There's a McDonald's in Zurich."

Even more convenient. Since hiking to Zurich wasn't in my travel plans for the afternoon, I retreated to the lobby and examined the contents of my shoulder bag. Kleenex. Lipstick. Nail file. Passport. Tic Tacs! I poured a half dozen into my hand and popped them into my mouth. Address book. Dental floss. A lone LifeSaver® hairy with fuzz.

Looked like pineapple. I didn't like pineapple. I dropped it into an ashtray. A bag of airplane peanuts. Yum. I'd save those for dessert.

Hearing the rumble of a diesel engine, I looked toward the side entrance of the lobby. The door flew open, and Nana trooped through, followed by the rest of the tour group. From the smile on her face, I guessed she'd just muscled past George Farkas again to be first off the bus. I waved her into the lobby and patted the seat beside me.

"You're back a little early, aren't you?" I asked.

"We skipped the last three sights on the tour because the Rhode Islanders were cold and the rest of us were gettin' antsy we'd miss the bus."

I shook my head. "The point of this trip is NOT to prove how punctual you are. The point is to see Switzerland, to sample the culture, to live a little."

"Tell you the truth, Emily, Bernice's hearin' aid was hummin' so loud, I couldn't hear a thing Sonya was sayin'. Sittin' on the bus wasn't so bad. At least we got outta the rain. And Wally conducted a nice sing-along." She tilted her head and gave me a quizzical look. "I don't recall your hair lookin' like that at breakfast this mornin', dear. Your mother's been hintin' that I'm losin' my memory. Don't tell her, but I think she may be right."

"Trust me. You're fine." I looked around the lobby. There were a few New Englanders milling around the front desk, but most people had headed back to their rooms so we were pretty much alone until Bernice spotted Nana and headed in our direction. She sat down at the end of the sofa and let out an audible sigh.

"I need to catch my breath before I head upstairs," she sputtered.

"Did you enjoy the tour?" I asked.

"What?"

"I said, DID YOU ENJOY THE TOUR?"

She gave me a vacuous smile. Nana caught my eye.

"She took her hearin' aid out, dear. If you want an answer, you'd have better luck talkin' to a kumquat."

That was handy. I exchanged vacuous smiles with Bernice and returned my attention to Nana. "I have something to tell you, and you have to *promise* to keep it to yourself."

She made a motion of locking her lips and throwing away the key. "I promise."

"I talked to Inspector Miceli this morning, and he told me that Andy's death looks suspicious. They think he might have been murdered."

"No."

"Yes. And the killer could be your Mr. Nunzio."

"No!"

"Yes. And what's worse, if it's not Nunzio, it could be someone on the tour."

"No kiddin'."

"And if the killer thinks we overheard something in Andy's room last night, he could be after us, too!"

Nana froze up like the Tin Man in a rain shower. "That's not good."

"So Inspector Miceli said we should watch our backs, and if we see anything suspicious, we should report it. And for heaven's sake, if you should see Mr. Nunzio again, don't stop to chat. Run!"

"But he seemed like such a nice man." She looked thoughtful for a moment. "You think we should arm ourselves?"

"With what?"

She gave her finger waves a slow, pensive scratch before pointing an excited finger at me. "Defense spray."

"Like mace?"

"Like hair spray."

Hmm. That might work. A blast of aerosol to the eyes wouldn't cause irreparable damage to anyone's eyesight, but it might slow them down. Slowing down was good. "Great idea. I have some in my suitcase."

"We better go up to the room then. I gotta figure out the best place to stash it—my fanny pack or my bra. I'm kinda leanin' toward my fanny pack though. My bra's pretty crowded already."

"With what?"

"Two thousand dollars' worth a traveler's cheques. But it's my own fault. I should've asked for somethin' other than twenties."

"About the room, Nana. We don't actually have a room right now." I gave her the scoop on my mad dash to pack our bags and the desk clerk's promise to have our luggage moved to our new room.

"Well, room or not, I need a potty break and fast. I'm an old lady. I got needs."

"There's a ladies' room down that way." I pointed toward the dining room. "You want me to go with you?"

"That's all right, dear. I'll take Bernice with me. She's probably caught her breath by now."

Fifteen minutes later, most of the Rhode Islanders had returned to the lobby, but many of our group were still missing, including Nana and Bernice. Concerned, I headed for the rest room.

I pushed on the door. It opened a quarter inch, then slammed shut. I tried again, and this time it didn't open at all. "Nana?" Could she have fainted . . . or worse? Was it her body that was blocking my entry? I pounded on the door. "Nana!"

I heard the toilet flush. Then I heard laughter. And clapping. "Who's in there!" I yelled. "Let me in!"

The door suddenly opened, and I was sucked into the crowd that was packed shoulder to shoulder in the small rest room. The toilet flushed again. More laughter. More clapping. Cameras flashing. "Nana? Are you in here, Nana!"

I came nose to nose with Helen Teig. "Have you seen my grandmother?"

"Stall number three," she said as she brushed past me.

I slithered through the crowd to find Nana holding open the stall door and directing traffic. "Time's up for you, Bernice. Come on now. It's Grace's turn."

What in the world? Was Nana giving toilet-training instructions to all of Iowa?

"Emily! Move aside there. Let my granddaughter through. You gotta see this, Emily." She flushed the toilet. The seat was shaped like a big doughnut, and when the water stopped running, it started moving in a clockwise direction all around the bowl, self-sanitizing itself as it passed through some kind of heating mechanism. "Just like a self-cleanin' oven, only quicker."

Grace Stolee pressed the button on her husband's camcorder. "Revolving toilet seat in the Grand Palais Hotel."

The city of Lucerne had to be a thousand years old. There were churches, and fountains and antiquities in Lucerne that most people would kill to see. But not my group. My group was squeezed into the rest room of the Grand Palais Hotel snapping photos of a revolving toilet seat.

You had to love a group that could find so much enjoyment in life's simple pleasures.

"The bus is getting ready to leave!" I hollered above the din. Gasps. Watch-checking. Louder gasps. Then I found myself being spun around and dragged forward as the ladies scrambled toward the door. Even the novelty of a revolving toilet seat wasn't worth being late over.

* * *

"Mark Twain called Lucerne's Lion Monument, 'the saddest and most poignant piece of rock in the world.'" Wally directed our attention to the mammoth dying lion that was carved in deep relief in the sandstone cliff before us. "The lion is twenty-seven feet long and is protecting a French fleur-de-lis. The monument was dedicated in 1821 and honors the Swiss Guards who died in Paris in 1792 trying to protect the life of Marie Antoinette."

The lion's massive paw hung over a shallow reflecting pool at the base of the cliff. I dug a penny out of my change purse and tossed it into the water.

"Did you make a wish?" asked Nana.

"Yup."

"What'd you wish for?"

I visored my hand over my eyes to shield the rain from my face. "Sun."

"Okay, people!" Wally called out. "This is your Kodak moment. Short people in front. Tall people in back. No umbrellas and no hoods."

"Did you notice it's raining?" Dick Rassmuson griped.

"You'll only get wet for a few seconds," said Wally.

"The photo's not gonna come out in the rain," Dick persisted.

Wally sighed. "We can digitally remove the rain."

I slatted my eyes and looked skyward. Too bad they couldn't digitally remove the fog.

The Rhode Islanders all clustered on one side and the Iowans on the other, as if the Great Wall of China stood between them. I stood between Nana and Lucille Rassmuson in the front row of the Iowa side, waiting for the photographer to snap his photo. "So who do you think killed Andy?" Lucille whispered to me.

I pivoted my head around so fast, I heard my spine

creak. "What?" How did she find out? No one was supposed to know.

"The police'll probably accuse one of us," Dick Rassmuson said from behind me. "When a fella dies, they always point the finger at his friends."

"Sometimes they blame the butler," offered Jane Hanson, who was sandwiched between Dick Rassmuson and Grace Stolee. "The butler does it in a lot of English mystery novels. Unfortunately, our store doesn't carry English mysteries anymore, but we still have a good selection of romance and male adventure novels."

"Andy didn't have a butler," came George Farkas's voice from somewhere to my right. "He had a housekeeper."

"And he sure as hell didn't have no friends," said Dick Teig. "He ran too hot and cold to have friends. He'd be all palsy-walsy with you one minute, and ignore you the next."

"All that theater business of his was the blame," Bernice said with authority. She'd obviously freshened the batteries in her hearing aid. "Community theater is just like Hollywood. You get real close to folks for a few weeks of rehearsal, then the production ends, and everyone goes his separate way. He didn't bond with anyone. All his friendships had to be disposable. Use 'em and lose 'em. Isn't that right, Helen?"

All eyes riveted on Helen Teig, who remained motionless for a beat before turning her head slowly to regard us. Helen had apparently remained in the rain too long because her right eyebrow had disappeared, leaving her with a grease pencil arch over only one eye. Not a good look for her.

"I'm not sure what you mean by that," Helen replied tartly.

"Your niece was in a play with Andy, wasn't she?" Bernice prodded. "The one about the London barber who gave his customers more than just a haircut and a shave. Didn't Andy pull the use 'em and lose 'em routine on her?"

Oh. My. God. Was Helen's niece the actress Andy wooed in *Sweeney Todd*? The actress who'd tried to commit suicide after he dumped her? I felt my spine prickle but didn't know whether to blame it on chills or the raindrops drizzling down my neck.

Helen turned back to the photographer. "I don't know what you're talking about, Bernice."

"Sure you do. Emily was in that play, too. You remember Helen's niece, don't you, Emily?"

"Ahhhh . . ." As my mouth was hanging open, Wally yelled, "Smile!" and a blinding light flashed from the photographer's camera.

"Jeez, I hate those flashes," complained Dick Stolee, who was looking pretty good with his toupee reattached. "I got spots dancing in front of my eyes now."

"Those aren't spots," said his wife. "They're floaters. I hope you haven't detached your retina again."

"Don't anyone move," instructed Wally. "We'll take one more picture."

"Waste of film," Dick Rassmuson grumbled. "Can't they see it's raining? Let's hurry it up. I need a cigar."

Nana looked up at me. "I think the rain's helped your hair, Emily. It's not so flyaway anymore."

Hard for hair to be flyaway when it's soaking wet. "You told," I accused in a stage whisper. "You told everyone what Inspector Miceli told us to keep under wraps."

Nana looked shocked. "I most certainly did not. You saw me lock my lips and throw away the key. That's good as swearin' on a Bible."

"Then how do they KNOW?"

"I thought you told 'em."

"I would *never* tell them."

"Well, I didn't tell 'em."

I pondered this. "If you didn't tell them, and I didn't tell them, who did tell them?"

We looked at each other. We narrowed our eyes. We swiveled our heads around to glare at Bernice.

"My hearing aid!" cried Bernice suddenly. "It's not in my ear anymore. It's gotta be on the ground someplace. Don't anyone move."

I glanced toward the ground and spied the device near the toe of Nana's shoe. "I'll get it." It probably wasn't even a real hearing aid. It was probably an ultrasonic eavesdropping device. She'd no doubt heard every word of my private exchange with Nana and lost no time spreading the news to everyone else. I bent down and picked it up.

"Smile!" yelled Wally. Snap. Flash. "Great pictures everyone. We're all done. You can get back on the bus now."

While I was still in my scooch with my palm open, inspecting the piece of plastic, Bernice walked past and snatched the thing out of my hand, as if she didn't want me to get too close a look. "Thanks, Emily." And before I could straighten up, the whole place emptied out in a mad stampede for the bus. I lost sight of Nana, but, as usual, from the depths of the crowd I could hear her yell something about saving me a seat.

I noted Helen Teig hustling around George Farkas and mulled over what I'd just learned. Helen's niece had tried to commit suicide because of Andy, which meant Helen could be out for revenge. She seemed the type who could hold a grudge, but was she the kind of person who could allow a grudge to lead to murder?

Hmm. Revenge was a definite a motivation for committing murder. Helen had a motive, and Andy's door being unlocked had provided her the opportunity.

I scuffled toward the waiting bus with a sinking feeling in my stomach. I wondered what I'd done with the card Inspector Miceli had given me this morning. I didn't want to make the call, but he probably needed to know that someone other than Mr. Nunzio had a reason to want Andy dead.

CHAPTER 6

"You're in room 4624, Miss Andrew," said the front desk clerk as she handed me the key. "I apologize for any inconvenience we might have caused you."

I grabbed Nana by the arm and sashayed her to the elevator. Three-quarters of our group had decided to be dropped off in town to shop, so only a handful of us had returned to the hotel.

"You seem awful excited, Emily. They must've given us a real spiffy room this time."

We stepped inside the elevator. I punched the button for level four. "It's not excitement. It's anxiety. I don't want to point fingers, but if Mr. Nunzio didn't murder Andy, I think I know who did."

"My money's on Helen Teig," Nana said. "She was probably holdin' a grudge against Andy for what he done to her niece, and it kept festerin' and festerin' until she couldn't stand it no longer. I can't say I like her doin' him in, but if Andy had hurt you like that, Emily, I'd probably wanna do him in, too. I can't figure out how she done it though.

There was no blood on the scene, so you know she didn't riddle him with bullets. I didn't see no ligature marks around his neck, so you know she didn't strangle him. She might a suffocated him, but they'll have to wait for the results of the autopsy protocol to decide that."

I stared down at Nana. "Autopsy protocol?"

"That's the file tellin' you everythin' there is to know about how someone died."

"How do you know about autopsy protocols?"

"*Investigative Report,* dear. You can catch it on A & E almost every night at eight o'clock Central Time, nine Eastern."

That did it. I was going to have to start watching more TV . . . and thinking like Columbo. I'd even cooked up a possible theory. "Do you suppose someone might have tampered with Andy's inhaler? I saw a movie once where a killer discharged the spray from a woman's inhaler so when the woman had an asthma attack, the apparatus was empty. She nearly died."

"That woulda been the most obvious way to do him in. And tidy, too. No screamin'. No fistfights. No splattered blood. Just release the spray or muck up the chemical balance in his Pirbuterol Acetate. But it don't do much good for all this second-guessin', does it? The police won't know a thing until the serology and toxicology reports come back."

Serology report. Right. I knew that.

"So who do you think killed him, dear?"

Considering all my years of higher education, it was deflating to be scooped by a woman with an eighth-grade education and a satellite dish, but not wanting to steal her thunder, I decided to take the high road. "Well, it could be one of several people, but maybe I shouldn't elaborate until I know more." After all, maybe I'd reached my conclusion too quickly. Maybe there was incriminating evidence about other people that hadn't surfaced yet. Maybe Bernice had mentioned the incident with Helen's niece to throw us off the scent. But *whose* scent?

"George Farkas was thinkin' a gettin' a pool together to guess the killer," Nana went on, "but he said he'd need more suspects than Helen to make it worth his while."

"That's terrible!"

"That's what I told him. Between you and me, Emily, I think George has a gamblin' problem."

"Why do you say that?"

"Because he shows up at Holy Redeemer every Thursday night to play bingo."

"So do you."

"But I have an excuse. I'm Catholic. Bingo's part a my religion. George don't have an excuse. He's Lutheran."

I shook my head. "I can't afford to be in a pool anyway. I have to buy a new watch."

"You just *bought* a new watch. Don't it keep good time?"

I coaxed my sleeve up my arm to regard my watch face. The hands had stopped at 10:13. "It'll give me great time twice a day, but when it's not ten-thirteen, I'm going to have a problem."

When the elevator stopped, I pushed open the door and escorted Nana into the hall. We struck out along a corridor to our right, the motion sensors causing overhead lights to blink on as we passed, and followed a maze of hallways until we reached the rooms in the 4620s. "It's right up ahead," said Nana. "That's my suitcase outside the door there."

Yup. There was Nana's suitcase.

"Where's your suitcase, Emily?"

Obviously not in the hall. I slid the room key into the slot, turned the knob and . . . CLICK. Okay. So I wasn't a fast study. But I was trainable.

The room was dark as a cave. "Hit the light, dear. I can't see a thing."

I fumbled for the switch on the wall and squinted when light diffused throughout the room.

"Well, would you look at that," said Nana. I suspected she was referring to the fact that this room was exactly like the other room, with one exception.

There were no windows.

And from what I could see in a quick visual scan, no luggage either. Delightful. I wheeled Nana's suitcase into the room and picked up the phone.

"Front desk," said the woman on the other end.

"This is Emily Andrew in 4624. We're in the wrong room again."

A pause. "What room are you supposed to be in?"

"A standard room."

Computer keys clicking. "Room 4624 *is* a standard room."

"N-no, no. I want the standard room with the four-poster bed, the little balcony, and the Jacuzzi."

"There are no standard rooms with those features. What you're describing is a prestige suite."

"Okay. I'll take one of those."

"There's a notation in our computer from your tour leader clearly specifying that you be assigned a standard room. If you wish to make a change, you'll need to contact him to change the request in the computer. Is there anything else, Madame?"

A slight pain started throbbing between my eyes. "Yes, there's something else. You were supposed to deliver two pieces of luggage to this room. Only one arrived."

Silence.

"Hello?"

"That's impossible. One moment please." Whispering.

Mumbling. "The bellman assures me he delivered *two* pieces of luggage to your new room, Ms. Andrew."

"He might have delivered two, but one is missing. Mine. It's a twenty-six-inch tapestried pullman on wheels."

"We'll look into it and get back to you immediately."

I hung up the phone and proceeded to massage my temples. "Is international travel always this difficult?"

"I never been outside the country before, dear, but it don't seem too difficult on *Lifestyles of the Rich and Famous.* Should I unpack?"

"You might as well. We can't go anywhere until Wally changes a notation in the computer."

Nana looked apprehensive. "I hope they find your suitcase soon. I'm gonna feel a whole lot better about defendin' myself when I can get my hands on that hair spray a yours."

I thought about calling Inspector Miceli to tell him my suspicions about Helen, but decided to hold off until I gathered more evidence. Bernice would probably offer Helen up on a platter during police questioning anyway, so Helen would be scrutinized at some point in time. However, if I was patient and said nothing, I'd be spared looking like a complete lunatic in front of Inspector Miceli if everyone, including me, was wrong.

I'd just unlocked Nana's suitcase when I heard footsteps in the hall, followed by an insistent KNOCK KNOCK KNOCK. I checked the peephole and threw open the door. I seized Wally's arm and yanked him into the room. "*How* could you think we'd want a room without windows?"

"Hey, you asked for a standard room. That's what I got you."

"You couldn't have *guessed* I was a little confused about the room rating system? You couldn't have *guessed* I was asking for an *up*grade instead of a *down*grade?"

"Go ahead. Blame me. You women are all alike. You think every man has the ability to read your minds."

My ex-husband used to accuse me of the same thing. He was right, of course. All women expect men to be mind readers. I figured it was biological. "Well, you might have asked!"

"And my mother wonders why I've never married."

"You need to change the room request you made in the computer."

"Sure. Why not? Are you going to tell me what kind of room you want this time, or am I supposed to guess?"

"We want a room like the Rassmusons and Teigs."

Wally shook his head. "They're in prestige suites. They requested standards, but their reservation got lost in some computer glitch, so the hotel was forced to give them upgrades. Moving to a prestige suite will cost you."

"That's all right," Nana piped up. "I'm rich."

He shrugged. "It's your dime." He handed me a large manila envelope. "These are the medical forms I mentioned earlier. All you Windsor City people filled them out, so you know what I'm talking about."

The bank had asked us to write down any medical conditions we had, what prescription and nonprescription drugs we were taking with us, and our primary physician's name, in case of medical emergencies.

"I hope I don't have to tell you these forms are very sensitive and should be held in the strictest confidence. If any of this information gets into the wrong hands, we could be looking at major litigation."

I'd written on my form that I have flat feet and was packing bottles of Excedrin and Advil. It was comforting to know that if word leaked out, I could sue the hell out of Triangle Tours. "What am I supposed to do with the forms after the trip is over?"

"Return the envelope to Mr. Erickson at the bank, and he'll see that they're destroyed. And speaking of Mr. Erickson, I just got off the phone with him. Apparently, when he went over to his sister's house to tell her about Andy, she wasn't home, so he tried her cell phone. You'll never guess where she was when she answered."

There was only one place I knew would be considered a surprise if Louise Simon were found there. "Wal-Mart?"

"Vancouver. She was about to board a cruise ship for Alaska."

"Vancouver? How did she get to Vancouver? She's afraid to fly. That's why she didn't come to Switzerland."

"She didn't come to Switzerland because she had plans to take a cruise with another man while Andy was away."

"No," said Nana.

"Yes," said Wally, "and furthermore, when Mr. Erickson told her about Andy's death, she said she wasn't going to fly halfway around the world to baby-sit a corpse. She said Andy might have ruined her life, but he wasn't going to ruin her vacation."

When a man spends his entire married life cheating on his wife, I guess he can't expect special treatment when he drops dead. "So what's going to happen now?"

"Mr. Erickson will make all the arrangements to have Andy's body flown back to the States, and Louise won't have to file for divorce after all."

"She was planning to divorce Andy?"

"That's what she told her brother. She said, and I quote, 'I'm through bankrolling this theater bullshit just so he can boink a bevy of buxom bimbos, then lie his buns off about it.'"

I was impressed with Louise's use of alliteration, especially given her pronounced overbite. But the revelation that she was ticked off about Andy's philandering caused a lightbulb to go on over my head. If she'd decided she no longer wanted to be married to him, would she entertain a way to get rid of him that would spare her having to fork over half her assets and putting herself through an embarrassing public divorce? Would she actually resort to murder? But how? She was an ocean away, which seemed like a pretty good alibi to me. The only way she could have caused his murder was if she'd gotten to him before he went away, or arranged for someone else to do the deed for her. Could *she* have been the one to tamper with his asthma medication? Or could she have hired someone who had a score to settle with him to pop him for her? Someone on the tour? Someone like . . .

Helen Teig? Oh. My. God. Had Louise and Helen joined forces in some kind of twisted triangle to give Andy his due? Did they both have a hand in killing him, like in Agatha Christie's tale of murder on the Orient Express? I hadn't read the book, but I'd seen the movie a really long time ago.

"I would have brought you the medications the bank gave Andy to take along with him, but the police confiscated all the drugs in his room. So if someone comes to you with a headache now, they're on their own, unless you brought extra aspirin and cold medication along with you. And I guess you'd know enough not to give appetite suppressants to someone on heart medication."

Appetite suppressants? Right. Like someone would actually need a pill to help them resist eating the food in this place. "I'll be sure to check out the medical forms before I dispense aspirin to anyone. And there's one more thing you need to look into. My luggage is missing."

Wally gave me one of those "Aw, go on" hand gestures. "They probably delivered it to someone else's room by accident. Not to worry. It'll show up. There's no crime in Switzerland, so you know wherever it is, it's safe."

When he'd gone, I threw the manila envelope onto my bed and returned to the task of unpacking Nana's suitcase.

"I wouldn't mind takin' a cruise to Alaska," Nana said as she gathered up some of her toiletries. "But I saw on one of them late-night shows on the Fox Channel how a woman flushed while she was still sittin' on the potty on one of them luxury liners, and the vacuum sucked her insides right out of her. They had a devil of a time stuffin' everything back into the right place again. That was a pretty good night for TV. Did you catch that one, Emily?"

BAM BAM BAM. Nana and I looked at the door, then at each other. It sounded as if someone was trying to kick our door down. "Maybe it's the bellman with your suitcase," Nana said.

I peeked through the peephole then opened the door.

Bernice. She'd kicked rather than knocked because she was hugging a dozen plastic shopping bags against her chest, all imprinted with the Bucherer name. My eyes narrowed into a suspicious squint. If I couldn't trust that she was deaf, could I trust anything else about her? "Been on a shopping spree, have you?" I said, as she shuffled into the room.

"Cuckoo clocks." She paused in the middle of the floor. "Would you help me put these things down? I think they're pretty fragile."

We unburdened her of her load, setting the parcels carefully on my bed. "I suppose you want me to help you to your room with your packages," I said coolly.

"I'm not taking them to my room. They're staying here."

I nodded as if I was following her logic. "Why are they staying here?"

"Because I don't have room for them in my suitcase."

"You're one up on me. I don't even *have* a suitcase."

"But you'll have access to Andy's coffin. Won't you?"

"What?"

"Here's the bottom line, Emily. Coffin's are pretty big, and Andy wasn't. There'll be a lot of empty space in that casket of his on the flight back to Windsor City, so I want you to cushion my clocks in there with him. Like bubblewrap. I figure the extra bulk will keep him nice and cozy so's his body won't be flopping all over the place if we run into turbulence. Louise will probably thank me. She wouldn't want him to get all banged up for the viewing."

The pain between my eyes grew worse. I regarded the mound of bags on my bed. I regarded Bernice. I forced myself to remain calm. "ARE YOU NUTS?"

She gave me a blank look, then tapped her right ear. "You need to speak up, Emily. I can't hear you."

Like I was going to fall for that again. "I have no authority to transport cuckoo clocks in Andy's coffin, Bernice. You probably need to have them shipped home."

She smiled that vacuous smile of hers. "I knew I could count on you, Emily."

"Bernice. Look at me." I enunciated very slowly. "I. CAN'T. HELP. YOU."

"Pack 'em real nice now." She headed for the door. "I paid a small fortune for those cuckoos, so I don't want anything happening to them. We shouldn't have any problem clearing Customs in Chicago. I bet they don't open coffins. And when we get home, as soon's you hear which funeral parlor Andy's going to be waked at, you let me know and I'll rush right down to pick 'em up. You're a natural at this escort business, Emily. Much better than Andy would have been."

The door closed. Nana shook her head. "She's tryin' to butter you up, dear. She actually paid you a compliment. I don't believe anyone on the planet has ever received a compliment from her before."

I stared at the packages on my bed again. "How can she afford to buy cuckoo clocks? I thought she was one step away from the poorhouse. How can she even afford to be *on* this trip?"

"When she heard who all was signed up to go, she didn't wanna miss out, so she pestered her son until he finally gave her the trip as a birthday present. He forked over a bunch a spendin' money, too. But he can afford it. He owns some big company in Ames."

"Who was she so fired up to be traveling with?"

"Me, for one. I don't wanna sound snooty, dear, but I think Bernice is a little jealous 'bout my lottery winnin's, so she needs to prove she can go anywhere I can go."

"She used to have money, didn't she? When she was modeling? What happened to it?"

Nana shrugged. "Don't know. But she's lucky to have a son generous enough to finance her holidays."

I couldn't help but wonder if the motivating factor was generosity or temporary relief from Bernice's nagging. I pressed my thumb to the bridge of my nose. "I need drugs. Ibuprofen. Acetaminophen. Aspirin. Anything."

"I never get headaches, so I didn't bring nothin' like that with me. I got Gas-X and Polident though. Will that help?"

The phone rang. I picked up the receiver. "Hello?"

"This is the front desk. Is this Ms. Andrew?"

"Yes, it is." I heard bottles clink together as Nana dumped the contents of her travel bag onto the bed.

"About your luggage . . ."

"Did you find it?" From behind me the sounds of rummaging, rattling, rustling.

"It appears your luggage may have been seriously misplaced, Madame."

"WHAT?"

"Well, I'll be," Nana chirped. "Did you know Dick Stolee has sleep apnea? Says here he has to wear some kinda mask at night. I wonder what he did before he got the mask? Do you s'pose poor Grace had to stay awake all night and smack him when he stopped breathin'?"

I motioned for Nana to quiet down so I could hear the desk clerk.

"In the history of our hotel, we have never had to deal with this kind of incompetence. This is a most unusual circumstance, Madame."

"A couple people have acid reflux," Nana mumbled. "Your grampa had that, too, but back then we called it heartburn. And would you lookit the people walkin' around with underactive thyroids? George Farkas. Bernice. Grace Stolee. Jane Hanson. Me."

"So what am I supposed to do until you find my suitcase? I have no clean clothes. No toothbrush." The enormity of the situation suddenly hit me. "No mascara!"

"We will do our utmost to remedy the problem, Madame. Until that time, I ask you to please bear with us."

I hung up the phone. "My suitcase has been seriously misplaced."

"Someone stole it?"

"Misplaced it. There's no crime in Switzerland."

"Here's somebody with gout," Nana marveled. "Is that still around? I thought they got rid a gout about the time they got rid a Limbo."

"You shouldn't be reading those forms, Nana. They're confidential."

"If somebody gets sick when you're not here, Emily, someone's gonna have to read them. Would you rather it be me or Bernice?"

She had a point.

"I'm sorry about your suitcase, dear, but don't let it

spoil your trip. I'll be happy to share my things with you. What's mine is yours."

I winced at the green-and-red-plaid polyester pants with the elastic waist lying in her suitcase. That's what I was afraid of.

Nana was out the door before I was out of the shower the next morning. When I walked into the dining room for breakfast, I saw that even though it was still early, Nana's table was full and the Iowa contingent was here in full force. I noted only one table of Rhode Islanders. I guess Easterners had mastered the art of sleeping in better than Midwesterners.

"Is this seat taken?" I asked as I wandered to the same table I'd occupied the night before.

"Emily!" Shirley Angowski flashed me a welcoming smile. "Sit down. Join us. We were just discussing our trip to Mount Pilatus today."

The Rassmusons and Teigs nodded to me over their coffee cups. Jane Hanson waved before returning her attention to her bowl of cornflakes. I stared at Helen Teig. She obviously hadn't had enough light to apply her makeup this morning because her eyebrows were fern green. One of the hazards of keeping your eye shadow stick and eyebrow pencil in the same cosmetic bag.

"Is that Alfred Dunner?" asked Helen.

I looked over my shoulder. "Where?"

"No. Are you *wearing* Alfred Dunner? I have a top just like the one you have on, and it's an Alfred Dunner."

There were two of these tops floating around? Bad news for the sighted world.

"Sleeves are kinda short," said Dick Teig. "Are they supposed to stop at your elbows?"

Of course the sleeves were short. The top belonged to

Nana. She was four-foot-ten. She had arms like a dwarf. "The hotel misplaced my suitcase, so I'm having to borrow. Nana was kind enough to lend me this Alfred Dunner creation this morning. It's her favorite." It was a polyester pullover in pale pink with teddy bears dressed in tutus dancing all over the front and back. WE LOVE OUR GRAMMA was embroidered in bold metallic floss across the front. My brother's kids had given it to her, which explained why it was her favorite. And since it *was* her favorite, how could I refuse to wear it when she'd offered it to me? I contemplated skipping Mount Pilatus this morning to run into town to buy something without teddy bears. Something sleek, black, and sexy. But I couldn't shirk my escort responsibilities, so I'd have to wait until later. I glanced past the velvet draperies to the darkness beyond. Maybe the sun would even be up by then.

"You're looking awful pale this morning," Lucille Rassmuson said to me. "Have you had a blood count taken lately? You look anemic. Or it could be leukemia. People your age get leukemia all the time."

Now there was a pleasant thought. The good news was, the day could only get better from here. I flashed a smile at Lucille. "I'm sporting the anemic look this morning because all my makeup is in my suitcase, which, let me repeat, has been misplaced."

"We'll be running a special on makeup around Christmas," Jane Hanson volunteered helpfully. "We're going to call it 'Jingle Bells Days.' Buy one product, get a second product half price. And we'll also be giving away midget lipsticks. Midgets make nice stocking stuffers."

"If I looked as bad as you do without makeup, I'd see a plastic surgeon," Lucille said to me. "They do a procedure now where they tattoo pink pigment onto your cheeks to give you a permanent rosy glow. They've been known to

screw up though. One woman ended up with two red rec-
tangles on her face. And she couldn't even tone them down
with foundation. Disfigured her permanently."

Yup. I was going to rush right out and do that.

"I always pack extra makeup," said Shirley. "Why don't I
pick out some things that'll match your color palette and
give them to you after breakfast. I owe you that much after
what you did for me the other morning."

"What did she do for you?" Helen asked.

"Emily was so sweet. After I found Andy's body, all I
could do was stand there screaming hysterically in the hallway. So she calmed me down and took me to her room.
And there it was only four o'clock in the morning."

Dick Rassmuson squinted across the table at Shirley.
"How'd you happen to find Andy's body at four in the
morning?"

"He invited me to his room. And it's a good thing, too,
because he might have been rotting there a long time if I
hadn't come by when I did."

A knowing look made its way around the table. "You
gotta give the little guy credit." Dick Teig laughed. "He
knew how to lure a woman into the sack." He toasted the
chair Andy had occupied that first night at dinner, then set
his coffee cup down. "Did you bring my pills, Helen?"

Helen reached into her Triangle Tour bag and placed
a small plastic container on the table. It was blue and
divided into compartments that were labeled with the first
letter of each day of the week.

"Is that the seven-day pill caddy?" asked Lucille. "Those
weekly models are so obsolete." She reached down beside
her and pulled out a larger plastic container with even
more compartments. "This is the deluxe model. It holds
two weeks' worth of medications and the lids are easy
opening, in case you're suffering from arthritis. They also

give you the first *three* letters for each weekday, in case you have predementia and can't remember if the *T* stands for Tuesday or Thursday or the *S* for Saturday or Sunday. Unfortunately, it doesn't help much if you're dyslexic."

Helen lifted her green eyebrows and smiled smugly. She reached into her bag again and held up a container that was larger yet. "This is the super deluxe model. It holds a *month's* supply of medications, has easy opening lids, spells out the *entire* day on each compartment, glows in the dark, and has a timing device that buzzes an alarm to remind you to take your next dosage."

I liked the idea of the thing buzzing an alarm, although if you were carrying a cell phone, I could see where you might not know whether to answer your phone or swallow a pill and could accidentally overdose.

"It also comes in five decorator colors," Helen added. "This particular color is called—"

"Melon!" cried Shirley, as excited as a game show contestant vying for a million dollars. "It's melon. I know it's melon because I have one just like it at home. I bought a new one for the trip, though." She rummaged in her bag and whipped out a container that was the size of a jelly roll pan. "This holds a month's worth of medications, too. It has the easy opening lids, an alarm, the day printed out, glows in the dark, *plus* it has two clocks—one for local time and one for the country you're visiting—a programmable calendar, a pager, and it plays a tune from a different Broadway musical every time you open one of the compartments. It's the ultra deluxe jumbo model."

I could tell from the sour looks on their faces that neither Helen nor Lucille appreciated the fact that Shirley's was bigger. So much for the myth that size doesn't matter.

"How come you don't eat with the people you're traveling with?" Helen asked Shirley in a frosty tone.

"I know all those people. When I travel, I like to meet new people. Half the fun of traveling isn't what you see, but who you meet."

"The rest of your group must think you're a pretty odd duck," said Dick Rassmuson. "I don't see none of them trying to follow your example. They all stick together like staves on a picket fence."

"That's because they're from New England. New Englanders never mingle."

"So what's your excuse?" he asked.

"I was born in Canada. Canadians are very friendly."

"Coffee!" yelled Dick Teig, brandishing his cup in the air. "More coffee! I need something to wash these pills down."

As if on cue, everyone flipped open the lids of their daily pill reminders. From Shirley's jumbo model came the strains of "Hickory Dickory Dock, The Mouse Ran up the Clock."

"What Broadway musical is that from?" I asked.

"This one might be off-Broadway."

While the waiter poured another round of coffee for everyone, I saw the perfect opportunity do some investigative work. I knew Helen would never open up to me about her niece in front of everyone, but this seemed a good time to gauge people's reaction to the most recent Andy Simon news. "Wally told me yesterday that Louise won't be flying over here to accompany Andy's body back to Windsor City because she's on an Alaskan cruise with another man."

"Old news," said Dick Teig. "Bernice told us last night."

Bernice? How had Bernice found out?

Dick Rassmuson held up a small, round, blue pill in a show-and-tell gesture. "Esidrex," he said. "Take it for my heart condition."

No appetite suppressants for him.

Helen looked at Dick's pill, then held up a yellow one of her own. "Vasotec. Two-point-five milligrams. For my hypertension."

"Mine's prettier," said Lucille, holding up a capsule that was marine blue on one side and sea-green on the other. "Minizide. Five milligrams. My hypertension is worse than yours." She left out the, "Na, na, na-na, na."

"Louise Simon was cheating on her husband?" choked out Jane Hanson. "*Uff da!* She probably won't appreciate the sympathy card I mailed her. And I had such a hard time finding one in English."

"Hell, they cheated on each other the whole time they were married," Dick Teig announced. "It was no big secret. Everyone knew. But he cheated a lot more than she did, and he wasn't so discreet about it."

"Louise and I had coffee together sometimes," Jane said, continuing to look shocked. "She was always trying to convince the pharmacy to donate prizes for her charity raffles. I had no idea she had this other life." I understood her reaction. It was upsetting to learn you didn't know a person as well as you thought you did. I'd been that route with my former husband, so I could sympathize.

"Now *this* is a pill." Dick Teig showed us a long, elliptical tablet the color of a Vienna sausage. "Dolobid. I get a touch of arthritis every now and again."

"Voltaren," said Lucille, flaunting a triangular pill the color of French's mustard. "I have osteoarthritis in my pinkie."

"Pravachol," said Helen. "For high cholesterol."

"Cotazym," said Dick Rassmuson, popping a pill that looked like a baby gherkin into his mouth. "My pancreas can flare up every so often."

I noticed that Jane assumed the look of a hovering

mother hen as she watched everyone pop the pills she'd probably supplied for them.

"Atarax," said Lucille, flashing a purple pill. "For anxiety."

She was probably worried the rest of her lips were going to disappear.

Shirley lined up all her pills on the table and pointed to each one in succession. "Dong Quai for hot flashes. Fo-Ti for high cholesterol. Gotu-Kola for poor circulation. They're not prescription drugs. They're herbal supplements."

Jane made a horrible gasping sound beside me.

"I believe in a more holistic approach to health," Shirley confided, even though to me it sounded more like the Chinese take-out approach to health.

"I take an herbal supplement, too," Dick Rassmuson offered. He held up the tablet, then looked as if he wished he hadn't.

"What's it for?" asked Helen.

"It's . . . uh . . . You know. Men take these pills sometimes when they want to improve their . . . their stamina."

"I know what it's for," cried Shirley, waving her hand in the air. "It's called Yohimbe, and it's for impotence. I know everything there is to know about herbals. But I'm not sure you should be taking a pill to boost sexual performance if you're on heart medication. Did you check with your doctor?"

The top of Dick's head turned scarlet. "Well, a man's gotta perform, because when he doesn't, there's no tellin' *who* the little woman is going to find to take his place."

This caused Lucille to grow red-faced. She slammed down the lid of her deluxe daily pill reminder and shoved it back into her canvas bag. "Men think it's all about sex. Well, it's not. It's about having someone make you feel special. It's about having someone actually *talk* to you without blowing cigar smoke in your face! Andy Simon may have cheated on his wife, but he knew how to make a woman feel like a woman."

Unh-oh. Was Lucille admitting she'd had an affair with Andy? Had Dick found out? Oh. My. God. Had Dick Rassmuson killed Andy for sleeping with Lucille? Or were Louise and Helen *and* Dick all part of the plot?

My twisted triangle was turning into a trapezoid.

Jane Hanson set her cereal spoon down. "We recently received a new video on marital fidelity in the store. It's in aisle two next to—"

"Oh, shut up," said Lucille. "Did anyone ever tell you you talk too much?"

I stood up and glanced at my watch. "Oops. Would you look at the time? The bus leaves at nine. Gee, I hope we're not all late."

The table emptied in five seconds, and when the other Iowa diners saw the rush for the door, they joined in. Twenty seconds later, Shirley and I and the three early risers from Rhode Island had the whole room to ourselves.

"My watch must be wrong," said Shirley in some confusion. "I have 7:19. What time do you have?"

"10:13."

"I think that's the wrong time, Emily."

"I know it is." But could I clear a room or what?

CHAPTER 7

"In medieval times it was thought the ghost of Pontius Pilate haunted the slopes of Mount Pilatus." We were gathered around Sonya in the welcome center at the top of the mountain. Outside, sunlight was streaming down onto the scantily clothed bodies of Swiss sunbathers, which meant our travel brochure hadn't been entirely wrong. There *was* sun in Switzerland. You just had to climb seven thousand feet to find it.

"Fearing trespassers would so enrage the ghost, he'd send violent storms thundering down into Lucerne, the city fathers forbade all foot traffic up the mountain. The ban wasn't lifted until centuries later, and in 1868, Queen Victoria proved she wasn't afraid of ghosts when she made the excursion up the mountain herself."

You had to admire the queen. Unlike our tour group, she didn't just slap her money down at the ticket counter and ride a couple of cable cars through the fog and clouds to the top. She made the hike on foot. And in a dress! Come to think of it, that's probably the way my ex-husband would have done it, too.

"Say, Sonya," Dick Rassmuson called out. "How much would it set me back to spend a night in that hotel over there?"

All heads turned toward the elegant building that was nestled against the sheer rock face of the mountaintop. It was fronted by a wide terrace beyond which was a drop-off into nothingness.

"You've already paid for the hotel in Lucerne, so you've no need to know how much this one costs. Any more questions?"

Wally joined Sonya in the middle of the circle we'd formed around her. "We'll be up here for about four hours, people. There are plenty of trails for you to follow and several restaurants in the Hotel Kulm and one here in the Hotel Bellevue where you can have a leisurely lunch. We'll meet back here at two o'clock to take the cog railway back down to the bottom. I think you'll enjoy the ride. The railway has a slope of 48 percent and is the steepest cogwheel railway in the world."

Nana tugged on the sleeve of my raincoat. "Bernice and me are gonna look for souvenirs, so we'll catch you later."

"*Small* souvenirs!" I called to their retreating backs. "Souvenirs you can pack in your *own* suitcases!" I walked out into the sunshine and stood for a moment with my face lifted skyward, soaking in the warm rays.

"You really should be wearing sunblock if you're going to do that," Shirley Angowski cautioned. "Though the foundation I gave you has an SPF of six, so that'll be some protection. And where are your sunglasses? Crow's-feet, Emily. You'll get them if you spend endless years squinting into the sun."

I opened one eye to regard Shirley. She'd been nice

enough to give me an entire makeover on the nine-mile bus ride to Kriens, so I probably owed it to her to stay out of the sun. I owed it to myself, too. She'd plastered so much makeup on me, if it got too hot, I'd have serious meltdown.

But I looked good. Really good. With a few strokes of the proper pencil and brush, she had given me eyebrows like Catherine Zeta-Jones, lips like Angelina Jolie, and cheekbones like Bo Derek. My eyelids wore a sooty smudge, my mouth a gleaming polish, my cheeks a blushing glow. I was gorgeous. I felt taller, thinner, more confident. I was sporting the kind of face that caused men to stare, or walk into walls, or off cliffs. I eyed the guardrail that was perched at the lip of the hotel terrace and worried it might not be high enough.

Shirley extracted a pair of dark glasses from her Triangle Tour bag and slid them onto my face. "I always carry an extra pair. Maybe the sun will stay out long enough for you to wear them a while."

Dick Stolee approached, panning his camcorder from right to left. "Top of Mount Pilatus. Hotel on top of Mount Pilatus." He angled the lens into my face. "Swiss babe wearing a red raincoat on top of Mount Pilatus." He held the camera in the same position for several seconds before adding, "Correction on the Swiss babe. It's Emily wearing sunglasses and too much makeup."

Ordinarily, a comment like that would have ruined the moment, but today, it rolled off me like water off a duck's back. I figured it had something to do with the altitude.

Shirley, however, took exception. She snatched a small automatic camera out of her bag and aimed it at Dick. "Top of Mount Pilatus." CLICK. The film advanced. She aimed again. "Rude old geezer wearing a cheap toupee on top of Mount Pilatus." CLICK.

"Cheap toupee? I paid three thousand dollars for this

rug!" Dick bristled. "And who are you calling rude? Hell, I'm being honest. She is wearing too much makeup."

"Emily's face is a work of art," Shirley fired back. "And applying makeup is an art form."

Shirley was probably wasting her breath talking about art. From my experience with men, it was obvious they knew only two things about art. During their college years, they knew all the bottles in their beer bottle pyramids had to match, and later in life, they knew the wood grain on their big-screen TVs kinda had to match the wood grain on their coffee tables.

Shirley seized my arm. "Come on, Emily. I don't like the view from here anymore." She whisked me away, and when we were out of earshot, she said, "That man is just like my first husband. Criticize, criticize, criticize. As if any man in all creation ever knew the first thing about what kind of makeup best enhances a woman's features."

"My ex-husband was pretty good with makeup," I said, recalling the two short years of my marriage to Jack Potter.

"Was he a makeup artist?"

"He was a gay stage actor."

"Wow." I could hear the respect in her voice. "They have a real gift for cosmetology."

"Yeah. He could apply eyeliner thin as a dime, and in a single stroke. And I won't even begin to tell you the miracles he could work with lip liner."

"Is he still acting?"

"He called me last year and said he was installing kitchen countertops and tile for a company in upstate New York."

"That's nice you've stayed in touch, but what a waste of talent."

"Not really. I guess he's dynamite with a caulking gun. And it's a really big one, too."

"Well." Shirley patted the camera bag that hung from her shoulder. "If we only have four hours, I'd better start snapping some pictures. I bought a new five-hundred-millimeter zoom lens, a kaleidoscope attachment, and a fisheye lens, and I'm dying to try them out. If I can catch the right light, I might even be able to use my sand grain and split-field filters."

I'd brought along a disposable Kodak FunSaver Outdoor camera with twenty-seven exposures. I'd thought about splurging and buying the panoramic version, but I didn't want to be too showy. "You know how to use all those filters and things?"

"Oh sure. I used to be a photographer for *National Geographic* years ago."

I tried to mask my shock as I imagined Shirley Angowski traveling around the world on photo shoots for *National Geographic*. I wondered why she quit. Probably ended up in the wrong country too many times.

"If I'm not back when it's time to leave, will you come look for me, Emily?"

"You bet."

She headed off on a trail that circled behind the hotel. I wouldn't have any trouble finding her if she was late. She was wearing a raincoat that was Tweety Bird yellow and hung down to her ankles. It'd be pretty hard to lose her in the crowd.

I longed to grab a table on the hotel terrace, order a fattening pastry and cup of coffee, and relax in the sun a while, but since every table was occupied, I decided to do some exploring on my own.

I skirted around the sun worshipers in their bikini tops and shorts in the front of the hotel and ended up on a narrow pathway that hugged the craggy rock face of Pilatus's summit. The trail was surprisingly isolated and overlooked a deep valley where evergreen forest, brown gorse, ava-lanched rock, and fractured sandstone sloped downward into a vast sea of cloud. In the distance, range upon range of saw-toothed mountain peaks punctured the cloud cover, while closer in, a jagged island of rock rose from the snow-white sea like a great spiny-backed reptile.

I removed my camera from my shoulder bag and looked through the viewfinder. The valley. CLICK. The mountain ranges. CLICK. The spiny-backed reptile. CLICK. I walked farther along the trail, snapping more photos of fractured rock, zigzagging trails, alpine huts nestled on tiny triangles of grass between impossibly steep inclines. The vista was so spectacular, I wished I *had* sprung for the panoramic camera, no matter how showy. But I kept well back from the guardrail because I found the view rather dizzying. Understandable, considering the highest point in Iowa is probably the top of Lars Bakke's grain elevator, and I'd never even climbed that.

I strolled leisurely down the path, pausing every so often to ooh and ahh to myself, to snap more pictures, to stand and listen to the quiet. After rounding a blind curve, I was surprised to find a storage area cut into the rock with the doors thrown wide open. It was a huge cave of a room that tunneled through to the other side. Inside were coils of rope dangling from pegs in the wall, shovels, picks, snowblowing equipment, fencing made of orange mesh, wooden barriers painted red and white. A sign on the door read AUTHORIZED PERSONNEL ONLY. I wasn't "authorized," but if I wanted to catch the sights from the other side with-out hiking all the way around the mountain, this would be the perfect shortcut.

I looked left and right. The coast was clear. Everyone was still back at the hotel drinking coffee and eating pastry on the terrace. I entered the cave and scurried through to the other side, shivering when the temperature seemed to drop twenty degrees. And it wasn't any warmer when I walked out into the daylight. Unfortunately, I'd left the sun and all its warmth on the other side of the mountain. But this wasn't so bad. At least I didn't have to worry about my makeup melting.

Ahead of me was a wooden guardrail. I inched toward it, peering down into a crevasse that bored its way downward into total blackness. I felt the bottoms of my feet tingle and inched slowly backward.

"Hi, Emily."

I wheeled to my left and looked up. The trail ended at this point and gave way to a set of wooden stairs that laddered up the rock face to the summit. Shirley Angowski was standing halfway up the staircase, her right leg hooked over the railing in what looked like an impossible contortion.

"Oh my God," I shouted. "Don't jump!"

"Smile." She aimed her big honking zoom lens at me and clicked her camera. "I'll mail that to you when I get it developed."

I breathed a sigh of relief. I'd misread her acrobatics completely. No one about to commit suicide would promise to send me photos. I mean, film processing could take as long as two weeks with some discount companies. "Thanks," I called up to her. "Just what I need. Another picture of myself with my mouth hanging open. You don't look too safe up there. Aren't you afraid you'll fall?"

"I used to teach gymnastics. You want to see me walk to the summit on the railing? It's just like the balance beam."

I was delighted by the number of job opportunities open to people who were geographically challenged, but no way was I going to encourage this kind of suicidal behavior. "I hope you're not serious!"

Shirley laughed. "Just kidding. Balance beam wasn't my specialty anyway. I was better at floor exercise."

"Well, be careful."

"You too."

I'd seen enough for now. Anxious to check in on Nana and to monitor the whereabouts of Helen and Lucille and Dick, I headed down the trail that flanked the shaded side of the mountain and eventually found myself walking through another tunnel. Along the thick outer wall, huge windows had been cut into the sandstone like embrasures in a castle wall to allow hikers unimpeded views of the mountainscape beyond. I stood at one lookout point, amazed to find a church perched at the very edge of a precipice on a flat of land below me. On a scraggly peak behind the church stood a solitary cross, dark against the endless bank of clouds. I found the sight of a church seven thousand feet up pretty inspiring, but I did wonder if they had an occasional problem with attendance.

I arrived back at the visitors' center to find Nana sitting alone on a bench on the flagstone belvedere outside the Hotel Bellevue. I sat down beside her and whipped off my sunglasses so she wouldn't confuse me with the other hot Swiss babes on the mountain. "Did you find any souvenirs?"

She checked over both her shoulders before removing a small plastic bag from a security pocket inside her rain-coat. "I got the stuff," she whispered.

"That's great," I whispered back. "What stuff?"

She eased one of her purchases out of the bag and cradled it in her hand. "The hair spray, Emily. Remember? I bought two. One for you and one for me. Travel size. Extra hold."

I regarded the container. The labeling was written in a language I couldn't read, but that wasn't the problem. "You bought a pump spray."

"Of course, dear. A pump is friendlier on the environment than an aerosol spray."

"But we can't stop a killer with a pump. If we spray this in his face, all we're going to do is give him a stiff upper lip. We need to blast him with an aerosol spray that has lots of chlorinated fluorocarbons to slow him down."

"I hadn't thought a that. Maybe I should try to exchange this."

I ran a hand over my hair, thinking that a shot of hair spray with extra hold wasn't a bad idea. "I'll tell you what. I'll pay you for both of these and you can go back to the shop and try to find the aerosol."

"My goodness, Emily, you don't need to pay me. I'm rich. Remember?"

I transferred the hair spray into my shoulder bag for later use. "Have you seen the Teigs and the Rassmusons by any chance?"

"I seen 'em in that little Swiss Express diner inside the hotel there. They were at a table beside the Stolees and Jane Hanson. They have a pretty tight little circle, don't they? Don't open it up to no one."

Yeah. And Dick Rassmuson had the gall to complain about the New Englanders not mingling. "I think Lucille might have opened up the circle to Andy Simon at some point in time, if you catch my drift."

"No," said Nana.

"It came out at breakfast. It sounded *very* much as if Lucille and Andy had been lovers and Dick found out about it."

"So you think maybe it was Dick Rassmuson who killed Andy?" Nana made a sucking sound with her lips. "Wasn't the Rassmuson company motto, *We get rid of what's buggin' you?* Sounds like Andy mighta been buggin' Dick too much, so Dick got rid a him. Dang. This is gettin' complicated'

"Just be careful when you're around them."

Nana stood up. "I'm gonna buy that aerosol spray right now, and if I have to use it, I'll offer up a novena about savin' the ozone layer. Bernice and me are gonna eat lunch in that Swiss Express when she's done in the souvenir shop. They're havin' a special on somethin' called Rosti potatoes. You wanna join us?"

"I feel like eating something more colorful. You go on without me. I'll catch you later."

I wandered over to the Hotel Kulm and found my way into a casual dining room that boasted a definite alpine flair. Shiny wood booths. Banners emblazoned with crests of arms flying from exposed rafters. Beer steins perched on display shelves. Rams' heads mounted on wooden plaques above the doors. Alpine horns and cowbells hanging on the walls. I found an empty booth next to a bank of windows and sat down. The sun was glaringly bright as it streamed through the window glass, so I left Shirley's sunglasses on as I looked over the menu.

"Hello, gorgeous." From the tail of my eye I saw a man standing beside my booth, his voice, low, breathy, seductive. I looked up.

"Hi, Wally."

He scrunched his eyes up like Superman doing his x-ray vision thing. "Emily? Is that you? I didn't recognize you. Wow. You look really good today."

I'm not sure what that said about how I'd looked *before* today, but I decided not to go there. "Must be the weather conditions," I suggested. "First time you've seen me in the sun."

"The sun. Right." He smiled. I smiled back. He gawked. I gawked back. If we did much more of this, I figured I'd never get to order.

"Would you care to join me for lunch?" I asked.

"I'd love to." He slid into the booth beside me.

And since he was here, "So how's that room change of mine coming?"

"It shouldn't be much longer. The Swiss are very efficient. Just cut them a little slack."

Easy for him to say. His room probably had windows. I returned my attention to the menu. "I suspect you've eaten here before. Do you have any recommendations?"

"Yeah. How about we get together for drinks tonight at the Hotel Chateau Gutsch? It's a really romantic spot, seventeen hundred feet up. There's a little railway that takes you up to the hotel and a belvedere platform that gives you a great panoramic view of the city at night. If the fog lifts, you might even be able to see something. I'll be free around nine o'clock. What do you say?"

Ordinarily, I'd leap at the chance to have a drink with a man who was a snappy dresser, had an exciting career, was kind to old people, and who was a flaming heterosexual, but my hormones were sending me signals that Inspector Miceli had ruined me for all other men. Miceli hadn't officially invited me to dinner yet, but what if he decided to invite me tonight? If I already had plans with Wally, I'd have to refuse him, and he might never ask me again. Was I prepared to suffer the consequences? I mean, I could be in danger of losing the love of my life by agreeing to climb seventeen hundred feet to ogle the same fog I'd seen by day, only darker.

"That's really nice of you to offer, Wally, but my grandmother already has me booked up for tonight."

"What about tomorrow night?"

I was flattered by his persistence. Boy, I must look *really* good.

A woman stopped at our booth at just that moment. Saved by the waitstaff, I thought. Only, I hadn't decided what to order yet.

"You'll please excuse my intrusion, but there are no other booths available, so I need to join you." Sonya slid onto the seat opposite us. Wally looked surprised, then irritated. Kind of hard to act the swain with an audience looking on. Whew.

"The food here is excellent," Sonya declared as she scanned the menu. "Natural food products. Unlike your country, there are no preservatives."

I guess that meant the Swiss had to eat their food really fast so it wouldn't rot. I ordered vegetable lasagna. Wally ordered Hawaiian pizza. Sonya ordered some kind of noodles with cheese.

"I ate some cheese at breakfast this morning," I said. "It tasted pretty good. Swiss cheese, I think." Okay, the cheese I'd eaten at breakfast didn't taste any better than the packaged variety I bought at the Fareway Foods in Windsor City, but I was trying to be nice.

Sonya slatted her eyes at me. "There is no such thing as Swiss cheese."

My mouth fell open. This was like learning there was no Santa Claus. "No such thing as Swiss cheese? Then what kind of cheese am I buying at Fareway that's full of holes and is labeled 'Swiss Cheese'?"

"It's called Gruyère or Emmenthaler. The same families have made Emmenthaler throughout the centuries. Their cows pasture in fields untouched by the pesticides that are used in your country. They ferment their milk in iron vats over wood-burning fires, which is best. In your country they use stainless-steel vats and everything is climate-controlled. The old-fashioned way is better."

Gee. Too bad she was so shy about rendering her opinion. "I suppose you make chocolate the old-fashioned way, too."

"Lindt and Sprungli are the finest chocolatiers in the

world. And unlike your country, they use no preservatives or artificial flavors. You can trust me on this. I'm a local guide. I know everything."

"I'm big into artificial flavors myself," I countered. "Strawberry licorice. Cherry lip balm. Green apple hydrating shampoo."

"Euw boy," Wally said under his breath.

Sonya's eyes grew smaller, her words more pointed. "Have you tasted the water in Lucerne? Even our water is better than in your country. We have no pollution. No chemical contamination. No lead pipes. Our water is the purest in the world."

The waitress came with our food at that point, which was a good thing, because I didn't know how much higher I could lift my feet to avoid all the manure Sonya was shoveling.

She dug into her noodles and cheese. "Is that Emmanthaler cheese?" I asked her.

She regarded the swill of melted cheese on her noodles. "It could be, but I'm not sure."

Imagine that. I guess she didn't know everything after all. I cut into my lasagna and shoved a forkful into my mouth. I bit down. *Scruuunch.*

Wally turned to me. "Did you hear something?"

Unh-oh. I moved the food around in my mouth, probing hesitantly with my tongue. Noodles. Unnamed veggies. A short metal object. Something that felt like a chunk of one of my back teeth. My tooth? I'd broken my tooth? I scraped my tongue on a jagged protrusion where a molar used to be attached. Great. This was just great. The first edible food I'd found in Switzerland and it was booby-trapped.

I spat what I'd been chewing into my napkin and plucked out a piece of one-inch metal that I brandished between my thumb and forefinger. "That was in your food?" exclaimed Wally. "God, what is it?"

"It lookths like the pwong of a meat fock," I slurred. I could understand why the Swiss had no lead in their water. They put it in their lasagna instead.

Sonya eyed the metal somewhat skeptically. "The kitchens in our restaurants are the cleanest in the world, but . . . sometimes things escape our notice." She shrugged. "What do you say in your country? Shit happens?"

Wally eyed what else was in my napkin. "Is that your tooth? You broke your tooth?" He waved his arm, calling for our waitress. "This young woman has broken her tooth on a piece of metal that was in her lasagna. What do you intend to do about it?"

Sonya explained the incident in a language the waitress could understand. For added effect, Wally lined up the metal prong and my tooth on the table and pointed maliciously to the lasagna as if to say, "Bad lasagna. Bad, bad lasagna." If he didn't make it as a tour guide, he had great potential as a mime.

The waitress nodded apologetically and cleared away the metal prong and my dish of lasagna. "More?" she said, indicating the lasagna.

Right. If I had more, maybe I could find the rest of the prong and nail the molar on the other side of my mouth. "I don't tink sho." I scraped my tongue on the remains of my tooth again and felt a throbbing pain swell in my jaw. I was just now realizing it hurt to talk, to swallow, to breathe.

"They'll compensate you," Wally assured me. "This is Switzerland. They have a strong sense of justice here, fueled by the fear of litigation."

"Eat your peechah," I slurred around the pain, nodding toward his untouched Hawaiian pizza. I didn't need to urge Sonya to eat her food. She'd already bolted down her noodles and slapped some money onto the table as she stood up.

"A pleasure dining with you. I'll see you back at the bus a little after two."

I cushioned my jaw in my hand, jealously watching Wally devour his pizza. The waitress appeared sometime later and placed a huge piece of chocolate cake in front of me. "Waths this?" I asked.

"To make up for your tooth," she said. "How do you say in your country? It's on the house."

"Crown's ah expensif," I complained to Wally after we left the restaurant. "Do dentishs in Swishlin take credit cahds?"

"I'll find out for you. Who ever heard of compensating you for a broken tooth with Black Forest cake. Though I have to admit, it was probably the best I've ever eaten. Maybe the best in the world."

That would make Sonya happy.

I returned to the Hotel Bellevue and entered the Swiss Express looking for Nana. If she had no objection, I was hoping we could leave early and catch a taxi back to Lucerne so I could find a dentist. I couldn't leave my tooth untreated. I was making hamburger of my tongue every time I opened my mouth to talk.

I found Bernice eating a piece of Black Forest cake at a table by herself. I wondered if she'd broken a tooth, too. "Wersh Nana?" I asked her.

She frowned at me. "What?"

"Nana." I pointed to the empty seat across from her. "Wheyr ish she?"

"YOUR GRANDMOTHER?" she shouted back. I guess she couldn't remember if her hearing aid was in or out, so she wanted to make sure she could hear herself. "She's out taking pictures. She's been back once already to buy more film. Said she found a cute little church in a place no one back home would believe."

I knew exactly where that was. "Tanks."

Bernice beckoned me closer with her finger. "Just a suggestion, Emily, but if I were you, I'd lay off the sauce this early in the day."

I found Nana at the lookout point where I'd stopped earlier. She was on tiptoes, leaning over the rocky sill at the base of the opening that was carved into the mountain, camera poised against her eye. "Be cahrful!" I shouted at her.

She angled around, surprised. "Have you seen this church, Emily? The Legion of Mary just started a thing where they give a prize to the best black-and-white photo used in the newsletter. If I can get a good picture a this church, I think I'll be a shoo-in. They give extra points for religious content. Did you have a good lunch, dear?"

"Tewwific."

"What?"

"I bwoke my toof."

"Have you been drinkin', dear?"

"MY TOOF!" I pointed to my jaw. "I BWOKE IT."

"No."

"Yath."

"How?"

"On a fock."

Nana's eyes widened for a moment before she flashed a sly grin. "Imagine. Havin' sex at this altitude. How nice for you, dear."

I waved off her comment and shook my head. "I need to fine a dentish."

"We'll go and look for one right away. Just let me get one more shot."

"You wan me to take it fo you? I'm tawler."

"I'm not sure what the rules say about someone else takin' the picture for you, so I better take it myself. I wouldn't want the Legion to accuse me a cheatin'. But you could hold my legs to keep me from doin' a nose dive."

She shimmied far out onto the sill, belly first. Marion Sippel. Also known as Little Egypt. I grabbed hold of her legs, envious that she had no fear of heights. Maybe it had something to do with her lower center of gravity. "Here we go," she said. "That's perfect."

I heard a click and a whir as the film advanced.

"Have I got time for one more? I wanna get a shot straight down from here to show your mother how far up I was when I took this."

"Go aheadt." I was from Iowa. Even in the midst of excruciating pain, I could be polite.

"By the way dear, I think I spied Mr. Nunzio while Bernice and me was eatin' lunch."

Nunzio? The police were supposed to drag him in for questioning. Did this mean they'd let him go? "Wheyre wazh he?"

"He was standin' in line to head back down the mountain. At least, I think it was him. Hard to tell with his trousers on. Well, would you look at that."

Oh, no. Now what?

"My eyesight's not what it used to be, but there's somethin' big and yellow on a ledge about a hundred feet down from here. It looks like some kinda Muppet."

"Maybe ish a kite."

"Do they have kites that look like Big Bird?"

I was pretty sure Big Bird was a *Sesame Street* character rather than a Muppet, but I didn't want to split hairs. "You beddah lemme see."

Nana wiggled backward until her feet touched ground

again. "It'd be too bad if someone lost their kite. It looks like a real nice one."

I squirmed forward over the sill an inch at a time, my heart pounding with the height, the bottoms of my feet tingling, again. With my fingers gnarled into the far end of the sill, I pulled forward just far enough so I could peek down into the depths below. My stomach somersaulted at the sight that greeted me.

It wasn't a Big Bird kite on the ledge below. It wasn't a Muppet at all.

It was a Tweety Bird yellow raincoat.

Unfortunately, Shirley Angowski was still wearing it.

CHAPTER 8

"Let me see if I have this down correctly."

I was seated in a small office in the Hotel Kulm, watching Inspector Miceli pace back and forth as he read aloud from his notes. My head throbbed, my jaw ached, and every time I said Shirley Angowski's name, I got a knot in my throat and tears in my eyes. In other words, I was a mess.

"The last time you saw Ms. Angowski alive, she was on the stairway to the summit, with her leg wrapped around the railing, shooting pictures."

I nodded.

"You initially thought she was about to commit suicide."

I nodded.

"But you later learned she'd assumed the ill-advised stance simply because . . . she could. She was extremely surefooted and flexible."

"A gymnisht."

"And the next time you saw her, she was at the bottom of the escarpment."

"Yath."

"So the victim might have chosen to shoot a picture from an extreme camera angle, climbed onto the sill, lost her balance, and fallen. Or, while she was perched on the sill, someone could have pushed her. Do you know of anyone who would want to harm the victim?"

"Nana tinks she sawh Mistah Nunzeoh outside the Swish Expwess, but she wathn't real surh 'cause he had on twowzers."

"Ah, yes, Nunzio. The gentleman who tried to pick up Ms. Angowski in the hotel lounge on the night Mr. Simon died. She called yesterday to inform us she'd discovered his name."

"Maybe he kilt them both. Why did you let him goh?"

"Because there *is* no Mr. Nunzio, Emily. He's vanished. He was never registered at your hotel or any other hotel in the city. It's not a question of letting him go. We haven't found him yet to question him. If you say your grandmother saw him this morning, that means he's still in the area, and I'll recommend we broaden our search. But other circumstances have come to light that suggest Nunzio may be nothing more than a love-starved Italian."

"Wat?"

"I'll share that with you before you leave. Meantime, do you know of anyone other than Nunzio who might have reason to harm Ms. Angowski?"

I shook my head. Her encounter with Dick Stolee earlier in the day didn't seem significant enough to mention. And the Teigs and Rassmusons had been miffed at her for displacing the Stolees at the dinner table, but I'm sure that wouldn't have incited them to murder her. Shirley Angowski had been a kindhearted, cheerful, guileless woman who didn't deserve to end her holiday by falling off a cliff. I felt tears sting my eyes. I'd only known her for a couple of days, but I'd grown attached to her in an odd sort of way. "I'll mith hur," I slobbered as my emotions let loose. I'd probably never be able to buy another bottle of Revlon nail polish without envisioning poor Shirley Angowski at the bottom of the mountain. I might never be able to wear polish again.

Inspector Miceli knelt in front of me and dried my tears with a crisply starched and folded handkerchief. "Poor, Emily. This has been terribly traumatic for you. It's never easy discovering a dead body, and in the space of two days, you've discovered two. I do hope you've reached your limit."

I nodded, which prompted him to lift my hand to his mouth and place a soft, lingering kiss in the center of my palm. If this was the Swiss way of dealing with trauma, I liked their methodology. Electric warmth radiated through my body. I stopped breathing. The little hairs on my arm stood at attention all the way to my elbow. My heart pounded in my chest, in my throat, in my ears. He studied my face intently as he traced the curve of my jaw with a slow, seductive knuckle, then he stood up and leaned against the desk that was behind him.

"For the record," he said in a husky voice, "that didn't happen."

I grinned numbly and gulped a mouthful of air. My tooth didn't hurt quite so much anymore. Maybe the lack of oxygen helped.

"On a more serious note," he continued, "we'll be sending a team of climbers down the mountain within the hour to recover Ms. Angowski's body, which leaves us with the question of her camera bag. You say she was carrying it earlier in the day, but from what I can determine, it's not on the ledge with her. She might have left it on the ground when she climbed onto the sill, and after she fell, someone could have picked it up, either to steal or to deliver to lost and found. Or the perpetrator might have thrown it over the cliff after pushing her so as not to draw attention to it. There's a deeper ravine below the ledge. If the bag is there, it might be our best clue as to whether Ms. Angowski fell accidentally or was murdered.

"And to that end, we'll be fingerprinting everyone in your tour group before they leave the mountain today in case we're able to retrieve the bag. If someone's prints other than Ms. Angowski's appear on the bag, I'll want to escort them to the station to find out why."

I held up my hands and wiggled my fingers. "Evhen me?"

"I'll fingerprint you personally tomorrow at the hotel, after you have your tooth looked after."

I didn't know if taking fingerprints would involve his lips coming into contact with parts of my body other than my hand, but I was hopeful.

He wrote something onto his notepad, then ripped off the page and handed it to me. "This is the name and address of my dentist. I'll call to tell him to expect you. And you needn't worry about the expense. Once I speak to the hotel management, I suspect they'll decide it's in their best interest to pay your bill in full. An officer will meet you at the bottom of the mountain to drive you to his office, and he'll wait to drive you back to the hotel."

"Wat about Nana?"

"I'm afraid she'll have to remain here with everyone else to be questioned and fingerprinted, but I can assure you, I'll see her safely onto the bus before it leaves."

"I'd kith you if I thaut it wount huht too mush."

He gave me a sooty look that made my toes curl. "I'll be happy to accept a rain check on that." He escorted me across the room.

"Wat were you gohing to tell me befaw I left?"

At the door he turned me around to face him, stroked my hair back from my face, and lazily fingered the lobe of my ear. I held my breath again. If I deprived myself of oxygen much longer, I probably wouldn't need a dentist at all.

"Two things actually." His voice dropped to a whisper. "You are the most desirable woman I have ever met, Emily Andrew. If Swiss women were more like you, I would have remarried years ago."

Gee, I'm glad I asked. I could hardly wait to hear what the second thing was. I looked at him expectantly.

"The second thing is, the serology and toxicology reports have come back on Mister Simon. They were positive for a substance called dimethyl sulfate."

"Wat's that?"

"Poison."

I shot up straight. "Poizun? Andy wath poizuned?" Oh. My. God. I'd been right. Someone had fiddled with his Piruter—Pirable—with his asthma medication. "Wath it in hiz inhalah?"

"His inhaler tested negative for toxins. It was pure Pirbuterol Acetate. We're uncertain how the dimethyl sulfate was introduced into his system, but whoever did it wanted to make sure Mr. Simon died an agonizing death, which suggests the killer had strong emotional ties to him and rather speaks in favor of Nunzio's innocence. Mr. Simon suffered crippling seizures the night he died. I suspect that's what you heard when you awoke that night. I've never known it to happen with a group of senior citizens, but it's likely someone on your tour is a cold-blooded killer."

I arrived back at the Grand Palais Hotel five hours later with a temporary crown glued into my mouth. The pain in my jaw was gone, replaced by a tingling sensation from all the Novocain the dentist had administered. At least I could talk again, even if I couldn't feel my lips.

"Room 4624," I said to the desk clerk. She looked up casually, then did a startled double take before checking the cubbyhole. I guess she didn't get too many hotel guests with lips the size of pontoons.

"That key is gone. Someone must have picked it up already."

That meant Nana was back. Good. I had lots to tell her. "Have you found my suitcase yet?" I needed my own clothes. I'd seen Nana's complete wardrobe, and it only went downhill from the teddy bears in tutus.

"We haven't located it yet. I'm sorry."

I drilled her with a damning look that sent her back a step. "Not *half* as sorry as you'll be if I have to wear teddy bears in snowsuits tomorrow."

I took the elevator up to the fourth floor and knocked on the door to room 4624. "It's Emily, Nana. I'm back."

The door cracked open an inch. Nana poked her nose through the gap to eye me, then threw the door wide. "Had to make sure it was you and not someone tryin' to sound like you. How's your tooth?"

I walked into the room and came to a grinding halt. "I have a temporary crown. What's all this?" A three-foot-high mountain of shopping sacks lay cluttered on my bed. Big bags. Little bags. White bags. Blue bags. Paper bags. Plastic bags. "Did Bernice go on another shopping spree? I told her anything else she bought would have to go into her own suitcase."

"It was because of the fingerprintin'," Nana explained. "Folks had nothin' to do while they waited their turn, so's they went shoppin'. All the gift shops were havin' blowout specials on cuckoo clocks."

"But why is it heaped on my bed?"

"Because Bernice told a few people you were such a dandy escort, you were gonna take care a shippin' her cuckoos back home for her. Word got around, and everyone decided you might's well take care a their cuckoos, too. I don't s'pose there's any chance you *could* jam all these packages in with Andy, is there?"

"Not unless they send him home in a UPS truck." I squeezed my eyes shut, hoping that when I opened them again, the packages would disappear and this would prove to be a bad dream. I opened one eye, then the other. Nope. Still there. "What am I supposed to do with all this stuff?"

"You might wanna think about movin' everything off your bed so's you'll have a place to sleep tonight."

I slumped into a chair. I looked at the cuckoos on my bed. I looked at the cuckoos on the floor. I wasn't a math whiz, but given the small area of the room, when we transferred what was on my bed to the floor, we'd be fresh out of floor space. "Do you suppose anyone would notice if I strangled Bernice?"

"With the way things've been goin', someone might do it for you."

I moaned. "Well, I'm sorry to disappoint everyone, but they can march right back here and gather up their purchases because I can*not* ship anything home for anyone." I gave my head an emphatic nod, then paused. "Or would it be better if I found out what room everyone is in and delivered their packages to them myself? Kind of a personal touch."

"Are you thirsty, dear? I bought lemonade while I was out. I'll pour you some."

I hung up my raincoat and kicked off my shoes while Nana disappeared into the bathroom. When she reappeared, she handed me a glass of pink lemonade. "Awful about that poor Angowski woman. Inspector Miceli asked me if I could account for my whereabouts this mornin', so I was real glad I was with Bernice most of the time, except when she had to wait in that long line to use the potty and I had to buy film. It's a real shame people keep dyin'. Our Swiss Triangle Tour seems to be turnin' into the Bermuda Triangle Tour. Maybe Shirley was the last victim, but you know what they say. Death always comes in threes."

Cheery thought. "Did Helen Teig and Dick Rassmuson have alibis?"

"I haven't heard, but I do know that Jane and the Dicks and their wives were all together most a the morning. I'm not sure what any of 'em would have against that Angowski woman though. They didn't even know her. Where's the motive?"

The only thing that popped into my head was that if Andy hadn't died, Shirley would have become his lover. Had a jealous *ex*-lover of Andy's punished her for making the attempt? Was the finger now pointing at Lucille Rassmuson?

I chugged some lemonade, frowning when my chin and neck grew suddenly wet.

"Did the dentist give you Novocain?" Nana asked.

I held my hand under my chin to catch the liquid that was dribbling down my face.

"Maybe you should hold off on the lemonade 'til you get feelin' back in your lips."

I handed her the glass and ran into the bathroom to wipe my face. The phone rang. Nana answered. I looked at myself in the mirror. "YEOW!" I had raccoon eyes from crying. My lipstick was smeared across my cheeks. My foundation was streaked with iridescent brown patches that had formerly been eyeliner and shadow. I looked like something from the *Rocky Horror Picture Show.*

"You don't say," I heard Nana say to the person on the phone. "Is that right?"

I grabbed the soap and scrubbed my face. I felt like a criminal having to wash away the beautiful face Shirley Angowski had created for me. She'd been such an artist. A modern-day da Vinci. But where da Vinci's work had lasted for centuries, Shirley's had only lasted the morning. I guess that was the downside of working with water-based products.

"I see," said Nana. "You bet. Thank you."

I dried my face and regarded myself in the mirror again. Even though I was still sporting Angelina Jolie's lips, I looked pretty ordinary without Catherine Zeta-Jones's eyebrows and Bo Derek's cheekbones. And then a horrible thought struck me. What if Inspector Miceli had found me desirable simply because of the magic Shirley Angowski had worked on my face? What if I never again looked as good as I'd looked this morning? Would he still find me desirable?

I stared fitfully at the sink. Unh-oh. Had my big chance at romance just washed down the drain with my SPF 6 foundation?

"That was the front desk," Nana announced from the bedroom. "They found a new room for us, so we gotta move."

I shot my head out the door. "Really?" Could I put the fear of God in people or what?

"They were real nice about it, Emily. Said they'd send a bellman up right away to transfer our luggage for us. We can even ride in the freight elevator with 'im to make sure our things actually arrive."

All right. Now we were getting somewhere. "Did they happen to say they'd found my luggage?"

"Nope. You want I should call 'em back and ask?"

"They might have moved it to the new room already. I'll just wait and be surprised."

We repacked Nana's suitcase and finished as the bellman arrived. He loaded everything onto his cart then escorted us down to the second floor. To room number 2248. He opened the door and switched on the light. "Well, would you look at that," said Nana.

This room was exactly like the last one, with one exception.

There was only one bed.

"What is this?" I asked.

"Your new room, Madame."

"N-no, no. Our new room is supposed to be a suite."

"This is the only room available at the moment."

I checked out the windowless walls. The carpetless floor. The narrow, solitary bed. I could feel myself start to hyperventilate. "If this isn't the suite we were promised, WHY ARE WE HERE?"

"Police orders, Madame. They've requested that the area surrounding your former room be cordoned off. The lady in the room adjacent to yours was apparently found dead atop Mount Pilatus today, so they need to conduct a full investigation."

I stood there in a semicatatonic state. If I didn't know better, I'd guess the dentist had shot Novocain into my brain rather than my mouth. I gestured toward the bed. "Does management realize there are two of us?"

"If you'd care to request separate beds, we can move you when something opens up."

They were wearing me down. I could feel my shoulders slump. My spine shrink. Maybe I was getting too old for this job. "We'll need a roll-away cot then."

"I'm sorry, Madame. All our cots are presently in service, but I'll make note of your request and see that one is delivered to you when it comes available."

"What are the chances one will come available before we leave?"

"Slim to none, Madame."

"That's what I figured."

By the time all the shopping sacks were piled on the floor, the room looked like the town dump. The only thing missing was seagulls. And the stench. Nana stood at the foot of the bed, observing it from all angles. "This won't be so bad, Emily. I'm pretty sure it's a double. See, it has two pillows."

Yeah. But they were stacked on top of each other.

Nana reached for her pocketbook and removed a small plastic bag. "You wanna see what I bought in that hotel gift shop to bring home to the boys?" 'The boys' were my brother Steve's five sons, ranging in age from two to eight. I baby-sat for them sometimes when I needed positive reinforcement that my life as a single female wasn't so bad.

"Watches," she said, lining them up on the bed. All five watches were identical—a vivid blue-and-green background with the head of a black-and-white cartoon-character cow in the foreground. "I got 'em all the same so's there wouldn't be any fightin'. Swatch. That's a good brand, isn't it?"

"It's a great brand," I said, blinded by the screaming wristbands stamped with psychedelic flowers and more cartoon characters. They looked like something that belonged in a toddler's playpen, but there was one thing that made them enviable.

They were ticking.

"The boys should love them, Nana." And they might have them a while, too, if they could refrain from feeding them to the dog.

"You wanna borrow one 'til you get your watch repaired? I don't think the boys would mind."

I regarded the Swatch with its hands keeping perfect time around the cow's little misshapen head. I eyed my gold-plated Gucci with its elegant hands stuck on 10:13. "Okay." Did I need to have my arm twisted or what?

I set my Gucci on the desk and strapped the Swatch onto my wrist. Okay, so the cow made me look like a dork, but at least I'd be a punctual dork.

Nana removed her toiletry bag from her suitcase and dug out her plastic soap container. "That fingerprint ink left an awful mess on everyone's hands. Lookit mine." She held them up for me to see. "They're still black."

I smacked the heel of my palm against my forehead. "Oh my God. I forgot to tell you about Andy. They know what killed him." I paused for dramatic effect. "Dimethyl sulfate."

"Die what?"

"Dimethyl sulfate. *Poison.*"

"No."

"Yes. But it wasn't in his inhaler. The police don't know how it got into his system, but you have to figure it was deliberate. They're treating his death as a definite homicide. And they're doubtful Mr. Nunzio is the perpetrator because poison suggests a close emotional bond with the victim, and Andy and Nunzio had a three-minute relationship, tops."

"What kind a poison is dimethyl sulfate?"

"I guess it's the kind that if it gets into your system, you die."

Nana rolled her eyes. "Where do you get it?"

"Oh, you mean, can you buy it over the counter or do you have to special order from someplace? I suppose if we can figure out who had easy access to it, we might nab our killer before he nails victim number three." I made a pointer of my finger and aimed it at Nana. "How about we fire up your laptop and do some surfing."

She yanked her computer out of her suitcase and set it on the desk. She sat down, flipped open the lid, powered up, then poised her fingers on the keyboard and began typing. I'd taken several computer courses in college, but my expertise in the field consisted of writing and retrieving E-mail and cursing really loud when AOL disconnected me. Nana had never attended college or taken a computer course, but she could hack her way into the files of any government agency with a few clicks of her mouse. Go figure.

After some humming and buzzing, the screen filled with text. Nana scanned the information and read aloud. "Dimethyl sulfate. Also known as sulfuric acid dimethyl ester. It's a highly toxic, colorless, odorless, oily liquid. Exposure can cause sore throat, runny nose, swellin' around the mouth and lips, tearin', pink eye, cyanosis, and death. After exposure, there may be a period of up to ten hours before symptoms manifest themselves. Dimethyl sulfate is used in the manufacture of dyes, drugs, perfumes, and pesticides."

"Dyes, drugs, perfumes, and pesticides?" I repeated. "Dick Rassmuson spent all those years running that pesticide business. Jane Hanson has access to all those drugs in the pharmacy. The Teigs were professional dry cleaners and dyers. And those are just the people at my table in the dining room! Dick Stolee used to work for that company that supplied chemicals to the perfume industry. If dimethyl sulfate is present in pesticides, every former grain farmer on the tour could have had easy access to it. Lars Bakke. George Farkas."

"I don't suppose they all had a hand in killin' Andy."

"The police seem to think one of them did." The question was, which one?

"Anything else you want me to check while I'm on-line?" Nana asked.

I looked at our room. I looked at the computer screen. I looked at Nana's nimble little fingers. A dormant synapse suddenly fired in the numbed gray matter of my brain. Duh? Why hadn't I thought of it before? If Nana could hack her way into a government agency, a Swiss hotel should be child's play. "Bring up the Grand Palais Hotel." I smiled. "There's more than one way to skin a cat."

Dinner that night consisted of roasted potatoes, peas, and a slab of meat that looked like chicken but had the consistency of squid. The places formerly occupied by Andy and Shirley Angowski were conspicuously vacant. The rest of us kept sneaking furtive looks at the empty chairs, and at each other.

"It's just like that story, *Ten Little Indians*," said Helen Teig. "Every time we eat dinner, someone else is missing. Someone else has been murdered. I wonder who'll be next? It happens in threes, you know."

I really needed to hear that again.

"No one knows if that Angowski woman was murdered," insisted Dick Rassmuson. "She might have fallen accidentally."

"They suspect murder," Helen countered. "Why else would the police have taken our fingerprints and asked us all those questions? They probably think Shirley was killed by the same person who killed Andy."

"Where were you when Shirley went over the cliff?" Dick Teig asked me.

"I was probably in the hotel restaurant foolishly ordering the vegetable lasagna."

"That's what I ordered at the Swiss Express," said Jane Hanson. "Mine was wonderful."

"You must have ordered the version without the metal prong."

"Someone said you were the last person to see Shirley alive," Helen said.

Was I? A chill raced up my spine. No, wait. That might not be true. "If Shirley was pushed to her death, her *killer* would have been the last person to see her alive. Not me." I waited, half-expecting someone to jump up and yell, "Okay! You got me! I did it!" But no one so much as twitched. What was wrong with these people? Didn't they ever watch old *Perry Mason* reruns?

"Was anyone with you when you saw her?" Lucille asked.

I shook my head. "I was by myself."

Cryptic looks passed all around the table.

"What? So what if I was alone? Since when is it a crime to go exploring by yourself?"

"You don't have an alibi," Lucille said, using her *na-na-nana-na* tone again. "The rest of us have ironclad alibis. If you have no one to corroborate your whereabouts, you could be the killer."

I could see them all inch back in their chairs, putting as much distance between me and them as was humanly possible. "I *liked* Shirley! Why would I kill her?"

"What time was it when you last saw her ?" fired Helen.

"10:13."

"That don't wash," said Dick Teig. "We didn't reach the top of the mountain 'til around 10:20."

"My watch has been stuck on 10:13 for two days now. It's broken!"

"That's pretty goddamn dumb," said Dick Rassmuson. "Why are you wearing a watch that doesn't work?"

"Because I like it," I snapped back. "And the band matches my favorite color lipstick."

Dick Teig studied my wristband. "Your wristband's blue. I don't recall seein' you wear blue lipstick."

He probably didn't recall seeing his wife wear green eyebrows either. Men could be really oblivious that way. "I'm wearing a different watch tonight. This one is unique. It works." I flashed my wrist in front of them for all to see.

"Is that supposed to be a cow?" asked Jane.

"I think it's a Holstein," I said. "They're the ones that are black and white."

"That's no cow," Dick Rassmuson asserted. "It has horns. That makes it a bull."

"It could be a steer," said Lucille. "Steers have horns."

Helen looked pensive. "Do steers have dicks?"

"Male cows all have dicks," Dick Teig scoffed, "but they don't all have testicles. Only bulls have balls."

Aha! I thought. Just like firemen.

"So how do you know Emily's cow is a bull when all you can see is the head?" Lucille demanded of her husband.

"Because he has horns," he repeated. "Bulls have horns."

"And they're supposed to have balls, but if you can't *see* his balls, how do you know he has any?"

"You don't always need to *see* someone's balls to know he has them."

Hmm. I wondered if Dick was making a commentary about bulls or himself.

Lucille did a sarcastic eye roll. "It's a steer."

"A bull," said Dick.

This is what happened when people raised on Iowa grain farms decided to talk animal husbandry. It seemed a good time to intervene. I raised my voice to be heard above the fray. "I told you where *I* was when Shirley fell off the cliff. Why don't you tell me where *you* were because I can't believe all of you were together every minute of every hour we spent on that mountain."

Silence. Followed by an exchange of more cryptic looks.

"I went to the ladies' room by myself," confessed Helen.

"So did I," said Jane. "The vegetable lasagna was good, but it didn't sit very well, if you know what I mean."

I arched my brow at the two Dicks. "All right," said Dick Teig. "I'll own up. Rassmuson and I followed Stolee around for a little while when he was filming the sunbathers in front of the hotel. And then we all headed off in separate directions to take a few pictures."

"Sunbathers?" said Helen, thwacking him on the shoulder. "You were ogling sunbathers?"

"What about you, Lucille?" I prodded.

"I can account for every minute I was on that mountain, and I was *always* with someone. So there."

"Even in the ladies' room?"

"I didn't use the ladies' room."

A collective intake of breath around the table. Either Lucille Rassmuson was a very cool liar, or she had the longest set of pipes known to man.

"And furthermore," she continued, "that cow on Emily's watch looks like he's been castrated, so that would make it a steer."

"It can't be a cow if it's been castrated," Jane Hanson spoke up. "You can only castrate bulls."

"That still makes it a steer," spat Lucille.

"So the animal on Emily's watch isn't a cow?" said Helen.

Jane's voice was strained. "It could be a heifer with horns."

"A heifer?" snarled Dick Rassmuson. "That's a bunch of bull."

Helen looked confused. "Are you saying there's no such thing as a cow?"

"A heifer becomes a cow after she's given birth," said Jane. "And *all* cattle are born with horns, but farmers remove them for safety reasons."

"How do you know so much about cows?" I asked.

"*Hoard's Dairyman.* Aisle five."

"Who said anything about cattle?" Lucille wanted to know.

"Could the animal on Emily's watch be an ox?" Helen asked. "Oxen have horns, don't they? I just don't know if they have balls."

I stabbed a few peas with my fork and shoved them into my mouth. Maybe tomorrow night we could discuss the gay and lesbian movement. I was dying to hear their take on that.

Nana had packed two nightgowns for the trip, which was a good thing because I found myself having to wear one of them to bed. I wouldn't have minded sleeping in the nude, but Nana stated quite emphatically that if two of us were going to share one bed, one of us *was not* going to be naked.

We lay in bed shoulder to shoulder—me, staring at the darkened ceiling, Nana, snoring like a lumberjack. I turned to look at her in the shadows and shook my head at the toilet paper she'd wrapped around her head. She said the toilet paper was a better alternative than a hairnet because it cushioned her hair without flattening her curls. As she slept, however, the tissue kept creeping down over her face, so as the night progressed, she was beginning to look more like Lon Chaney in a twenties version of *The Mummy*.

I couldn't sleep. I kept thinking about Shirley Angowski and the way she'd looked at the bottom of the precipice and wondering if the police had recovered her camera bag from the ravine. What if she *had* plummeted to her death accidentally? If that was the case, I was wasting a lot of energy worrying about who was where and when. But if someone had pushed her, I wanted to know who, and I wanted to know right now. What person who had access to dimethyl sulfate also had a grudge against Shirley Angowski?

There were only three people I could cross off my suspect list. Me. Nana. And Louise Simon. Even if Louise had had the opportunity to poison Andy before he left Iowa, she hadn't been on top of Mount Pilatus, so she couldn't have pushed Shirley. Although, after I thought about that for a minute, I frowned at my logic. The fact that Louise hadn't killed Shirley didn't mean she hadn't killed Andy. What if someone else had killed Shirley independently of Andy? What if there were *two* killers?

I rubbed my throbbing temples. If there *were* two cold-blooded murderers, at least I could take comfort in the fact that one of them was on a boat in Alaska.

"EHHHHH!"

The shriek had me jackknifing into a sitting position in a fraction of a second. I swung my legs over the bed and landed on my feet.

"EHHHHH!"

A woman's scream. Coming from the room next door. Oh, no. Not again. I HATED people saying death happened in threes.

"STOP IT! GET AWAY!"

I jumped as something *thunked* into the wall. I hoped it wasn't a body. I groped for a weapon. My shoe.

"EEEEEEK!"

I thought about my shoe. Was this wise? This was the mate to the only pair I had left. If I ruined this shoe, I'd have to go barefoot.

I dropped the shoe and grabbed my pillow instead. More thunks against the wall. More screams. Footsteps pounding across the room. A scream echoing in the hall. I raced to the door and threw it open.

Grace Stolee was in the hall jumping from foot to foot and screaming like a madwoman. The door to her room was open wide and she kept jabbing her finger toward it in utter hysteria. Oh my God. Had someone tried to kill Grace?

I ran toward her. "Who attacked you?"

She pointed toward the door again. I spun around to follow her gaze.

A man stood within the shadows of her room. He was big, and hulking, and lumbering straight toward us. When he came into the light, I saw his face. Kind of. His forehead and nose and mouth were hidden behind a mask that fit over his head so that only his evil little eyes were visible. Oh my God! It was Hannibal Lecter.

"EHHHHH!" I screamed.

"EEEEEK!" Grace screamed.

He had something in his hand. A gun? A knife? I didn't wait to find out. I rushed at him and whammed him in the midriff with my pillow. He doubled over with a loud, "OOHFF!" My pillow burst. Feathers sprayed everywhere. Hannibal dropped his weapon. Onto my foot.

"OW!" I cried.

"EEEEEK!" Grace screamed like a banshee. She jabbed her finger toward my room. I turned around. A hideous dwarf with toilet paper tacked to its face charged at us with the ferocity of an avenging angel. "It's the Mummy!" shrieked Grace. BOOM. The floor shook as Grace went down like a ton of bricks.

PSHHHHHHT! "Take that, sucka!" yelled Nana as she power-blasted Hannibal with a shot from an aerosol can.

"Get him again," I yelled. "He eats people!"

PSHHHHHT!

Hannibal waved his arms through the air. He coughed. He wheezed. He dropped to his knees. I stuck my nose into the air and took a whiff.

"What kind of hair spray is that? It smells really good."

Nana peeled a layer of toilet paper off her face and held up the can. "They didn't have hair spray in an aerosol so I had to get room deodorizer. Alpine Meadows. You like it?"

I inhaled again. "That's really nice. You suppose they sell that back home?"

Hannibal groaned, gasping for air. Returning to the task at hand, I found the snap on the back of his mask and ripped it off.

The guy was bald, red-faced, and weeping uncontrollably. Oh my God! It was Dick Stolee! Had he been about to kill Grace? Was the mask his signature? Did he always don it when he attempted to kill people? Had he been wearing it when he poisoned Andy? When he pushed Shirley off the cliff? Just like Jason in the *Friday the 13th* movies. Or was Jason the one in the *Halloween* series? Whatever. Filled with indignation and rage, I grabbed the aerosol can out of Nana's hand and conked him on the nose. He crossed his eyes stupidly and collapsed onto the floor.

Nana looked at Dick. She looked at his mask. She looked back at Dick. "Hmm," she said.

"What?" I dangled the mask from two fingers and gave it the once-over. Some mask. It looked more like a jock strap to me, which made me wonder where else it had been. Yuck. I flicked it off my fingers.

"You remember me sayin' Dick Stolee has sleep apnea?"

I searched my memory banks. "Yeah. Kind of. You read it on his medical form."

"You s'pose that mask could be the sleep apnea mask he has to wear at night so's he won't stop breathin'?"

I looked at Dick. I looked at the mask. I looked back at Dick. Unh-oh. "But Grace was screaming. She yelled at him to get away. He had a deadly weapon in his hand. He was going to attack us!"

"What kinda deadly weapon?"

I did a visual search of the floor and plucked it out of the feathers. I held it up as evidence. "A curling iron. Looks like one of those travel models."

"Where's the cord?"

"This one's cordless."

"No kiddin'?" She lifted it out of my hand for a better look. "I could use one a these."

Doors finally started to fly open up and down the corridor. Heads popped out. Slippered feet wandered into the hallway.

I scratched my head. "This makes no sense. Why was Grace screaming if Dick wasn't attacking her? What was she so afraid of?" I caught sudden movement from the corner of my eye and ducked as something *whooshed* out of the Stolee's room straight past my head. "EHHH!" I screamed, swatting my hands through the air.

Nana watched the thing wing its way down the corridor. "Well, would you look at that. It's a little bat. You s'pose that's what was causin' all the ruckus next door?"

A bat? I looked at Dick lying unconscious on the floor, a welt already starting to form on the bridge of his nose.

Oops.

CHAPTER 9

"Mr. Stolee says if you'll agree to move to a room that isn't adjacent to his, he won't press charges."

The next morning, I was seated in the now-familiar office of the Grand Palais Hotel, wiping fingerprint ink from my hands. Ever the fashion plate, today I was wearing Nana's best Sunday sweatshirt—a lemon yellow pile pullover with lace at the collar and cuffs. Lace. Oh God. Etienne leaned against the office desk with the grace and elegance of a leopard. He looked very Swiss in his black suit and black turtleneck, but with his black hair falling rakishly onto his brow, he reminded me of one of my childhood fantasies. Zorro. I'm not sure if I'd been more enamored with Zorro's mask, cape, or sword, but the result was that to this day, men in black still make my hormones jump.

"I'm not sure why he doesn't appreciate my efforts," I objected. "I was only trying to help." I wadded the paper towel into a ball and tossed it into the wastebasket.

"I take it you haven't seen Mr. Stolee's nose."

I winced. "Did I break it?"

"It's the color of a zucchini and twice the size it was yesterday. You didn't break it. However, if I were you, I might accept his invitation to move to another floor."

"He probably wishes I'd move to another planet." I threw my hands up in surrender. "All right. I'll go quietly."

"Just for the record," Etienne said, a smile hitching up the corners of his mouth, "you hit him with a can of room freshener?"

"Our first choice was hair spray, but room freshener was the only thing Nana could find that didn't come in a pump."

He shook his head. "If Mr. Stolee had been the real killer, it could have gone very badly for you last night, Emily. I cringe to think what might have happened had he been wielding a knife instead of a curling iron. Your bravado was admirable, but I fear, foolhardy."

Etienne had me all wrong. I wasn't brave. I was only a hapless victim of circumstance who was having a hard time getting a good night's sleep.

"The next time you hear someone screaming in the hall, will you promise me you'll call the front desk instead of handling the situation by yourself?"

"I wasn't handling it by myself. Nana was helping."

"Which is even more reason why you need to pick up the phone. Think how bad it makes us look when seventy-eight-year-old grandmothers are taking down guests in the hall."

"What happened to the bat?"

"Apparently, Mr. Stolee only stunned it with the curling iron when it was inside his room, so it flew down the hall and got away."

Which was exactly what was happening with our killer. "Do you have any more word about what happened to Shirley Angowski?"

"We recovered her body late yesterday afternoon and autopsied her last night. There's no indication she died from causes other than falling."

An unwelcome chill crept down my spine. So we were no closer to answering the question of whether she'd been pushed or not. "What about her camera bag?"

"We haven't found it yet, but we've assembled a climb team to search the ravine below the ledge. Weather permitting, they should begin their search today."

"Weather permitting." I glanced at the gray, rainy mist outside the window, feeling tired and a little depressed. "Does the sun ever shine in Lucerne?"

"Occasionally." Then in a low seductive voice, "But I find the mist and rain quite tolerable . . . especially when it allows a man to engage in more provocative indoor activities." He drilled me with a look that sizzled all the way to the back of my skull.

A delicious sensation tingled all my erogenous zones. I even tingled in places that hadn't been zoned yet. Not only was the man gorgeous, he was good. I mean, he was *really* good. This would have been the perfect time for him to drop to one knee and kiss my palm again, but my hands were totally black with ink, so I figured it wasn't going to happen. Unh. I could really use a kiss right now.

"Forgive me, Emily. It wasn't my intent to make you blush. Swiss women never blush."

"They never blush. They never kid. They never smile."

He laughed aloud at that, a wonderfully soothing sound to my ears. I couldn't remember Zorro ever laughing with so much animation. "You're quite right. Perhaps that's why I prefer American women. You're much more given to laughter than the Swiss. And you do smile more." He zeroed in on my mouth. "You smile a great deal more."

Okay. MAJOR erotic thoughts going on here. I didn't

want to get ahead of myself, but I wondered if that confident look in his eye meant he was even more skilled with his blade than Zorro. Hmm. One could hope.

"This is going to be a long day for me," he said. "I'm not even sure I'll have time to eat dinner, but if you'd be willing, I'd like to take you out for a drink later on this evening at the Hotel Chateau Gutsch. It's a wonderfully romantic spot with a belvedere that affords a superb view of the city at night. If the fog lifts, you might even be able to see it; although, I find there's something incredibly intimate about the fog. The way it envelops your body. Caresses your face. Dampens your skin. It's almost like—" He stopped short, seeming to remember himself. "If I planned to pick you up at nine, would you be free to accompany me?"

"Yes." I wanted to keep things short and to the point to avoid any cultural miscommunication between us.

"Yes? That's splendid. I hope you won't be disappointed."

If he was planning to demonstrate his prowess with his sword, I didn't see any possible way I could be disappointed. From where I was sitting, even the sheath looked pretty spectacular.

"And now for the more tedious part of our interview. You know most of the people in your tour group, Emily. You've had a chance to observe them since Mr. Simon's death. Is there anything you can tell me that might shed some light on who might have wanted both Mr. Simon and Ms. Angowski dead?"

I guessed it was time for me to fess up about all the theories I'd formed. "How much time do you have?"

I ticked each item off on my fingers. Helen Teig's suicidal niece. Louise Simon's affair with another man and her rumored divorce from Andy. Lucille Rassmuson's affair with Andy. Dick Rassmuson's herbal supplements to keep him potent and his wife interested. Dick Stolee's run-in with Shirley Angowski on Mount Pilatus. The dimethyl sulfate connection to everyone on the tour. When I finished, he ran his knuckles along the curve of his jaw and gave me a long look.

"In other words, there's circumstantial evidence to support *everyone's* guilt."

I shrugged. "That's my guess."

"Lovely. And, Emily?"

"Yes?"

"Nice sweatshirt."

After breakfast I hurried back to the room to scrub the rest of the ink off my hands, all the while trying to ignore a pain that had started to throb around my temporary crown. It wasn't too bad though. I could live with it. We were scheduled to take a boat tour of Lake Lucerne at eleven, so I had a little time to myself before I headed down to the lobby. Probably just enough time to throw Nana's things back into the suitcase before we moved again.

As I repacked her slacks and pullovers, I realized with sudden horror that unless my suitcase showed up, my attire for my romantic evening with Etienne would consist of my black wool pants and any of a number of Nana's tops that were appliquèd with cuddly animals. I could see it all now. The intimate bar of the Hotel Chateau Gutsch. Candlelight. Soft music. The Swiss patrons dressed in their dark Italian suits and close-fitting black sheaths. Me, in a pastel blue sweatshirt with a litter of kittens frolicking on my chest.

I shivered at the thought. I needed my stuff.

I glared at the phone, picked it up, and dialed the front desk. "This is Emily Andrew in room number—" What room was I in now? Nuts. "Just one moment please." I opened the door, checked out the number, and returned to the phone. "This is Emily Andrew in room number 2248. Have you found my suitcase?"

"We're still working on it, Madame."

"I *demand* you find my suitcase. And if you haven't found it by five o'clock today, you will cut me a check that will cover loss of goods, inconvenience, and mental distress."

"That's not hotel policy, Ms. Andrew."

"Then change your policy! I've been invited out this evening by Inspector Etienne Miceli of the Lucerne police department. If I have to appear at the Hotel Chateau Gutsch with him wearing *pastels*, I guarantee you, heads will roll. Do I make myself perfectly clear?"

"We've never known Inspector Miceli to wear pastels, Madame."

"No. *I'd* be the one wearing pastels. Not him."

"That's not what you said. You misplaced your modifier. It would have been more correct for you to say—"

"Well, *you* misplaced my luggage and I want it back! Today!" I slammed down the receiver and smiled to myself. All those years of phone solicitations for Playgrounds for Tots had really paid off. I'd sounded downright fearsome just now. And what about that ultimatum? *If you don't have my luggage back by five o'clock . . .*

Wait a minute. Had I said five o'clock? No! I should have said *three* o'clock. The stores all closed at five. If my suitcase never showed up, I'd have nowhere to shop for a new dress. I knocked my fist against my forehead. Brilliant, Emily. Truly brilliant. I stared at the phone. I could call the front desk to ask them if I could change my ultimatum, but that would probably gain me nothing more than a snicker from the clerk. Snickering wasn't good.

Okay, I'd simply have to have faith that they'd find my suitcase. If they didn't, I was screwed.

The pain in my tooth increased as I resumed packing. When I couldn't stand it any longer, I went into the bathroom, stood in front of the mirror, and peered into my mouth. My temporary crown looked like a big clump of Juicy Fruit gum planted between my teeth. Ick. I poked it with my finger. It wasn't loose or anything, so I wasn't sure why it was aching, but I knew I couldn't go through the day without getting some kind of relief. If I had my toiletry bag, I could pop a couple of Excedrin, but my toiletry bag was in my suitcase, and who knew where my suitcase was, so I was going to have to improvise.

I dug out the packet of materials Wally had given me and thumbed through the medical forms that listed the medications each tour member had taken with him. When I reached Jane Hanson, I stopped. Good Lord, she'd brought the whole pharmacy with her. Everything from Aspercreme to Zantac. Maybe a druggist's motto was like that of a Boy Scout. *Be prepared.* Looked like Jane was prepared to treat any malady from athlete's foot to brain tumors.

I scanned her list of pain relievers, called the front desk to find her room number, and hiked up to the third floor. I rapped on her door and practically did handstands when she answered.

"Emily. What a nice surprise. What can I do for you?" She was dressed this morning in a navy-and-white gingham blouse, gray polyester pants with an elastic waistband, and penny loafers. Probably a good thing she wore a lab coat at work. Poor Jane needed to spend less time leafing through *Hoard's Dairyman* and more time leafing through a *Spiegel* catalog.

"The dental work I had done yesterday. My tooth is killing me. Do you have something I can take for the pain?"

"You bet. Come on in. I'll see what I have for you. That sweatshirt is so cute! Did you buy it in Windsor City or did you order it out of a catalog?"

"It's Nana's." I guess that said it all. Her room was huge. Of course, it would have to be huge to accommodate a four-poster bed, armoire, chaise lounge, and three upholstered armchairs. She even had a window dressed with the same kind of posh velvet drapes I imagined Mammy had used to sew that gown for Scarlett O'Hara after the war. "Wow. Nice room." I could handle a room like this. "Is this a prestige suite?"

"It sure is. I didn't know when I'd ever get back to Switzerland again, so I wanted to do it right the first time."

I smiled a secret smile. "I don't have a nice room yet, but I have sources who are working on it."

"I would have preferred a room with a balcony, but the weather's been so bad, I'd probably never get to use it anyway, so why complain?"

Good philosophy. Jane Hanson might not have the best taste in clothing, but her attitude certainly gave me something to emulate.

"Let's see what I have to offer you, Emily."

She'd set up a mock pharmacy on her desk along with her Apple iBook computer in a muted tangerine color. "Nana has an iBook just like that," I said, "only in blueberry."

"I can't be far from my computer," Jane stated as she scanned her array of medications. "I have to stay on top of the FDA alerts on recalled drugs. You know how it is. One day a drug is working just fine and the next day it's shown to have killed thirty people. That happened a few weeks ago with one of the popular cholesterol medications. I had to phone both Helen and Bernice to tell them to stop taking it." She plucked a bottle from her stockpile and read the label. "My first choice for you would be Motrin. I'd recommend twenty-four hundred milligrams a day, and if that doesn't help, we can increase the dosage to thirty-two hundred. Do you have nasal polyps?"

Gross. "No."

"Any sensitivity to ibuprofen?"

"No."

"Angioedema or bronchospastic reactivity to aspirin or other nonsteroidal anti-inflammatory agents?"

"What?"

"I'd guess that would be no, too." She popped the cap and dispensed several pills into her hand. "I'll start you out on six eight-hundred-milligram tablets for today and tomorrow. When you need more, come back and see me. I have some snack-size plastic bags you can put these in. They're in the bathroom."

As she headed for the bathroom to fetch the bag, I crossed to the window and looked out. Her room faced the same inner courtyard our first room had faced. Yellow brick everywhere. Row upon row of windows. Service area and waste disposal unit directly below. I leaned across the sill to peer into the Dumpster but saw nothing that resembled a twenty-six-inch tapestried pullman amid the ordered neatness of black plastic trash bags. Okay, so thinking someone might have accidentally misplaced my suitcase in the trash was a stretch, but let's face it, I was desperate. Not only didn't I have a dress for tonight, the only footwear I had was what I was wearing—my clunky Nubuck walking shoes that didn't fit right unless I wore heavy socks with them. I stared down at my feet. Not exactly the ideal footwear to complement the short, clingy black dress I imagined I was going to have to buy when my luggage didn't show.

"I seem to have buried the bags under a few things, Emily. I'm sorry to keep you waiting." I heard the echoes of plastic crinkling and pills rattling. I jumped at the sound of glass shattering on the tile floor.

"Are you all right in there?" I asked.

"*Uff da!* My drinking glass."

"You need help cleaning it up?"

"No no. It'll only take me a minute. I hope you're not in a terrible hurry."

I checked the face of my little cow watch. "I have plenty of time." I wandered over to her desk to look over her stash of drugs. Amazingly, she'd taken the time to arrange the items in alphabetical order, which sure made it easy to find things. It also made me wonder if the ability to alphabetize was a major requirement of the profession. But this sent up a flag of warning in my head. What if Jane had invited the Rassmusons and Teigs and Stolees to her room? That would have given them easy access to a whole raft of drugs. What if Helen or Dick or Lucille had used some of Jane's drugs to commit murder? Could the interaction of several different drugs cause a reaction that mimicked dimethyl sulfate poisoning? Oh. My. God. What if Jane had unwittingly aided the murderer? Had her pharmacist's sense of order allowed her worst nightmare to be realized?

"Have you been socializing with the Dicks and their wives at night?" I asked in as neutral a tone as I could muster.

"Sure have." I heard toilet paper being ripped from the roll. Pipes groaning. Water running. "We met here the first night. And since it was my room, I decided to invite the Bakkes to join us. And George and Bernice. Since they're traveling by themselves, I thought they might enjoy getting together with the group, at least for one night."

I wondered how the Dicks and their wives had reacted to the expanded dynamic of the group. Good for Jane! Mother Hubbard watching out for the loners in the group . . . all the loners, I suddenly realized, except one. "Did you invite Andy to join you that first night?"

"Of *course* not. That wouldn't have worked. You know how the Stolees felt about Andy."

I felt a trill of anticipation bunch my stomach into knots. I looked toward the bathroom. "Actually, I don't know how the Stolees felt about Andy."

She appeared at the door, her hands full of moist toilet paper. "It was because of that dance school business years ago."

"What dance school business?"

She leaned her shoulder against the doorjamb. "Grace used to run that Arthur Murray dance studio on Main Street, in that brick building between the shoe store and the dress shop. Do you remember? A real nice location. Lots of parking. First-floor access. Well lit. Andy apparently signed up for ballroom dance lessons, but from what they tell me, he took the 'ballroom' part too literally because Grace couldn't get through a rumba or a jitterbug without Andy hitting on someone. She lost a lot of clients because of it, so she ended up banning him from the class."

"For how long?"

"For life! Grace was really angry, but so was Andy. He didn't like being humiliated. Unfortunately, he owned the building the studio occupied, so when Grace went to sign a new lease, Andy refused to renew it. She was forced to relocate at the other end of town in that seedy building near the grain elevator. A third-floor walk-up. No parking. No streetlights. Her business really dried up. Then one night when she was closing up, she tripped over a loose board and fell down a whole flight of stairs. That pretty much ended her dance career. She broke her leg in four places. And it never mended like new. She still suffers a lot of pain.

You wouldn't believe the scrip she brings in every month for painkillers."

I stood there in a stupor, wondering what other gossip I'd missed while I'd lived away from home. Okay. I could see how Grace and Dick might blame Andy for the accident. But had Andy's conduct enraged them enough to kill him? Geesch, was there anyone on this tour who *didn't* want him dead? "So there was bad blood between the Stolees and Andy. I had no idea."

"That's what I heard."

Which further piqued my curiosity. "Who did you hear it from?"

"Bernice. She told me about a month ago when she came in to fill a prescription." Jane disappeared into the bathroom again.

Bernice? The knots in my stomach tightened. Funny how Bernice was always so Johnny-on-the-spot to divulge damning information. How she always managed to overhear conversations despite her supposed hearing loss. How she always seemed to glide in and out of our presence as if she were invisible.

"Here you go, Emily." Jane emerged from the bathroom and placed a small packet in my hand. "Six Motrin tablets in a Ziploc bag."

Funny? At one time, maybe, but suddenly it wasn't so funny anymore.

"Watch your step, please. Step down into the boat." A blonde-haired deckhand greeted us as we crossed the plank onto the cruise boat. On a sunny day, I imagined people would be jockeying for seats on the exposed upper deck, but given the spitting rain and heavy mist today, everyone was filing down to the enclosed lower deck, where they could stay warm. Iowans might not be given credit for having the brashness of New Yorkers or the sophistication of Californians, but they sure know enough to get in out of the rain.

Dick Stolee was ahead of me with his camcorder glued to his eye. "Cruise boat on Lake Lucerne." He panned the length of the boat. "Life preservers strung along the upper deck. Long-handled fishnet lashed under the rail." He panned left. "Fog on Lake Lucerne." He continued turning in a circle, sucking in his breath when he zoomed in on my face. "Crazy woman who tried to kill me last night."

"I did not!" I protested. "I was only trying to help!"

"Stay away from me," he shouted back. "And that goes for your grandmother, too!" He lowered his camcorder so he could glare at me with both eyes. That's when I saw his nose.

EHHH! It didn't look like a zucchini. It looked like a malignant lump growing in the middle of his face. If the antigun lobby ever saw what I'd done to Dick's nose, they'd probably start a drive to ban room freshener instead of assault rifles. But I was looking at Dick a little differently this morning anyway. Yesterday, he'd been just another tour member. Today, he was a tour member who'd had a plausible reason to want to make Andy suffer. And he'd had words with Shirley on Mount Pilatus. Good God. Could either he or Grace be responsible for Shirley's death? Could they be the kind of people who took offense at the smallest slight? If Dick could knock Shirley off for a little tiff, I shuddered to think how he planned to deal with the person who may have permanently disfigured his nose.

"Hey, Stolee," Lars Bakke called out from behind me. "What happened to your nose? You forget to open a door or something?"

I shrank down into the crowd, trying to make myself invisible.

"Did you see how bloodshot his eyes are?" Solvay Bakke whispered to her husband. "I bet he's been tippling in his room at night. I've always suspected he had a drinking problem."

I didn't want to point out that Dick's red eyes might suggest some kind of ocular sensitivity to Alpine Meadows room freshener. He'd probably be okay with other room fresheners, especially ones that weren't sprayed directly into his eyes.

The real shame here was that if Dick *had* been trying to kill Grace, everyone would be congratulating me this morning for clobbering him in the hall last night. Instead, the hotel manager had confiscated my room spray, and Dick seemed about to slap a restraining order on me. Could anything else possibly go wrong?

The lower deck was set up like a diner with long booths and tables flanking both starboard and port sides. I walked to the far end of the boat and slid into the last booth, hoping to be spared further discussion of the incident in the hall last night. To my right, a sliding window opened onto a vista of rain plinking onto Lake Lucerne and layers of fog hanging over the water. Yup, we were sure going to see some sights today.

"Well, if it isn't Annie Oakley," Wally said as he slid into the seat opposite me. "Nice job on Dick's nose. What caliber aerosol spray were you packing?"

I shot him an exasperated look. "I don't want to talk about it."

"Hey, you're not lisping anymore. You must have gotten your tooth fixed. Gotta admit, though, that lisp was pretty cute. I'm kind of sorry it's gone. But, now that you're back to your old self, what about that drink at the Hotel Chateau Gutsch tonight?"

"Tonight?" Could I tell him I was going out with

another man? Would the revelation hurt his feelings? I didn't want to do that. Better play it safe. "Did I tell you the hotel still hasn't found my suitcase? I'm not sure how I can go anywhere without the proper dress clothes."

"*Still* no suitcase? This is ridiculous. Okay, when we get back to the hotel, I'll rattle a few cages. They're usually so fastidious about transporting luggage. I can't understand what's happened."

"Ladies and gentlemen," said a voice over the loud-speaker, "vee velcome you aboard the *Vilhelm Tell* for our excursion of Lake Lucerne. If you vould kindly take your seats. Hot drinks vill be on sale in the bow of the boat once vee are under vay. Vee hope you enjoy your tour."

The engines revved and sputtered. Diesel fumes wafted through the air. Nana slid onto the seat beside me, with Bernice in tow.

"Have you seen Grace Stolee's hair this mornin'?" she asked under her breath. "Three booths back on the other side of the boat. Go ahead and take a peek."

I snuck an inconspicuous look over my shoulder. EHH! Her hair looked worse than Dick's nose. Her normally styl-ish coif resembled a field of windblown ragweed. "I didn't do it," I said in defense of myself. "I didn't get anywhere near Grace with my aerosol can."

"I know, dear. It's because of her curlin' iron. Dick tried to fend off that bat with it, but since bats are a pro-tected species, there's laws against thwackin' 'em with hairstylin' equipment. Dick's lucky he didn't end up in jail. He got off with a warnin', but they still confiscated the curlin' iron 'cause he'd tried to use it in the commis-sion of a crime. If you ask me, the real crime is Grace's hair. Lookit her. That's the worst case a bedhead I ever did see."

"You're our escort," Bernice piped up. "I think the

responsibility falls on you to get Grace's curling iron back for her."

"I'll get right on it," I said without missing a beat. I'd had such good luck with luggage, I could hardly wait to see my results with small appliances. I regarded Bernice offhandedly, trying to recall a visual memory of her that was flirting with my subconscious. What was it? Unh.

"Why are you looking at me like that?" asked Bernice.

I shook myself out of my reverie. "Sorry." Had I gone over the top with my suspicions about Bernice? She was one of Nana's closest friends. Nana was a great judge of character who had better intuition than to hang out with a cold-blooded murderer, didn't she? Of course, she did. So why did I still have a niggling doubt in my mind?

I saw the lines being cast off from the pier, heard more chugging and sputtering from the engine, then we were angling out of our berth and heading into open water. "Lake Lucerne is the fourth largest lake in Svitzerland," our guide said over the microphone. "It is tventy-four miles long, and at its broadest point, is two miles vide."

I peered out at the fog, thinking this would be a good time for it to lift. Nana and Bernice excused themselves to buy coffee at the snack bar, and Wally excused himself to make the rounds. "Chitchat is part of the job," he said. "A good tour guide is attentive to every member of the group. Besides, if you ignore someone, they'll probably give you a lousy evaluation."

"Evaluation? Guides get evaluated?"

"Yeah. At the end of the tour I'll hand out a sheet that all the guests are supposed to fill out. It asks questions like: Was I courteous? Was I informative?"

"Are escorts evaluated, too?" It would be just my luck. I could imagine what Bernice would write about me when I dumped her cuckoos back in her lap, or the Stolees after the incident last night. If the evaluations were too bad, maybe the bank wouldn't even reimburse me for the trip. Then what would I do? How would I pay back all those credit card bills that would be landing in my mailbox?

"I don't know if bank escorts are subjected to the evaluation process, but I can find out for you."

I nodded my thanks and as we nosed farther away from the shoreline, felt myself slip into a semivegetative state. I'd wondered what else could go wrong, but hadn't expected the answer to come so quickly. It looked like I was going to have to redeem myself, and fast, but the problem was, how?

"Out the vindow to your right is the snowcapped, seven-thousand-foot mountain named Mount Pilatus," the guide announced.

Heads turned to the right. Cameras clicked. Film whirred. It didn't seem to matter that we couldn't actually *see* the mountain. People obviously wanted to capture the *moment* rather than the mountain. I could hardly wait for the picture exchange.

"Some kilometers in the distance to your left is Mount Rigi," the guide continued.

Heads to the left. Cameras clicking. Film whirring. I rolled my eyes. I wondered who was going to be the first person to realize we could only see twenty feet in front of us.

"If you had been here *last* veek, you might have been able to see Mount Rigi," joked the guide. "Last veek there vas no fog."

Laughter. Giggling. Sounds of mirth. I was delighted the group was so happy to be taking a scenic cruise on a lake where they could see nothing. Who knew? Maybe I'd reach a point in my life where I could be happy about paying big bucks to see nothing, too. But I figured I had a long wait.

When the guide began to talk about the four cantons surrounding the lake, I put my brain into neutral and nested into a comfy corner of my booth, relieved at how much better my tooth felt. The Motrin really worked. I'd have to do something nice to repay Jane for her kindness. Hmm. Maybe a fashion consultation.

After a while, the sound of the guide's voice blended into the sound of the engine in a hypnotic serenade that started to put me to sleep. But I was cooking inside my raincoat and from what I could see, the fog was growing worse. Boy, we were really getting socked in.

I squinted out the window, then on a whim, rubbed my hand across the glass, making a surprising clear spot. My imagined fog wasn't fog at all. It was condensation. There were so many people on the lower deck, and the ventilation was so poor, we were fogging up all the windows. Lovely. Now we couldn't see inside *or* out.

The stuffiness was so oppressive, I felt as if I was starting to smother. I needed fresh air. With the door to the companionway directly ahead of me, I slipped out of my booth and escaped to the upper deck.

Okay, so it was a little drizzly. A little misty. The air felt good on my face, and it was really quiet in the fog. Even the engine seemed muffled. And I was all alone up here. Almost. George Farkas was sitting on a bench that faced the prow. I guess he couldn't handle the stuffiness either.

"How are you doing today, George?" I called out as I headed in his direction.

He looked over his shoulder and gave me a finger wave. "I've been better," he said. "This cussed dampness is making my stump ache something fierce. Thought I'd come up here out of the crowd and unstrap my prosthesis for a spell. Didn't want to do it downstairs. Makes some people uncomfortable when you take your leg off in front of them." He'd set his prosthesis on the deck in front of him and was massaging his stump with both hands.

"Do you have anything you can take for the pain?" I asked.

"Pills are for sissies. Besides, this isn't so much a pain as it is a nuisance."

I guess I wouldn't tell him how many milligrams of painkiller I was taking for a simple toothache. "Well, I'm going to wander the deck for a while, George, but if there's anything I can do for you, you let me know."

"I sure will. That's nice of you to offer, Emily. Thanks."

I walked over to the starboard rail feeling much better about myself as an escort. Maybe I wasn't a total washout. Maybe there was hope for me yet.

Without the condensation hampering my view, I could see the vague contours of the shoreline and some private piers jutting into the water. I could only imagine how lovely the scenery would be on a day with blue sky and the sun reflecting off the water. I decided I'd have to visit Switzerland again one day. In the summer.

Somewhere in the fog I heard the muffled sound of another engine, and I turned to see a smaller cruise boat emerging from the mist on a parallel course to ours, heading in the opposite direction. Hard to believe there were *two* boats conducting scenic cruises on the lake today. I wondered what the volume of traffic was like on days when you could actually see something. Must be like rush hour in Chicago.

I waved at the other boat, but since no one was standing outside, no one waved back. Someone might have waved from belowdecks, but their windows were as fogged up with condensation as ours, so I didn't see them either. The two boats blew their horns at each other in what I figured was a gesture of greeting, then the other boat disappeared into the mist once again.

Well, that was exciting. I turned back to the rail, and

after a few seconds, felt the deck tilt beneath my feet as we quartered into the other boat's wake.

BOOM. The first wave hit our prow. BOOM. We dipped into a trough and smacked into the second wave. BOOM. The deck pitched left and right. I clung to the rail for balance and hoped that everyone had remembered to take their Dramamine.

"SHIT!"

I spun around. George Farkas had hopped one-legged to the rail and was flailing his arms wildly toward the water. "My leg," he screamed. "It slid overboard!"

I rushed to his side and looked down into the lake. There was George's leg, bobbing just below the surface like a little nuclear submarine. "At least it's floating. We'll have to turn the boat around and pick it up."

"There's no time!" He ripped off his jacket. "I have to jump in after it!"

"WHAT?"

"That shoe is steel-toed. It's gonna drag my leg down like a sinker."

"Are you CRAZY? I bet you can't even swim!" What was *wrong* with these guys? Did they all have death wishes?

"Don't try to stop me, Emily. That leg is irreplaceable. It's made from the same material as the shields on the space shuttle. It's bulletproof. It's termite resistant. It can withstand heat up to 180 degrees Fahrenheit."

But the important question was, "Is it waterproof?"

"It cost twenty thousand dollars. Medicare doesn't cover it! I've gotta save it!" He thump-hopped to the nearest bench to remove his other steel-toed shoe. I shot a look into the water. He was right. His leg was starting to sink. Nuts.

I scanned the upper deck. Not a harpoon in sight. Probably not too many whale sightings on Lake Lucerne. Portable tables. A fire extinguisher. Trash cans. Ashtrays.

Life preservers. I pondered the doughnut-shaped pre-servers strung along the rail. These were great for saving people, but they might not work so well on an artificial limb, especially if the limb wasn't attached to anything.

I peeked down into the water again. I caught a glint of metal in the tail of my eye and redirected my gaze to the rail, where I found a pole. An aluminum pole. It was as long as the device used by pool cleaners and secured by straps to the outside panels of the rail. At one end hung a mesh fishnet that was as deep as a giant's sock. *Fishnet?* Eureka!

I leaned over the rail and wrestled with the straps.

"Outta the way, Emily," George yelled as he threw his shoe aside.

I released the pole, zeroed in on the leg, and plunged the net into the water. George thump-hopped to the rail beside me.

"What are you doing? You're gonna hurt it!"

I maneuvered the pole to the left. To the right. "My grampa used to take me fishing with him up in Minnesota when I was little. Gull Lake. I wasn't thrilled about sticking the bait on the hook, but I loved using the fishnet." Bracing myself against the rail, I scooped the leg out of the water. "I got pretty good at it, too."

"You did it! You did it!"

And best of all, I'd stayed dry.

"I'm gonna give you a really good evaluation, Emily. All fives. All outstandings."

"How do you know you'll be asked to evaluate me?"

"Because I'm the one who's supposed to pass out the forms."

Using the hand-over-hand method, I raised the net higher and higher out of the water.

"Careful," coached George. "Oh crap!"

"What?"

"There's a hole in the bottom of the net. Look. The toe of my shoe is poking through. I think the whole thing's ripping!"

"There should be a net on the other side of the boat."

THUMP-HOP. THUMP-HOP. THUMP-HOP. "I found it."

"Bring it here. We'll double net." I hand-over-handed faster. And faster.

"I can't work the straps loose! Hold on. Maybe if I lean over—"

With a final grunt of exertion, I swung the net over the rail, muscling the leg onto the deck like a Pacific tuna. "Forget it, George! We snagged it!"

I heard a loud plunking sound nearby. I looked cross-deck. "George?"

No George. Where'd he go?

Unh-oh.

I ran to the rail and looked down. George's little bald head was submerged beneath the surface. Arms flailing. Body thrashing. With a burst of strength he rocketed himself upward to yell, "I can't swim!" then disappeared beneath the waters of Lake Lucerne.

Of course he couldn't swim.

As I hurdled the rail, I heard footsteps behind me and a man shout, "Don't jump! Maybe vee can talk about it!"

SPLAAAAT!

CHAPTER 10

Squish. Squish. Squish.

George was transported by ambulance to a local hospital after his near drowning. "For observation," the medics said. The tour bus had dropped everyone else off downtown to shop, but I had walked back to the hotel and could feel my socks squishing inside my shoes as I approached the front desk. "I'd like the key to room 2248, please."

The clerk looked at me with the same horror Vera Miles had shown in *Psycho* when the chair spun around to reveal the decayed remains of Norman Bates's mother. In my head, I could hear the frenetic sound of Bernard Hermann's screeching violins. But unlike Vera Miles, the desk clerk didn't scream. She merely slanted one of her perfectly penciled eyebrows into a disapproving arch and stared.

Water trickled from the hem of my slacks and puddled onto the floor. Water beaded the ends of my hair and dripped into my eyes. I swiped at my face with my hand. "I took a dip in the lake."

"At this time of year?"

"Very bracing. You should try it. Have you found my suitcase yet?"

"Ah. The guest with the missing suitcase. Ms. Andrew, isn't it? Unfortunately, we're still unable to locate it. But you did give us until five o'clock to produce it, and right now it's only two. We still have three hours."

I knew I'd be sorry I'd given them that five o'clock deadline. "No suitcase." No surprise. "How long before you list it as stolen and report the theft to the police?"

"It's not stolen, Madame. There is no crime in Switzerland."

Of course there wasn't. That's why people were dropping like flies around here. "Do you at least have a key for me?"

She turned around and plucked a key from one of the cubbyholes behind her. "We were told you needed to be moved off the second floor, so we took the liberty of moving your belongings to room number 5111. I hope you don't mind."

Room 5111. If I was any farther away from the second floor, I'd be in another country.

"And please accept our regrets about this ongoing dilemma with your luggage. The staff feels so bad about your plight, we took up a collection for you." She handed me a white envelope.

They were spoiling everything. How could I be angry with them if they decided to be nice to me? I peeked inside the envelope.

"It's not much," the clerk apologized. "But it's out of our own pockets."

I poked my finger at the lone banknote and collection of coins inside. "This is very kind of you. I don't know what to say." I tried to decipher the numbers on the coins.

"It's twenty-two Swiss francs. In American dollars that would be thirteen dollars and fifty-four cents." She graced

.ne with a genuinely sympathetic look. "Perhaps you could use it to help defray the cost of surgery on your nose."

I fingered the bridge of my nose to find it swollen like a walnut. Great. I could hardly wait to see what color it was. But $13.54 might almost be enough to buy my nephew a new Swatch cow watch to replace the one I ruined when I rescued George. And I swore, that would be my *last* purchase of a timepiece in Switzerland. I wasn't going to strap on another wristwatch until I reached the landlocked bliss of Iowa once again. I could be dense at times, but I knew when to throw in the towel.

Room 5111 was in another wing of the hotel, down a labyrinth of long corridors and angled into a maze of shorter ones. I opened the door, ready to switch on the overhead, but there was no need. The drapes were pulled back from a bank of French doors, allowing daylight to fill the room. I stood with my mouth hanging open for a full minute.

Nana's suitcase lay on a luggage rack at the foot of a canopy bed that was as big as a football field. Bernice's cuckoos and everyone else's sacks formed a tidy mound in the far corner of the room, on a carpet that was thick as attic insulation. The boudoir chairs were covered in peach taffeta and arranged in conversational groupings around the room. The fireplace was carved from marble with a gargantuan rococo mirror hanging over the mantel. There were two armoires, an antique desk, a crystal chandelier, and beyond the French doors, I could see the intricate wrought iron railing of the balcony. If the fog lifted, I might even be able to see across the street.

Yes! And I felt no guilt at all about the tactics we'd employed to effect the upgrade. If the Grand Palais Hotel was too cheap to buy a state-of-the-art security system for their computer, they deserved to be hacked into by seventy-eight-year-old grandmothers.

I ran into the bathroom, shedding clothes as I went. Huge Jacuzzi bath. Glass-enclosed shower. Plush towels on a heated rack. Vanity. Lighted makeup mirror. Blow-dryer. Little basket of scented soaps, shampoos, and body washes. Now *this* was my idea of a deluxe room in a four-star hotel. I spun around in a circle with my arms thrown wide. Yes! I didn't care what kind of mayhem went on in the room next door tonight, I was *staying* in this room. They'd need the Swiss guard to get me out of here. I glanced toward the mirror.

"EHHH!" My mouth dropped to my chest. That couldn't be my nose.

I rushed closer to see my reflection. Oh my God. It *was* my nose. Just my luck the deckhand had appeared when he did. In an attempt to save me, he'd thrown the life preserver from hell at me. And he'd been dead on. Clonked me right across the bridge of my nose.

I dimmed the light over the sink, but it didn't change anything. My nose was blue. I looked like I had a Smurf wedged between my eyes. I'd done a really good deed today. Was this fair that I should end up with a blue nose?

An hour later, shampooed, showered, and blow-dried, with a half pound of concealer on my nose, I slipped into one of Nana's plain black skirts that looked okay other than the fact that it was four inches too big at the waist. Since she hadn't packed suspenders, I rolled up the waistband and hid the lump it made beneath a white sweatshirt with a huge photo of a thirty-pound muskie lying on a bed of ice stamped on the front. I guess I was lucky Nana had decided to take a picture of the muskie instead of a picture of Grampa at the wake. Sporting a deceased relative on my chest was even less appealing than sporting a dead fish.

I power-walked along the promenade by the lake, past the casino and the Wilhelm Tell Restaurant, across the *Schweizerhofquai*, and along the *Rathausquai* by the River Reuss. My hair was starting to frizz in the drizzle, but I figured I'd wear it up tonight and plaster it with the extrahold hair spray Nana had bought on Mount Pilatus. I entered the sparkling glass doors of an upscale shop named Spengler, found women's wear on the directory, and took the elevator straight up.

The little black dress was *in* in Lucerne. The salesclerk showed me what was available in my size, and without noting the prices, I gathered up the sexiest of the lot and scurried to the fitting room. I'd determined the first one wasn't skimpy enough and was zipping myself into the second when I heard familiar voices in the room beside me.

"Do you think she suspects anything?" asked Helen Teig.

"How could she?" replied Grace Stolee. "She doesn't know any of the details."

"But I'm worried she might put two and two together. And then the jig would be up. Is that dress your size, Grace? It looks too small for you."

"I've lost weight since I've been on this trip. I'm sure it'll fit."

I stood very still, wondering who "she" was and what "she" wasn't supposed to suspect.

"Will it go just the same as we planned for Andy?" asked Helen.

"With one exception," said Grace in a sinister voice. "After last night, I think we should plan a little something extra for Emily. Something . . . special."

I sucked my breath in so hard, I sounded like a Hoover vacuum cleaner. I wanted to yell out, "Emily who?" But since I was the only Emily on the trip, it was fairly obvious

"Emily who." Oh my God. I'd been right. I was next on the "To Kill" list!

"Help me with this zipper, Helen. I think it's stuck."

"It is. I can't get it past this roll of fat at your waist."

"That's not fat. I'm retaining water."

I could almost see Helen rolling her eyes. "My niece said that used to be Andy's favorite line. He swore he wasn't fat. He was just retaining water."

Retaining water. Right. Andy Simon had been short and stout. Just like the Little Teapot.

"How *is* your niece?" asked Grace. "Is she on the mend?"

"With the help of Prozac and therapy. It's terrible the effect a man can have on a woman. Poor girl didn't realize Andy Simon wasn't worth trying to kill herself over. But he got his, didn't he? If I'd had my way, though, he'd have suffered a lot more before he died."

I shivered at Helen's words. Was this an admission of guilt or just wishful thinking? Oh, geesch. What I wouldn't give for a tape recorder right now.

"So how come you went along with our idea?" asked Grace. "You should have told us how you felt. Maybe we could have altered our plans a little."

"Everyone was so enthusiastic. Besides, you're the one who'd been hurt the most, so if you still wanted to do it, I didn't want to be the fly in the ointment. And I liked Lucille's plan. She has a real knack for these things."

Lucille? Was Lucille the gang leader? It *was* like *Murder on the Orient Express.* Everyone had a hand in killing him. I sucked in my breath again.

"Did you hear something?" asked Helen.

"Sounded like a faulty vacuum cleaner," said Grace.

I slithered out of the dress I was trying on and reached for Nana's skirt. I needed to make a fast getaway before I was discovered.

"Funny thing about Lucille," Grace continued. "I didn't think she had it in her to mastermind something like this. She really surprised me."

Yeah. It was freaking amazing what a woman with no lips was capable of doing.

"So what do you think of this dress?" Grace asked.

"It's a smidgen tight, but I think it's you. Buy it."

I grabbed all the little black dresses and dashed to the register.

"Did you find anything to your liking, Madame?"

I flipped through the dresses and selected one that looked good. "I'll take this one."

"An excellent choice. And may I help you find shoes, hosiery, an evening bag, or other accessories to complement your selection?"

I slapped my VISA card onto the counter. "Just the dress. And could you speed it up. I'm in a hurry."

"Very good. Were you aware your nose is blue?"

"I missed you at supper," Nana called out to me from the bedroom. "Where did you eat?"

It was 8:45 P.M. and I was in the bathroom, putting the finishing touches on my makeup before my date with Etienne. "I found a little tearoom up the street from Bucherer."

"We had mushy vegetables and some kinda meat in white sauce again. What'd you have?"

"Four different kinds of luscious pastry." If I was going to get whacked, I didn't want my last meal to consist of nondescript meat in white sauce. I wanted to go out the American way—crazed out of my mind on carbs.

"I wish I'd gone with you. I could use some luscious pastry. My triglycerides could use a boost."

I checked myself out in the vanity mirror one last time,

then made a sweeping entrance into the bedroom. "Ta da!"

"Well, would you look at you," said Nana. "Just like Loretta Young. She used to make them grand entrances through fancy double doors on her TV program years ago. Just once I was wishin' she'd get her train caught between the doors so's I could see the surprise on her face, but all the times I watched, it never happened. It was my biggest disappointment of the fifties. But now *your* dress. There's not enough of it to get caught in the door. Turn around. Lemme see the whole thing."

I spun around on one black stiletto heel and kicked up my other foot in an ingenue pose. Luckily, the dress I'd selected fit like a latex glove. The neckline was low enough to show cleavage. The hemline high enough to show lots of leg. And in between, it was all sexy black shimmer. I'd bought strappy heels, black hose, and pinned my hair up into a French twist with a few wispy corkscrew curls tickling my neck. "I'm a knockout, right?" I asked Nana.

"Yup. A real knockout. Is your nose blue?"

"Unhhhh!" I ran to the mirror. "But I bought foundation. I bought more concealer. How can it still be blue?"

"It'll probably be dark where you're goin' tonight. Maybe your young man won't notice."

"But what if he does?"

"Then tell him the truth."

"The truth?" Hmm. I hadn't thought of that. Nana always had the most original ideas.

"You shouldn't be ashamed a your nose, Emily. You should be proud of it. You done a real brave thing today, and George is real appreciative. I'm sure he'll do something special for you to show his appreciation when he's released from the hospital."

Yeah. Maybe he could save me from the death squad that was out to get me.

"Are you plannin' to bring your young man back to the room with you tonight? If you are, I could make myself scarce and go visit Bernice."

Bernice. Unh. I sighed deeply. "About Bernice, Nana, how much do you really know about her?"

"She's the undefeated champ a the five-yard dash in the Senior Olympics. She's lived in Windsor City all her life. Loves to gossip. Don't have much of a sense a humor. She's treasurer a the Legion a Mary, but I'm not sure why 'cause her math's not real good. We keep comin' up short. I think we need to buy her a calculator. She was widowed real young. Would like to have some plastic surgery but can't afford it. I think she preferred the days when she modeled for that magazine. She still has old issues lyin' all over her house. They're the first thing you see when you visit her. She don't much like havin' a dowager's hump and wrinkles. She'd rather look like you, or maybe blond, like that Angowski woman. Why are you lookin' like that, dear? You look like you just seen a ghost."

Oh. My. God. Could Bernice have pushed Shirley off the cliff out of jealousy? Was she so bitter about getting old that she'd resorted to killing women who were younger and prettier? How twisted was that? "Nana, you may not want to hear this, but I think Bernice may somehow be involved with the deaths."

"No."

"Yes. I know it may sound crazy to you, but hear me out." So I told her how distrustful I was of Bernice's always trying to make other people look bad. How she might be casting suspicion on others to cover her own tracks. How she'd had access to Jane Hanson's drug supply the night Andy died. How she might have lied about the length of the rest room line on top of Mount Pilatus to provide herself an alibi while she pushed Shirley Angowski off the cliff.

"You said yourself she's the reigning champ in the five-yard dash," I said, driving home my point. "That makes her one fast cookie."

"Only when there's a blue ribbon involved."

I gave Nana a pleading look. "So what do you think?" I still hadn't figured out Bernice's connection to the death squad, but I figured I could tackle that angle later.

Nana sucked a little on her teeth. "I don't buy it, dear."

"Why not?"

"Three reasons. Number one, I never seen her speak to that Angowski woman. Why would she kill someone she don't know? Number two, she didn't have no good reason to wanna kill Andy. What's her motive?"

I shook my head. "I haven't worked that out yet, but I have a feeling something happened between the two of them that we don't know about yet. What's your last reason?"

"Bernice is my friend. She might be whiny, and snippy, and crabby, but she's no killer. The killer's gotta be someone else."

I'm glad she could be so confident. I wasn't so sure. "Will you promise to stay away from her?"

"How am I gonna do that without havin' her put me through the third degree? She's not gonna hurt me, Emily. I done nothin' that'd make Bernice wanna kill me."

"You won the lottery."

"My money's no good to Bernice, specially if I'm dead."

I hoped Nana was right. Bernice could schedule a lot of face-lifts with seven million and change.

"I went shoppin' today," Nana said, effectively closing the door on our discussion of Bernice. "Seein's how they took away our defense spray, I figured we needed to rearm ourselves, so I got somethin' even better." She removed an object from a white plastic Casa Grande sack and held it up for me to see.

"A Swiss Army knife? Cool."

"I bought two. This one's yours. See, it even has a little clock in the housin'. And it has all these cute little dinguses inside." She began flipping so many metal gadgets out of the housing, she looked like the stunt double for Edward Scissorhands. "Isn't this somethin'? All these jiggers can perform twenty-nine different functions. I don't know what they all do yet, but if this doesn't scare the killer, it'll sure as heck confuse him."

"I went shopping today, too. I picked up another cow watch to replace the one you lent me. It got a little water-logged when I dived in after George."

"I shoulda mentioned it wasn't waterproof."

Probably wouldn't have helped.

The phone rang. I answered. "Etienne's waiting for me in the lobby," I said when I hung up. "Keep your knife close to you this evening. Okay? Do you have any big plans?" I slipped into my raincoat and stashed my new Swiss Army knife in the outside pocket.

"Don't know yet. I might try out the Jacuzzi. Or I might set up my laptop and send some E-mail to your mother. If her mailbox isn't full, she can go into a full-blown depression. I'm afraid I created a monster when I give her that computer last Christmas. She's sufferin' major addiction."

"You think she does chatrooms and forums and things like that?" I'd once hit the wrong key and landed in a chatroom with "Stud Master" and "Power Prick." Obviously, too many men were spending far too much time at Home Depot these days.

"I don't think she's advanced beyond E-mail yet, but we was talkin' at one of our Legion a Mary meetin's about how

people was havin' electronic romances these days. Imagine."
She shook her head. "Time was, a fella come to your front
door with candy and flowers and courted you real proper.
Now he types a couple a sentences into a computer and
that's s'posed to be good enough. There's no hand holdin'.
No smoochin'. Where's the romance? When I grab a man by
his gonads, I wanna see his face while I'm doin' it."

Eh! If my tongue hadn't been attached, I would have
swallowed it. "How often did you grab men by their
gonads?"

"I only did it with your grampa. And only when I was
feelin' frisky."

That was a relief.

"In later years I never did it more than a couple a times
a day."

"A couple of times a *day?*"

"I slowed down some when I hit seventy."

I wondered if I'd inherited Nana's nymphomaniac gene.
I hadn't seen any evidence of it yet, but who knew? Maybe
I'd be a late bloomer.

I left Nana locked up safely in room number 5111. I suspected she was going to be perfectly fine by herself. After all,
the death squad wasn't after her. They were after me.

The Hotel Chateau Gutsch sat like a castle high above
the city of Lucerne, clinging precariously to the side of a
mountain. Trees and darkness hovered at its outer edges
while floodlights illumined its turrets and whitewashed
stone. After parking his car, Etienne led me through a car-
peted vestibule beyond which I could see small, candlelit
tables set with white linen and gleaming china. For the first
time since the incident in Spengler's dressing room today, I
felt safe. No one in the tour group could ever get to this
place without a car, so I could let down my guard and relax.

At the end of the vestibule, Etienne ushered me through a glass door and into the bar area. It was a cozy room with floor-to-ceiling windows, round tables, a grand piano, and ice sculptures perched on a table with bowls of munchies. He pulled out a chair for me at a secluded table for two in the corner. "Shall I take your coat?"

I slipped my coat off and felt that familiar tingling in my stomach when he did a slow look up and down my body. "Nice." His voice washed over me like warm honey. "Very nice."

Okay. So I'd be paying off my credit card bill for the rest of my life. It was worth it to see that titillating look in his eye. I sat down and opened the wine and cocktail list. Whoa! Twenty francs for a daiquiri? Twenty-two francs for the house wine? I wondered what the incidence of alcoholism was in Switzerland. Probably zero percent. At these prices, a person would fall into bankruptcy before he ever had a chance to fall off the wagon.

"Have you decided what you'd like?" Etienne moved his chair close beside me. Our legs touched casually beneath the table in some kind of unannounced foreplay, and then his pant leg brushed my knee so intimately, I thought my kneecap would have an orgasm.

"I'll have whatever you're having," I said, trying to keep the quiver out of my voice.

He ordered two martinis, then returned his attention to me. "You look lovely tonight, Emily. Absolutely lovely. The dress is exquisite. The hotel must have found your suitcase."

"It's still lost. But the staff collected thirteen dollars and fifty-four cents to see me through until they find it."

He smiled. "Generous of them. That should be just enough to buy yourself more contraband room freshener."

"We're not doing room freshener anymore. We found something better."

"Dare I ask what?"

Since I didn't know if the Swiss had laws against carrying pocketknives concealed, I decided not to press my luck. "I'd prefer not to tell you."

"I hope this doesn't mean you've graduated to something more lethal."

"How do you define lethal?"

He stroked the shimmery cloth at my shoulder then feathered a lazy finger down my inner my arm. "An M-16 is lethal, but in your hands, I suspect a wand of lipliner could become deadly."

Only if it was in a color I didn't like. "I hope you're not laughing at me, because I know for a fact that *I'm* the next victim on the list. They're going to pop me. And I got the impression it was going to be sooner rather than later."

"Who is 'they?'"

"The Dicks and their wives, and maybe Bernice. They're all in cahoots with each other. They killed Andy, and now they're going to kill me."

"You're making some serious charges, Emily."

"I know. But I'm not making it up. Something happened today in the changing room at Spengler."

"Is that why your nose is blue?"

I shook my head. "That happened when a deckhand hit me in the face with a life preserver."

His demeanor suddenly screamed "Inspector Miceli" rather than "Etienne." "Did you report the assault? Do you want to press charges?"

"He didn't mean anything by it. It was just a lucky shot. He thought I was trying to kill myself. But that's not important. I overheard a conversation between Grace Stolee and Helen Teig in the fitting room today, and they practically announced they were going to kill me."

The waiter arrived with our drinks. I stared at the martini glasses that were filled to a third of their capacity and wondered if the bartender had run out of mix. "Is this normal?" I asked Etienne.

"Is what normal?"

"The glasses aren't full." I mean, I'd knocked back more liquid out of the little plastic cup that held an adult dosage of Nyquil than was contained in the cocktail glass in front of me.

"They're full by Swiss standards."

I nodded. Definitely no alcoholism in Switzerland. I raised the glass to my lips, making a special effort not to accidentally swallow the whole thing in one sip. "About Grace and Helen," I continued. "They said they had the same plan for me that they had for Andy."

"Did you hear them say specifically that they were going to kill you? Did they use the words 'kill' or 'murder' or 'poison'?"

"Uh—not exactly. They said things like the jig would be up if I suspected anything. And then Helen said she wished Andy had suffered more. And Grace said Lucille had been the brains of the outfit. And Helen said Grace had a roll of fat at her waist."

"And you put all the pieces together and concluded they're going to kill you."

"Well, what would you conclude?"

"From that conversation? I would conclude that Grace needs to be on a salad diet."

"You didn't hear Grace's voice. It was really sinister. Especially when she mentioned my name."

"I'm afraid we have no law against saying someone's name in a sinister voice. Grace or Helen will have to threaten you with bodily harm before I can make a move, Emily. I'm sorry."

"Okay. But when I end up at the bottom of a cliff like Shirley Angowski, don't say I didn't warn you."

"There's still a chance Ms. Angowski's death was accidental. We've located her camera bag, but it's wedged between two rocks halfway down a chasm. The climbing team won't be able to retrieve it until tomorrow. If neither Grace's nor Helen's fingerprints appear on the bag, perhaps that will calm your fears." He lifted my hand and pressed his mouth gently to the inside of my wrist. I could feel my pulse gallop wildly. "You didn't overhear them *say* they pushed Ms. Angowski off the cliff, did you?"

I watched his mouth whisper across my flesh, causing gooseflesh to rise on my arms. "Unh-uh."

"You didn't hear them *say* they poisoned Mr. Simon, did you?"

I shook my head.

"Then for the moment, my hands are tied."

If his hands were tied, then whose forefinger was tracing the neckline of my bodice, dipping tantalizingly beneath the border and lingering at the place where my bosom swelled above the cloth? Unh. His eyes were so hot on my mouth, I thought my lips might burst into flames. He inched closer. He cupped his hand around the back of my neck and drew me to him, then pressed his lips against the corner of my mouth. "Your dress is driving me insane. If we were alone right now, you'd be up on this table, and I'd be peeling the clothes from your body."

My idea of relaxation exactly. Having someone else undress you. "Maybe the bartender and those people at that other table will leave."

"Or perhaps they would be kind enough not to notice us." He crushed his mouth against mine.

I heard bells. I heard whistles. I heard a door bang open, followed by an intrusive chorus of excited voices. I opened one eye to find Wally leading a contingent of the Golden Swiss Triangle Tour group into the bar. AARRRRRGH!!!

"Hey look!" someone shouted. "There's Emily!"

They swarmed around us like bees. "Imagine finding you here," said Wally in a frosty voice. "I guess when I asked you this morning if you were free tonight, it must have slipped your mind that you already had a date."

Oh, this was going well.

"Official police business," said Etienne, staring Wally down. "Miss Andrew had no choice but to accompany me here this evening. I'm sure you understand."

I worried that someone would ask what kind of police business required Etienne's sticking his tongue down my throat, but no one bothered. They were too busy looking out the window and grabbing munchies from the serving table. "Drinks!" I heard Dick Teig yell. "We need drinks over here."

Nana slithered through the crowd with Bernice. "You wouldn't believe what it took for us to get here, Emily. We hopped a bus outside the hotel, then an electric car at the terminal, then we rode a little cable car up here to the top."

"It's not a cable car," corrected Bernice. "It's a counter-balanced elevator with windows. It's called a funicular."

"I thought you were going to stay in the room this evening," I said to Nana.

"I was, until I got a better offer."

"Emily!" George Farkas fought his way to the table. I guess they didn't want to observe him anymore at the hospital. "There's my little hero. Don't know what I would have done without you today. Your young man won't mind if I buy you a drink to thank you, will he? Maybe I could buy him one, too. Hell, I'm so happy, I'll buy *everyone* a drink. Drinks on the house!" he shouted to the room in general.

I suspected he didn't realize he'd have to take out a small loan to pay for a single round of drinks in this place.

"You don't mind if I join you, do you?" George asked us as he pulled up a chair.

Maybe that was a good idea. I knew CPR. I could probably resuscitate him after the bartender presented him with the bill.

"Marion. Bernice. Jane. Lars. Solvay," said George. "Grab yourselves a chair. Come join us. Maybe we can convince Emily to tell us how she rescued me and my leg today."

Etienne squeezed my knee beneath the table. I flashed him a hopeless smile, then caught sight of the three Dicks and their wives at the next table. They were looking this way, and for whatever reason, they weren't smiling.

CHAPTER 11

"The Black Forest is named for the dark pine and fir trees that cover a mountainous region that is one hundred miles long and twenty miles wide. Throughout the centuries, the forest has been the setting for many fairy tales, but in the most recent decades, nearly half the trees in the region have been damaged by acid rain. And the source of much of that toxic rain is from factories in the United States. In Switzerland we are kinder to the environment. We are the most environmentally conscientious nation in the world."

I yawned as I stared out the window at the forest Sonya was describing over the loudspeaker. Two seats ahead of me, Grace Stolee punched a button on Dick's camcorder and aimed it out the window. "Trees," she said. Grace could really cut to the chase.

We were on a day-trip today, heading for a little spa town called Titisee-Neustadt, which was located at the point where Germany, France, and Switzerland converge. We had already stopped for picture taking at the Rhine

Falls, which I considered a major water hazard, but since Dick Stolee's toupee didn't fly off his head, I was spared having to fling myself into the raging water to save it.

I didn't have to worry about George Farkas losing his leg today. George wasn't with us.

Nana and I were sitting on the long bench seat at the back of the bus, she at one window and I at the other, with a good six feet of space between us. I eyed the space longingly and thought about a nap. Not a bad idea considering how little sleep I'd gotten last night.

I looked over at Nana to find her snoring quietly with her chin slumped onto her chest. I guess she wasn't too interested in Sonya's dissertation on acid rain, which didn't mean she was antigreen. It just meant she hadn't gotten much sleep last night either.

When Sonya finished her spiel, Wally navigated to the front of the bus and took over the microphone. "You've probably noticed that George Farkas isn't with us this morning. George suffered what we all thought was a major heart attack last night at the Hotel Chateau Gutsch after the bartender presented him with his bill. Emily had the presence of mind to throw him to the floor and begin resuscitation measures, but luckily it only turned out to be a panic attack."

I'd suspected he wasn't having a heart attack when he tried to give my lip a hickey during mouth-to-mouth.

"Emily and her grandmother were kind enough to accompany George in the ambulance to the hospital, and to stay with him until he was released, so let's have a round of applause to show the ladies our appreciation."

Scattered applause. A few whistles.

"George decided to stay at the hotel today to recuperate," Wally continued. "But you have to ask what he's recuperating from? The panic attack or the excitement of Emily's mouth-to-mouth!"

Hoots. Guffaws. Giggles.

Dick Rassmuson stood up and clutched his hands to his chest. "I feel the big one coming on, Emily. I need oxygen. I need mouth-to-mouth!"

"Take an aspirin!" one of the men shouted.

I hunkered down in my seat and began counting the number of days left on our Golden Swiss Triangle tour. I didn't know how much longer I could play the part of the escort extraordinaire. Last night had started out so perfectly. The intimate room. Etienne's kiss. The prospect of getting naked. Hanging out in a hospital waiting room for five hours hadn't been part of the plan. I didn't even get a chance to kiss Etienne good-bye. I'd merely had time to wave to him from inside the ambulance as we drove away. There was *no* justice in the world. With the way I'd looked last night, I should have spent the evening doing something that would have caused me to wake up this morning feeling satisfied and glowing. Instead, I'd broken the heel of my strappy new shoes in an altercation with the hospital's vending machine and I had bags under my eyes. Was I the poster child for today's successful woman, or what?

"We'll be stopping in the town of Titisee-Neustadt for two and a half hours," Wally announced. "There are plenty of places to have lunch along the main street and lots of boutiques and shops in the town center."

It was becoming apparent that a Golden Swiss Triangle tour revolved around driving really long distances to eat lunch and shop. But I didn't mind the drive today. The weather had broken the moment we left Switzerland and crossed the border into Germany, which made me think we would have been wiser to book the Golden Deutschland

Triangle Tour. Switzerland might have Alps, but Germany had sunshine.

I rested my head against the window, letting the sun wash over my face, and the next thing I knew, Wally was standing above me, shaking my shoulder. "We're here, Sleeping Beauty. Do you want to join us?"

I rubbed the sleep from my eyes. "We're here?" I looked down the length of the bus to find it empty. "Where is everyone?"

"Walking down to the lake to board the boat."

"Boat?" Unh-oh. "You never said anything about a boat."

"I did so. About a half hour ago. You must have been sleeping."

"We *can't* board another boat! We can't go anywhere *near* water!"

"It's on the itinerary. We take a one-way boat trip from the southern end of Lake Titisee to the town at the northern end, and the bus meets us there. It's not a long boat ride. Only about ten minutes. Are you coming?" He headed off down the aisle. I chased after him.

"But I didn't bring any dry clothes with me!"

"What makes you think you're going to get wet?"

"When have I been around water on this trip and not gotten wet?"

He stopped for a beat. "Are you wearing a watch?"

"No."

"Then what are you worried about?"

We were the last people to board the boat. Much to my relief, the vessel was a sightseeing boat, enclosed in glass, with no upper deck, so there would be little opportunity for anyone to lose anything overboard. I slid into the first booth with a space and took a deep breath, hoping my knees would eventually stop knocking together. Wally was right. I had nothing to worry about. So why did I feel as if I was waiting for the other shoe to drop?

"I'm having the big one!" Dick Rassmuson yelled out from the stern of the boat. "I need mouth-to-mouth, Emily! You did it for George. You can do it for me!"

I threw him my "Get real" look, then settled in for the journey across the lake.

Sonya began a narration over the boat loudspeaker. "Lake Titisee is named for the Roman general Titus, who once camped here with his troops, but the first authenticated reference to the name is found in documents dating from the year 1111."

The lake was a sparkling gem, with a forest of golden-leaved trees marching from high, steep slopes down to its shore. It was kind of neat to imagine the lake had looked exactly like this two thousand years ago, only without the powerboat.

"How deep is this lake?" Lars Bakke called out to Sonya.

"Why do you need to know that? Are you going scuba diving? There is *no* scuba diving allowed in Lake Titisee."

"How cold's the water?" asked Dick Teig.

"Why don't you stick your head in and find out?" hissed Sonya.

"No!" I leaped out of my seat. "No one sticks anything in the water! Do you hear me? No piggies. No pinkies. No heads. Stay in your seats and don't move a muscle!" Okay, so maybe I was a little over the top, but it seemed to work. No one was moving. That was a good sign. Besides, if Dick Teig stuck his head in the water, we'd be looking at a major tidal wave.

"It's the big one, Emily!" shouted Dick Rassmuson. "I can feel the palpitations. I'm getting short of breath. You better get back here and start puckering up!"

Laughter exploded throughout the cabin. High-pitched

giggles. Earsplitting hysteria. I looked from bow to stern. Dick Rassmuson might be a cutup, but he wasn't *that* funny. What in the world was going on? Then I noticed the fingers pointing out the window. I pivoted my head around. A man was wading into the lake near the beach area at the opposite shore. There was nothing noteworthy about that, other than the fact that he was buck naked.

The uproar grew louder. Hoots. Wolf whistles. I guess that meant the men had spotted the naked women lounging on chairs in a glass-fronted building behind the beach. I executed a major eye roll. I'm so glad everyone was being so adult about this. Wally wandered over to my side.

"What's with all the laughter? They've never seen naked people before?"

"I'm sure it's because they've never seen a public beach before. Remember. They're from Iowa."

Sonya's voice came over the loudspeaker again. "Titisee-Neustadt is a spa town. The glass-fronted building you see ahead of you is where people are treated for obesity, asthma, chronic bronchitis, allergies, metabolic diseases, and physical and emotional exhaustion."

"Is that place coed, or do you have to get naked in a room with your own kind?" yelled Dick Rassmuson.

Sonya blew a disgusted breath into the loudspeaker and clicked it off in an obvious snit. I suspected that marked the end of her narration. I heard the engine cut as we neared the shore, and we got jostled a little as the vessel bumped against the rubber tires on the dock. The captain assisted each of us out of the boat and as we followed Wally toward the town center, I breathed a sigh of relief that the excursion across the lake had gone off without incident. All that concern for nothing. I'd become too much of a worrywart. I needed to chill out more.

Wally stopped in the middle of the pedestrian walkway

with instructions. "Those of you who are interested in see- ing how cuckoo clocks are made can see a demonstration with me in five minutes. The rest of you can explore the town and meet the bus in the parking lot at the end of this road at two o'clock."

I didn't want to know how cuckoo clocks were made. If I got curious, I could dismantle one of the clocks Bernice had stockpiled in my room. She'd never miss it. I did want to do some shopping, I wanted to eat, and I wanted to keep tabs on the Teigs, Rassmusons, Stolees, and Bernice. If they had any surprises planned, I wanted to be three steps ahead of them.

"Bernice and me are goin' to that cuckoo clock demon- stration." Nana tugged on my sleeve to make sure I heard. "The place is probably gonna be really crowded, but we'll try to wrestle our way down front so we'll be *in full view* of everythin' and you won't have to worry 'bout us missin' nothin'." She waggled her eyebrows in an overstated ges- ture which I took to mean, *There's safety in numbers, dear. Don't worry about me.* And she was right, of course. She wasn't a child. I couldn't tether her to my wrist to appease my anxiety.

"You gonna be all right on your own?" she asked me.

I gave her a thumbs-up and patted the pocket that con- tained my Swiss Army knife. "I'll be fine." But the cuckoo clock business reminded me that I hadn't heard a word about the disposition of Andy's body. Had they shipped him back to Iowa already or was he going to fly back with the rest of us? I made a mental note to ask Etienne. It would give me the perfect excuse to call him. Maybe he'd have the fingerprint results on Shirley Angowski's camera bag today. I hoped so. All these unanswered questions were making me as cuckoo as some of the clocks around here.

The streets and sidewalks were crowded with tourists

eating ice-cream cones, pushing baby strollers, and toting shopping bags. Most of our group followed Wally to the cuckoo demonstration, but the Rassmusons, Teigs, Stolees, and Jane Hanson ventured off down the street toward the spa, so that's where I ventured, too. I'd never tailed anyone before, but it was pretty much a no-brainer. All I had to do was mingle with the crowd and stay far enough behind them so I wasn't being too obvious.

They wandered into a couple of shops specializing in wine, cheese, and sausage. I got hungry smelling sausage fumes, so I bought an ice cream and sat on a bench on the opposite side of the road. When they reappeared, they caught my eye, waved, and continued down the road. I was a little concerned about the wave. Were they feigning friendliness or were they on to me? Whatever. I headed down the road behind them.

Near the Spa they detoured into another shop. When I got close enough, I saw that it was a cafeteria-type eatery, which meant, they were going to be in there for a long time. I gnawed on my cone, wondering what to do. Should I go in there after them, or should I look for a pair of shoes to replace the ones I'd ruined last night? Hmm. The ice cream hadn't filled me up. Maybe I should have some Black Forest cake to top it off. That sounded good. And if they accused me of following them, I could tell them it was a free country. I thought about that for a moment. Germany was free. Wasn't it? I entered the cafeteria, promising myself I'd brush up on international politics when I got back to Iowa.

I grabbed a tray and wandered around the many colorful food islands, having no idea what much of the food was since it was labeled in German. No pizza. No spaghetti. No fried chicken. No Iowa pork chops. They did have serve-yourself soft-serve ice cream with sprinkles, and cherries, and nuts, but since I'd already been the ice-cream route, I loaded my tray with some other awesome-looking desserts and headed for the cashier.

The Dicks et al had pushed two tables together and were digging into their food when I passed them on my way to an empty table. Dick Stolee looked up at me with his hideously deformed zucchini nose. Ouch. He was making the Elephant Man look good. "Are you following us?" he asked.

I smiled nervously. "Of course I'm following you."

"Why?"

"Because you're stopping at all the places where I want to stop. Would you rather have me get ahead of you? Then you can follow me."

Lucille and Helen exchanged glances as if they wished they'd thought of the idea. Dick narrowed his gaze at me. "Just don't get too close," he warned.

I smiled again. "Enjoy your meal."

I kept my eye on their table as I plowed through my plates of pastry. They sampled each other's food a lot and took turns snapping pictures of each other at the table. Dick Stolee wandered around the food islands with his camcorder and came back with a tray of coffee for everyone. They drank, talked, laughed, and drank some more. Then Jane and Grace disappeared for several minutes and returned with a tray of ice cream sundaes.

"I've changed my mind," I heard Lucille say. "I'd rather have sprinkles than nuts."

Her husband plopped the sundae in front of her. "If you change your order, everyone else's order gets messed up. You ordered nuts, you eat nuts."

She skated the bowl back at him. "I don't want nuts."

"There's no keeping you happy, is there? Too damn bad. Nuts is what you're getting." He shoved it back in her direction.

"Excuse me?" she snapped. "I don't remember anyone making you emperor. Does someone else want my nuts?"

"I'm kind of a cherry man myself," said Dick Teig.

"Me too," Dick Stolee added quickly.

I suspected both Dicks preferred nuts over cherries but were too homophobic to admit it.

"Jane?" Lucille implored.

Jane shook her head. "I'm allergic to nuts."

"So's Lucille," said her husband. "At least *my* nuts. She didn't seem to have a problem with Andy's though."

Gasps all around the table. "That was uncalled for," said Helen.

Lucille propelled the sundae back at Dick. "I wouldn't eat that now if you *paid* me, you miserable lowlife."

"Two-timer."

"Skinflint."

"Slut."

I watched the sundae shoot back and forth between them and wondered what was going to break out first: a fistfight or a food fight.

Lucille shot out of her chair, causing it to crash backward onto the floor. "Slut? How dare you!" She picked up the dish of ice cream. She glared at her husband. Okay. My money was on the food fight. Dick Stolee reached for his camcorder.

"Press one button on that camcorder, and I'll break your arm," Grace threatened. She got to her feet to join Lucille. "It's bad enough Dick Rassmuson has to air his dirty laundry in public, but you're not going to encourage him by getting it on tape!"

"The hell you say," said Dick, who whipped the camera up to his eye and aimed it at his wife. "No one's going to tell me what I can or can't record. This is Grace under pressure. Boy, she looks like she's gonna blow."

Grace picked up her coffee cup and fired the contents at the camcorder. "Grace!" screamed her husband as he sloughed coffee off his face. "You idiot! If you've ruined my camera, I'm going to be *so* pissed! Napkins. I need napkins!"

"Why don't you use your toupee?" said Lucille. "It's the closest thing to a mop around here."

Grace gave Lucille a high five. Helen and Jane stood up in a show of force. "I saw a pharmacy a few doors down," said Jane to the ladies. "I recommend we wander over and check out the prices."

Lucille dropped her dish of ice cream back onto the table. "I don't know who you think you're going to sit with on the trip back to Lucerne," she spat at her husband, "but it's not going to be me. Come on, girls."

"Don't flatter yourself!" Dick Rassmuson raved, as the women huffed away from the table. "I'd rather *walk* back to Lucerne than sit on the bus beside you!"

Unh-oh. Wally was *not* going to be happy about the change in seat assignments. The Dicks, on the other hand, looked thrilled about the sudden change in seating. Or maybe they were just happy about all the unclaimed ice cream in front of them. Before the women were out the door, they'd divvied up the seven sundaes among themselves and began scarfing down sprinkles and cherries. They weren't completely out of touch. Even in Iowa, soft-serve tended to melt fast.

Dick Rassmuson caught my eye and held up the odd bowl. "Last one. You want it?"

I waved him off. "Couldn't eat another thing."

He shrugged and ate it himself. When they got up to leave, he caught my eye again, clutched his chest, and hung his tongue out the corner of his mouth. This was getting old *real* fast. "You need another schtick," I called out. "Go away. Leave me alone."

With the group in fragments, I didn't feel so impelled to keep my eye on them. I suspected they were too annoyed with each other to implement their plot against me. A successful murder attempt would require both cooperation and coordination, and cooperation wasn't what was happening with the Dicks and their wives this afternoon. Gee. What a shame. I guess I'd be forced to fritter away the rest of my day in some of the little boutiques that lined the main street.

A half hour later, armed with a stack of postcards and some souvenirs for my nephews, I found my way onto the lawn of the spa and dug my camera out of my shoulder bag. No sense letting the sun go to waste. I put a bead on the lake and the surrounding mountains. CLICK. The sightseeing boat that was docked at the pier. CLICK. The base of a hooped barrel that looked as if it might be used for outdoor baths. CLICK. Three men sneaking around the corner of the spa with cameras at the ready. Hmm. I lowered my camera. What a surprise. The three Dicks. I could imagine the headlines of the *Windsor City Register* should someone catch them—"Snoopy Dicks Branded Peeping Toms in German Spa Town."

I let fly a whistle that spun them around and had them scampering across the lawn toward me like wayward puppies. Stolee and Teig arrived first. "How's the scenery down there?" I asked. "Finding a lot of Kodak moments, are you?"

Dick Teig spoke under his breath. "Look, Emily, it's not every day you stumble across naked babes like this. The guys back home won't believe it. So if you could keep it under your hat until we show them the pictures."

"What about your wives?"

Dick Rassmuson pulled up the rear. He must have seen something that scared him because his hands were trembling. "What about our wives?" he asked.

Duh? "What do you think they're going to say about your extracurricular activities?"

"They'll never find out," he rasped. "Not unless you tell them. You're not gonna do that, are you? Man, is it hot out here or is it just me?" Dick Rassmuson was sure out of shape. A little jog like that had gotten him all out of breath.

Dick Teig elbowed him in the ribs. "Probably the scenery that has you so worked up. Hubba hubba."

I gave them my sternest schoolmarm look. "Okay, you guys, if you leave right now, I won't tell your wives. If you don't, all bets are off."

"Party poop," said Dick Teig.

"Might as well go," groused Dick Stolee. "My camcorder's not working right anyway."

Dick Rassmuson urged the two along. "Go on without me. I'll catch up as soon as I catch my breath." He placed his hand over his heart. "My chest's really pounding, Emily."

"You suppose it's the big one?"

"I need to sit down. Maybe I need a cigar."

The man never gave up. "You do that. But you better not stay long because I'll be back to make sure you're not doing any more snooping."

He sat down on a nearby bench and massaged his abdomen. "I don't feel so good. I could use some serious mouth-to-mouth."

How gullible did he think I was? Did he think I'd been born yesterday? "Nice try, Dick. You might want to consider some daily aerobic exercise though. It might help with the shortness of breath thing."

I spent the next forty-five minutes in a ladies' boutique named Toni Heim, trying to convince myself not to buy a cute little boiled wool jacket that cost more than the national debt. In the end I bought it anyway. The exchange rate made it cheaper than it would be back in the States, so I reasoned it was more like the national debt of Liechtenstein than the United States. Liechtenstein was a small country. I could afford Liechtenstein.

I practically had a head-on collision with Nana when I walked out the door of the boutique. I grabbed hold of her so as not to knock her down. "You're going someplace in a hurry," I laughed.

"I'm headin' back to the bus for a nap. I'm all used up. But I can't figure what did me in—sittin' in the hospital waiting room 'til the wee hours a the mornin', or those three Shirley Temples I knocked back at the chateau last night. Don't tell your mother about the cocktails. She don't think a woman a my advanced years should be drinkin' ardent spirits."

I made a gesture of buttoning my lip. "It'll be our secret. But, Nana, a Shirley Temple is nonalcoholic. It's not that potent."

"At seventy-eight, strawberry Ovaltine can be potent."

"I'm not sure the bus will be open if you head back to the parking lot." I yanked my Swiss Army knife out of my coat pocket to check the time. "We still have another hour before we leave. I'm going to head over to the spa grounds, sit on a bench, and write out a few postcards. You're welcome to come with me and take a nap on the bench."

"Lead the way."

"Where's Bernice?"

"She's staked a claim on a table at a little outdoor café where she says she's gonna stay 'til just before the bus leaves. She's been doin' too much walkin'. Her bunions are killin' her."

We dodged tourists and scurried out of the path of strollers as we headed toward the lake. When the spa came into view, I noticed a man on the bench where Dick

Rassmuson had been sitting when I left. As we drew closer, I realized my lecture had fallen on deaf ears because the man sitting on the bench *was* Dick Rassmuson. He'd probably been getting an eyeful for the last forty-five minutes and acting like a real jerk.

I stomped in front of him. "Okay, Dick. Hand over your film." I was probably overstepping my bounds as an escort, but it was worth a try. Maybe I'd catch him in a weak moment.

Dick didn't respond. His head was hanging forward on his chest, like he was taking a nap, but his eyes were wide-open. Unh-oh.

Nana bent down to look at him. "You s'pose he knocked back one too many Shirley Temples last night, too?"

His skin looked kind of purple and waxy, his lips were really pale, and his hands were tinged blue. I tapped him on the shoulder. "Dick?"

No response. I was getting a very bad feeling about this. I pressed my fingers to his neck. His skin was still warm, but he had no pulse. I stepped back from the body and grabbed Nana's hand. "I don't want to jump to any conclusions, but what does this look like to you?"

"Looks like a dead Dick."

CHAPTER 12

"That's what it looks like to me, too." I sucked in a resigned breath and struggled to remain calm. "He's dead." When I said the words aloud, the full impact of the situation hit me. "OH MY GOD! HE'S DEAD! This is all my fault! He said he didn't feel well. He said his chest was pounding. He said he needed mouth-to-mouth. I didn't believe him! I could have saved him! Oh my God. I killed him!"

"The man dropped dead, Emily. We're old. It happens."

She had a point. But still, "You don't think I'm to blame?"

"I think all those cigars he smoked was to blame."

That made me feel a little better. I cocked my head to look at him from another angle. "What do you suppose killed him?"

"Looks like he had the big one."

Nana was probably right. There was no blood. No visible bruising. No obvious gunshot wounds. He had a heart condition. He'd probably suffered a heart attack. I mean, according to Shirley Angowski, he'd already been playing with fire by taking pills for impotence with his heart medication. That made him a prime candidate for a heart attack. Unless . . .

I sucked in my breath again. Unless someone had poisoned him with the same dimethyl sulfate that had killed Andy and made his death *look* like a heart attack. Oh my God! Was Dick Rassmuson the killer's third victim?

Okay. I was really creeped out now. "I need to find Wally," I said in a rush of breath.

"He had lunch at the same outdoor café that Bernice and me ate at. Maybe he's still there."

"You want to come with me?"

"I better stay here with the body."

"Are you sure you want to do that?" It wasn't like Dick was going anywhere, and guarding a corpse wasn't one of the highlighted activities on Nana's holiday itinerary.

"I'm the Legion a Mary's official representative for visitations at Heavenly Host Funeral Home, so I'm pretty used to hangin' around dead people these days."

I dumped my purchases onto the other end of Dick's bench. After getting directions from Nana, I sprinted down the street toward the café. Wally was seated at a table drinking café latte. He was sporting what looked like a new green alpine hat to keep the sun out of his eyes. I grabbed him by the arm and urged him to his feet. "Nice hat. You need to come with me. We have a crisis."

"What kind of crisis?"

"You need to come now. Leave some money for the bill."

He slapped some coins onto the table and stumbled behind me as I dragged him into the street. "This had better be good," he complained. "I was only halfway through that café latte."

"Dick Rassmuson is dead."

"WHAT?"

"Can you walk a little faster?"

"How do you know he's dead?"

"Because he's not breathing!"

"Shit," he said, doubling his pace. "SHIT!"

"It looks like a heart attack."

"Great. This is just great. We'll never get him out of Germany if he's dead."

"Why not?" I hurried him toward the spa grounds.

"Because it's Germany! They don't like foreigners dying in their country. You wouldn't believe the paperwork. This happened to one of my colleagues a few years ago. An elderly man died, and the authorities kept the whole tour group confined for over a week asking questions, administering polygraph tests. It was a disaster. Triangle Tours lost a lot of money on that one because they had to reimburse everyone for the inconvenience plus pay for their lodging in Germany. If the same thing happens to us, Triangle is out a lot of money again, and I'm probably out a job. Shit."

It seemed this information might have warranted a footnote in the brochure. *Triangle Tours strongly suggests you not die while visiting a foreign country, Germany in particular.* Of course, there was no guarantee Dick Rassmuson would have heeded the warning, especially if it had been written in fine print.

Nana was sitting on the bench beside Dick when we arrived, shooing away flies with her handbag. I admired her courage for daring to sit that close to him. "I thought if we both sat here sayin' nothin' to each other, people would think we were married and wouldn't pay us no nevermind."

Wally felt for a pulse.

"Well?" I asked.

"Shit. He's dead."

"So now what do we do? Call the police?"

"NO! No police. We gotta get him out of here. We gotta get him back on the bus."

I thought about that for a full millisecond. "ARE YOU CRAZY?"

"Look, Emily. He can't stay here. We have to get him back to Switzerland and *then* we can call the Swiss police. The Swiss are much more understanding about people dying on them than the Germans. We'll tell them he died in his sleep on the bus."

"But that's a lie! We could end up in jail for obstructing justice, for perjury, for—"

"You better decide what you're gonna do fast," said Nana. "These flies are gettin' thick." She swatted Dick's arm with her handbag. He fell sideways and toppled off the bench.

"Oh geez," hollered Wally. We both seized an arm, hiked him up, and heaved him back onto the bench.

"You're lucky rigor mortis hasn't set in yet," said Nana.

Wally looked apoplectic. "Okay, Emily, here's the deal. You help me get him back on the bus, and I'll take full responsibility for the consequences. I won't mention your name. You won't even have to talk to the Swiss police when we get back. But we have to get him out of here before anyone else notices he's dead."

I didn't feel real comfortable about this, but I supposed the bottom line was, Dick was dead, and there was nothing we could do to bring him back. We wouldn't know how he died until an autopsy was performed, and since all the other autopsies had been performed in Lucerne, this one might as well be too. I just hoped we wouldn't be leaving vital evidence behind when we moved him. "All right," I conceded. "I'll help you."

"When are you gonna tell Lucille?" asked Nana. "She's bound to notice he's not breathin' at some point on the bus ride home."

Wally's eyes glazed over. "Shit. I forgot about his wife."

"Lucille won't be a problem," I assured him. "They had a big fight in the cafeteria. They're not speaking. They had no intention of sitting with each other on the way back to Lucerne anyway."

"Good. That'll buy us some time."

But it did nothing to solve our immediate problem. "Okay, how do we get him back to the bus without attracting attention?"

Wally executed a 360-degree turn, looking, assessing. He snapped his fingers. "The spa. You two sit tight. I'll be right back."

Fifteen minutes later he reappeared in a four-passenger motorized golf cart with a canopy. "I told the spa manager who I was and explained that one of my tour members was ill and needed to be transported back to the bus. They're keeping my passport as collateral until I bring it back. Okay, ladies, let's load our passenger into the backseat."

I grabbed an arm. Wally grabbed an arm. "On the count of three," said Wally. "One. Two. Three!" I yanked. Wally yanked. We clean-and-jerked him off the bench. Momentum sent him flying forward. SMACK! Face first into the canopy of the golf cart. BOOM! Flat on his back onto the ground.

"This is going well," I said.

"Shit," said Wally.

"What's this gizmo on the back of the golf cart?" asked Nana. Wally and I took a peek.

"Looks like some kind of hydraulic lift," I said. Coloradans knew ski lifts. Californians knew face-lifts. Iowans knew hydraulic lifts, especially Iowans like me, who'd been raised on grain farms around heavy machinery. I hopped into the driver's seat and fidgeted with a few toggle switches. HRRRMMMM! The lift hummed into action. Ah, the genius of German engineering. I backed the cart up to the body and we hoisted Dick onto the lift. I hit the toggle switch again and Dick levitated upward like an oversize sack of seed corn.

"All right!" said Wally.

We swung his legs around and slid him onto the backseat in a sitting position, then stood back to assess our handiwork. Nana had closed Dick's eyes, but it hadn't helped much.

"What do you think?" Wally asked me.

"It looks like we have a dead guy sitting in the back of our golf cart."

"Maybe you need to gussy him up a bit so he don't look so dead," said Nana.

I looked at Wally. Wally looked at me. I stared at Wally's new green alpine hat and smiled. He swiped it off his head and stuck it on Dick's at a cocky angle. We assessed again.

"Better," I said. "But he's still too exposed." I snapped my fingers with sudden inspiration. I dug into my shoulder bag and pulled out the sunglasses Shirley Angowski had given me atop Mount Pilatus. I slid them onto Dick's face. We assessed again. "What do you think now?"

"Perfect," said Wally. "Hop in. I'm driving."

"You're driving?" I objected. "How come you get to drive?"

"Because I'm the one whose passport is on the line if anything happens in transit."

I looked at Nana. Nana looked at me. One of us was going to have to sit in back with Dick. "You wanna flip a coin to see who gets to ride shotgun?" asked Nana.

Two minutes later we were whizzing across the spa lawn

at the breakneck speed of eight miles per hour. Wally shot out onto the pedestrian walkway and banged a sharp left turn. Dick lurched forward and fell over into my lap. "You wanna watch the corners!" I yelled from the backseat as I propped him back up. I straightened his hat and sunglasses and batted a few flies away. "How far to the bus?"

"Be there in a few minutes," assured Wally.

The driving was slow, with all the tourists crowding the walkway. "S'cuse me!" Wally kept shouting. "We're trying to get by here!" We spied Bernice as she hobbled in the direction of the parking lot, and when Wally slowed to let a stroller pass, she flagged us down.

"I can't walk another step. You got room for another passenger?"

"NO!" we yelled in unison. Bernice winced and grabbed her head as if she'd been zapped by chain lightning. I suspected if she wasn't deaf before, she was now.

Wally zoomed around the baby stroller and gunned the cart. Lars and Solvay Bakke were standing by a bench on the walkway and waved as we passed by. "New hat, Dick?" Solvay called as we slowed for more foot traffic.

Being dead, Dick said nothing.

"Yoo-hoo," Solvay persisted. Sweat beaded my upper lip. Sweat bathed my palms. We were about to be found out.

"Hey," Solvay shouted. "Are you too good to talk to us?"

I waved to Solvay, then slid my left hand under Dick's elbow and popped his arm up so he could wave, too. I figured Dick would have wanted it that way. He wasn't a snob. He couldn't help it if he was dead.

We found the bus at the far end of the parking lot. It was completely empty. It was also locked.

"Damn!" said Wally. "We gotta find Max before people start drifting back." He checked his watch. "We only have a half hour."

"More like two minutes," I corrected. "Remember? Iowans are always early."

Max, our bus driver, was a big bull of a man who looked as if he might have been a Gestapo commandant before he made the big career move to tour bus driver. I gave the parking lot the once-over and noticed a small group of tidily dressed men standing by one of the other tour busses. "He could be over there," I said, pointing.

Wally took off like a shot. "He'd better hurry," said Nana. "Bernice will probably wanna chew on him for not givin' her a lift, so I expect she'll be showin' up any minute."

I looked over my shoulder to find Wally and Max locked in a heated discussion as they headed back toward the golf cart. Arms flew. Spittle flew. Max unlocked the door of the bus, then headed in our direction.

"We gots to get body to hell into bus," said Max. English obviously wasn't his first language. "Man can't die here. Better he die in Switzerland." He shoved Dick's hat and sunglasses at me, then in one motion lifted Dick over his shoulder and carried him up the stairs of the bus. He made his way down the aisle to the back of the bus and unloaded Dick on the rear seat. Whew. Now that the hard part was behind us, maybe I could breathe a little easier.

"I'd better get his hat and glasses back on him," I said to Wally.

"Right. And we'll be making some hairpin turns on the way back to Lucerne, so you need to make sure he doesn't fall over too much. Try to keep him propped against the window."

"Excuse me?" My part in this was over. I'd helped get Dick back to the bus. What was this propping him against the window business?

Wally looked surprised. "You need to sit with him on the way back."

"ME? Why me?"

"*Someone* has to!"

"What about you? *You're* the tour guide. I'm only the escort!"

"You've done such a good job with him so far, Emily. Can't you be a team player and follow through?"

"NO!"

"Well, you have to do it anyway because there *is* no one else. I have to sit at the front of the bus and conduct the sing-along on the way back."

"I could conduct the sing-along," I protested. "I have a good singing voice. I was in *Joseph and the Amazing Technicolor Dreamcoat.*"

Wally smiled. "Nice try. I don't think so. You better get back there and get settled before people start arriving. I need to get the cart back to the spa."

"But it's a long drive back to Lucerne," I shouted, as Wally hopped into the cart. "Shouldn't Dick be in a cooler or something? What happens if he starts to—you know— smell bad?"

Forty minutes later, as the bus headed out of the resort town of Titisee-Neustadt, Wally made an announcement over the microphone. "Due to a malfunction in the ventilation system, I regret to inform you that the back half of the bus will be a little cool on the drive back to Lucerne. There are blankets in the overhead compartments if you need them. I apologize for any inconvenience this might cause."

A *little* cool? We weren't even on the main road yet and the tips of my ears were starting to freeze. I grabbed two blankets from the overhead compartment and tucked one around Dick and one around me. I know I'd said earlier that I needed to chill out, but this wasn't exactly what I'd had in mind.

* * *

The weather deteriorated steadily as we headed south. Arriving back in Lucerne, we were welcomed by the normal fare of heavy drizzle and dense fog. I was so cold, I no longer had feeling in my extremities, and my lips were completely numb. I felt like Emily Andrew, human Sno-Kone.

"After dinner this evening there'll be a group meeting in the lobby for the Iowa contingent," announced Wally over the mike. "It's extremely important that all of you attend, so please be there."

The bus emptied amid grumblings from everyone about the trip home. The people at the front of the bus had been too hot. The people at the rear of the bus had been too cold. I'd have thought the people in the middle would have been just right, but even they had started to complain about an unpleasant odor wafting about the bus. Fortunately, my nose was a cube of ice, so I couldn't smell a thing. My only problem was hypothermia.

Wally made his way to the back of the bus and clapped me on the shoulder. "Good job, Emily. We pulled it off. I'll contact the authorities, and they can take it from here. Geez, you look awful. I hope you don't have frostbite." He hugged his arms to himself. "Man, it's freezing back here. No wonder your nose is purple. I'm heading inside the hotel. I'll wait for the police in there."

Nana helped me inch my way off the bus and into the hotel. Every bone inside me creaked with each step. "How come you're not cold?" I asked her.

"The change, dear. I haven't been cold since nineteen-seventy-two."

We picked up the room key at the desk and took the elevator to the fifth floor. "You may wanna take a long, hot bath in the Jacuzzi," Nana suggested when we were inside the room. "It might take the chill off. You want me to run the water?"

I nodded. My jaw was too stiff with cold to answer. My teeth were ice pellets inside my mouth. And through the cold, I could feel the area around my new crown start to ache again. Ah, yes, another banner day in the life of Emily Andrew.

I hung up my raincoat, kicked off my shoes, collapsed into a boudoir chair, and thought about what a horrendous day I'd had. The trickery. The deceit. The cold. Of course, my day hadn't been as horrendous as Dick Rassmuson's. I shot up a little straighter with that thought. All things considered, my day had been considerably better than Dick's.

Nuts. I hated when that happened. I hated having my pity parties interrupted by the voice of reason.

KNOCK. KNOCK. KNOCK.

I stared at the door. Not the police. They couldn't get here that fast, and besides, Wally promised he wouldn't drag my name into the investigation.

I tiptoed to the door and looked through the peephole. A man wearing a bellman's uniform was in the hall. I opened the door. "Ms. Andrew?"

"My suitcase!" There it was. Sitting on its little wheels beside him. My twenty-six-inch tapestried pullman. I suppressed the urge to scooch down and hug it. "You found my suitcase! This is wonderful! Where was it?"

He wheeled it into the room. "Apparently, a member of our housekeeping staff noticed a rend in the material when it was sitting outside your room, so she took it to luggage repair to have it mended. We have our own mender in house."

"So it was here all the time?"

"In the basement."

"It was in the basement, and you couldn't find it?" Incredulity in my voice.

"You should have told us there was a rend in the material, Madame."

"I didn't *know* there was a rend in the material."

"Yes, but if you had noticed, that would have clued us to check the repair room rather than the storage room and lost and found."

"I didn't know you *had* a repair room."

"Every hotel in Switzerland has a repair room, Madame. It's rather a necessity considering what the airlines do to luggage these days." He broke into a smile that stretched ear to ear. "The Grand Palais prides itself on keeping their guests' luggage in perfect repair. It's hotel policy."

I thought about the pink teddy bear sweatshirt. The Sunday sweatshirt with lace. The dead muskie sweatshirt. My words squirted out of my mouth between clenched teeth. "Does the hotel have a policy about guests being forced to run around without their clothes . . . WHILE YOU REPAIR A MICROSCOPIC TEAR IN THEIR LUGGAGE?"

"As far as I know, Madame, the hotel has no policy concerning nudity."

I was busy emptying my suitcase when Nana came out of the bathroom a few minutes later.

"Well, would you look at that," she marveled. "Your suitcase is back. Where'd they find it?"

"In the basement being mended."

"Did it need mendin'?"

"*Someone* seemed to think it did."

Nana shrugged. "They must have better eye care here than we do back home."

By the time we hung up the rest of my clothes and put away my toiletries, the Jacuzzi was full and the jets were percolating. Nana checked her watch. "Supper's in fifteen minutes, Emily. We gotta hurry."

"You go on without me," I insisted. "I plan on soaking until my skin wrinkles like a prune. But I'll meet you in the lobby around seven for the group meeting." I failed to mention that my tooth was aching so badly, I probably wouldn't be able to eat anyway.

I set my Swiss Army knife on the side of the bathtub so I could watch the time, then sank down into the bubbling water to warm my frigid bones. I tried to let my mind drift toward happy thoughts, but Dick's sudden death kept intruding. I wondered how Lucille was taking the news. It was sad her last words to him had been so harsh. She'd have to live with that for the rest of her life, which was a good lesson for me. No matter how angry you are, some things are better left unsaid, because once the words are spoken, there's no taking them back.

Dick's death reminded me so much of Shirley Angowski's. Shirley could have either fallen accidentally or been pushed. Dick could have either died from natural causes or been poisoned. At least, that was my take on it. Neither Wally nor Nana had seemed surprised by Dick's death, so maybe I was out in left field about my poison theory. But it had happened to Andy. Why not Dick? Except, who would want to kill Dick? He wasn't sleeping around. Other than being a little loud and boisterous, he wasn't a bad sort. What could be the motivation?

I stared at the ceiling, completely confused. Here I'd thought Dick was part of the death squad to get me and he ends up dead himself. Boy, I'd called that one wrong. Maybe that would teach me not to be so suspicious. But that still left a big question unanswered. What *had* Helen and Grace been discussing yesterday in Spengler's dressing room if not how to eliminate me?

I put it out of my mind as I felt my bones start to thaw. In fact, I put my brain in neutral and concentrated on the positive forces that were making inroads in my life. I had my suitcase back. I was staying in the room of my dreams. Etienne wanted to see me naked. Maybe I'd rounded a bend in the road of life and my future was on the upswing.

I was humming the second verse of "She'll be Comin' 'Round the Mountain When She Comes" when I heard the knock on the door.

I decided to ignore it.

It sounded again, loud and persistent.

I checked my knife. Six-thirty. Maybe it was housekeeping to turn down the covers and leave the mint on the pillow. Sigh. I supposed it was time to dry off and get ready for the meeting anyway. "Just a minute!" I yelled.

I hopped out of the tub, slid into the thirsty terry cloth bathrobe that was hanging on the door, and scurried into the bedroom. "Who is it?" I called as I crossed the floor.

"It's the police, Madame. Please open the door."

CHAPTER 13

The police?

My knees liquefied. So much for life taking an upswing. Wait until I saw that turncoat Wally again. Not going to drag my name into the investigation, was he? He set me up! He stuck me with the dead body all the way home, and now he was going to feed me to the police. My list of possible offenses flashed before my eyes in big neon letters: OBSTRUCTION OF JUSTICE. PERJURY. FLEEING THE SCENE OF A CRIME. LITTERING. I was hoping they might overlook the littering charge though since I hadn't *intended* to leave my bag of postcards behind on the spa bench.

But wait a minute. The police? Maybe it was Etienne.

I raced to the door and glued my eye to the peephole. Not Etienne. But he was wearing a police uniform, so it looked pretty official. Unh-oh. I opened the door.

"Ms. Andrew? Ms. Emily Andrew?"

"Yes." He was carrying a small pewter vase that he thrust

at me. Unprepared for the handoff, I bobbled it for a moment before cradling it like a football in the crook of my elbow. "What's this?" I asked.

"Inspector Miceli instructed me to deliver this to you."

A gift? For me? From Etienne? I took back all the spiteful thoughts I'd just had about Wally. "Why, it's beautiful," I said, smoothing my fingertips over the brushed satin sheen of its deep curves. Oh yes, life was definitely looking up. I imagined setting this on the mantel of our first house and filling it with tulips. "Is he at work? I should call him and thank him for it."

"I'm afraid you won't catch him at the station this evening. He's at the Forensics Lab." He removed a paper from his breast pocket. "You'll need this certificate to expedite the parcel through Customs."

I blushed at Etienne's extravagance. The vase was so expensive, it needed separate papers. "Tell him he shouldn't have."

"It's a requirement, Madame. All bodily remains passing through Customs need to be documented."

My hand froze on the vase. "Excuse me?"

He regarded the paper. "According to the documentation, the urn bears the remains of Mr. Andrew Simon, late of Windsor City, Iowa."

I plucked it from the crook of my elbow and held it at arm's length away from my body. "THIS IS ANDY?"

"Yes, Madame. What's left of him."

"What happened to the idea of a coffin? What happened to the idea about one of his former wives flying over here to escort the body back?"

The officer shrugged. "He was cremated, Madame, and Inspector Miceli indicated you would be the one to take responsibility for the urn. You *are* the escort for the tour group, aren't you?" He looked suddenly concerned. "Should I tell the Inspector you'd prefer to pass the responsibility on to someone else?"

Oh, sure. That would be a great way to impress Etienne. Shirk my responsibility. Be uncooperative. Whine. Smart people hid those parts of their personalities until *after* the wedding vows were spoken. "I'll do it," I said reluctantly, "it's just that, it comes as a surprise."

"Death always comes as a surprise, Madame, even when you're expecting it."

I turned back into the room and eyed the heap of packages I was supposed to stuff into Andy's coffin on the trip home. I held the urn up to gauge its measurements.

By my calculations, it was going to be a tight fit.

At seven o'clock I walked into the lobby of the hotel to find the entire tour group huddled around coffee tables and sitting shoulder to shoulder on the settees and sofas. Lucille Rassmuson was absent, as would be expected, but the other two Dicks and their wives were there, which indicated to me that they hadn't heard the news about Dick Rassmuson's death yet. I waved to Nana, then sauntered over to one of the lobby's marble columns to use it as a backrest.

"Looks like we're all here," announced Wally. "After the meeting you can purchase the group photo we had taken at the Lion Monument in the bar area."

"How much?" asked Dick Teig.

"Fourteen American dollars."

"That's too much," replied Dick.

"Then don't buy the damn thing!" snapped Wally.

I suspected Wally had been spending a little too much time around Sonya.

"You don't have to get crabby about it," Dick shot back.

"We could buy one copy and have it reproduced in the Pills Etcetera photo machine back home," offered Jane. "That would only cost four ninety-five per photo, not including tax."

Wally fanned his hands through his hair. "Look, I'm sorry. It's been a stressful day, and that's part of the reason I called this meeting. I have some tragic news to report to you, people. Dick Rassmuson appears to have suffered a massive heart attack on the way back to Lucerne today. I'm sorry to have to tell you that he has passed away."

A collective gasp. Hands flying to mouths. Then silence as the news sank in.

"Lucille is with the authorities at the moment. She's been sedated and will probably need someone to stay with her tonight if any of you would like to volunteer."

Helen and Grace allowed tears to stream unashamedly down their cheeks. George Farkas hung his head. Jane tented her hands over her face. Dick Teig and Dick Stolee sat in stunned silence, probably realizing there were only two of them now. It had to be hard to lose a Dick. Bernice sat quietly watching how everyone else was reacting.

Lars Bakke stood up. "I'm only speaking for myself, but I think this tour has been cursed from the beginning. The weather's been foul. The food's been inedible. Three people have died." He paused for effect. "I don't know about anyone else, but I say we get the hell out of here before anyone *else* dies. I say we get on the first plane heading home and cut our losses while we still can!"

"Hear, hear!" yelled Solvay.

Nods of approval. Whispers. Mumblings.

"You want to go home?" asked Wally to the group in general.

Home? Wait a minute! *I* didn't want to go home. I just got my clothes back. I had the good room. The good view.

At least, I'd have the good view when the fog cleared. I had another week with Etienne! I couldn't leave. He hadn't even seen me naked yet.

"Okay, let's have a show of hands," said Wally. "How many of you are ready to cancel the rest of the tour and head home?"

Hands flew up all over the room. No! This couldn't be happening. This was a trip of a lifetime! How could they be throwing it all away?

"I guess I don't need to ask how many opposed."

I raised my hand. Wally looked in my direction. "One opposed," he said. "You're way outnumbered, Emily."

"Things could start to get better," I reasoned. "The food isn't *that* bad. The fog could lift. And since people die in threes, we've already met our quota."

"You can say that because you're young," shouted Bernice. "You're not worried about dying. You probably don't even know what your cholesterol level is."

"Yeah," said George Farkas. "Three gone already. What's to say we won't start on *another* set of three? I agree with Lars. I say we head out to the airport in the morning and camp out until they find a plane to take us home."

More nods of approval. "Is that what everyone wants to do?" asked Wally.

"You bet it is," barked Lars.

"Get us out of here," agreed Bernice.

Since I was the lone dissenter, it seemed futile to protest the decision. Majority rules. We were going home, and there was nothing I could do about it. I couldn't even stay behind on my own because *I was the freaking escort.*

Wally quieted everyone down. "I'll still be continuing the tour for the people from Rhode Island, but I'll call the airport right away to see what I can arrange for flights for the rest of you. If there's anything available, you'll have to be prepared to have suitcases outside your doors at five o'clock tomorrow morning and be ready to leave the hotel by seven."

I'd just unpacked my suitcase and now he wanted me to *re*pack it before I went to bed tonight. Typical.

"I'll call each of you tonight to let you know the plan, so please don't stray far from your rooms. And don't forget about the photos in the bar."

Nana walked over to me as the group broke up. "Are you disappointed we're leavin'?"

I nodded. "I didn't even get to send any postcards."

Dick Teig walked past us in a daze. Helen touched my arm on her way by. "When Dick and Lucille didn't show up at dinner, we called their room, but there was no answer. We thought they were probably still miffed at each other and not in the mood to socialize." She shook her head. "We had no idea."

"I wasn't at dinner either," I said, wondering why they hadn't bothered to call me.

"You weren't at dinner?" Helen said, looking perplexed. "Isn't that odd? I guess I never noticed."

"I'm gonna have a peek at that group picture at the Lion Monument," Nana interrupted, taking a step toward me.

"OUCH!" wailed Helen.

Nana looked perplexed. "My goodness, was that your foot, Helen? I'm sorry. I guess I didn't notice you standin' there."

I rolled my eyes at Nana's need to even the score.

"You wanna come with me, Emily?" Nana asked.

If this was the group photo where I was bending over for one shot and had my mouth hanging open for the other, I'd rather have a root canal. "I don't think so. I need to head upstairs. I have some unfinished business to take care of."

Nana understood unfinished business. She'd just taken care of hers.

Back in room 5111 I contemplated the problem of the extraneous purchases lying in shopping sacks in one corner of the room. One way or the other, they had to go, and they *weren't* going with Andy. I hefted one of the bags into my hands, wondering what it was and who it belonged to. I should have made an announcement at the meeting instructing people who'd left shopping bags in my room to pick them up. Unh. Why was hindsight always twenty-twenty?

As I went to set it down, I noticed a name in Magic Marker in the corner of the sack. *George Farkas Room 2115.* Checking another sack, I found a notation in the same place. *Solvay Bakke Room 3008.* I shuffled through several more to find them *all* like that. This had to be Nana's doing. She must have had everyone write his or her name and room number on their sack before they left it. The woman was brilliant! Absolutely brilliant. I could only hope I'd turn out just like her. Only taller.

I separated all the sacks by room number, gathered up several, and took the elevator down to the second floor. I knocked on George Farkas's door and when he answered, I stuck his shopping sack in his face. "You'll need to find some other way of getting this back home."

"But Bernice said you were going to ship it home in Andy's casket."

"Andy isn't going home in a casket. He's going home in a jar. He was cremated."

"A jar?" He looked crestfallen. "Hell, I can't take it with me. My suitcase is packed to the gills. How big is the jar?"

"Not big enough. I suggest you call the front desk to inquire about shipping services."

I conducted similar conversations with the occupants of

two other rooms, then headed back to the fifth floor for another batch. Nana was waiting outside the room for me when I arrived. "I'm sorry you had to wait," I apologized as I unlocked the door. "I'm delivering all the shopping sacks back to their original owners."

"That's the spirit, dear. I didn't think Bernice's idea was such a good one in the first place. Was there a problem with the coffin?"

"Big problem. There *is* no coffin."

"No coffin? Oh, dear. How're we s'posed to get him home without one?" She narrowed her eyes in suspicion. "Is Wally behind this? I don't mind tellin' you, Emily, I hope we don't have to go through that business with the hat and sunglasses again. It might a worked with Dick, but Andy's been dead a few days. We'll never get him past the agent checkin' photo IDs at the airport."

I gathered my sacks into my arms and headed for the door. "No disguises this time." I nodded toward the pewter urn on the desk. "Say hello to Andy."

"Well, would you look at that," said Nana. "They cremated him. Bernice is *not* gonna be happy about this."

"They did *what* to him?" Bernice complained ten minutes later.

"Cremated him," I replied. "He's in a little urn about this big." I indicated the general dimensions. "You'll probably have to call the front desk to inquire about other shipping arrangements."

The elevator was overcrowded and headed in the wrong direction, so I decided to take the stairs back to the room. As I sprinted up the staircase, I moved away from the handrail to avoid colliding with a platinum-haired woman who was struggling with a huge Bucherer sack. No doubt another traveler looking to have her cuckoo clocks shipped. I eyed her as we passed, wincing at the thick layers of poorly applied makeup that masked her face. Her rouge and eye shadow highlighted all the wrong bones. Her lipstick appeared dry and flaky, as if she'd forgotten to use conditioner. Her feet looked really elegant in a pair of strappy black velvet heels like the ones I'd bought yesterday, but she was wearing them with a *dark navy* coatdress, ugh, which illustrated a stunning truth about women and fashion: any female with halfway decent taste could pick out stylish separates, but knowing how to coordinate them was a gift many women lacked. Including this one. Poor thing.

I reached the top of the stairs feeling gloomier than ever about the end of what could have turned into the perfect holiday. I'd have to phone Etienne to tell him about our change of plans, but since he wasn't at the station this evening, I probably wouldn't even get a chance to talk to him in person. I'd have to leave a message on his voice mail, or with a stranger who might not even speak English. The situation was so depressing, my head started to ache as badly as my tooth.

"Wally just called," Nana informed me back at the room. "Looks like he might be able to fit all of us on the plane tomorrow, so we need to pack tonight." But she didn't seem quite herself. Her eyes looked terribly sad, as if she'd just lost her best friend.

"Are you okay?" I asked gently.

She shook her head, then sat down in one of the boudoir chairs, head drooping, shoulders slumped. "I think you may have been right, dear."

I sat down opposite her. "Right about what?"

"I just got an E-mail from Alice Tjarks back home. You remember the other day when you asked how Bernice lost all her money? Well, you put a bee in my bonnet, so I sent a message to Alice, tellin' her what all's been happenin' here, and I asked real casual-like if she knew why Bernice was in the financial straits she's in now." Her head drooped lower.

Unh-oh. "Did she?"

Nana nodded. "The way Alice tells it, Andy was doin' financial plannin' back in the early eighties, and one a the portfolios he managed was Bernice's. But he didn't give her real good advice. Told her to put all her eggs in one basket. Real estate. 'Buy farmland,' he tells her. 'It's worth a mint.' So she buys the land and the next thing you know, the government reduces grain subsidies and the price a land bottoms out. She lost everythin'. What was worse, at the same time Andy's tellin' her to buy, he's sellin' off the land he'd bought years earlier. So he ends up rollin' in dough while Bernice can't rub two dimes together. When she caught wind a what he done, she marched into his office and told him she didn't care what she had to do, or how long it took, but one day, she'd see he got his comeuppance."

"No!"

"Yes."

"How did Alice know all this?"

"She was the file clerk in Andy's office. She was right there when it happened. And I trust her memory, Emily. She's secretary a the Legion a Mary, and she remembers so good, she don't even have to take notes at the meetin's to write the minutes."

I leaned back in my chair, stunned. Even though I'd suspected Bernice, it didn't delight me to know my suspicions had been on target.

"You was right, dear, and I was wrong. All along I figured she wanted to visit Switzerland 'cause she was a little jealous I was goin', but thinkin' back, she didn't get real fired up to go 'til she seen the entire list. The one with Andy's name on it. She signed up 'cause of Andy, not 'cause a me."

Nana looked so miserable, I suddenly found myself defending Bernice. "But how did she get hold of dimethyl sulfate?"

She boosted herself out of her chair, crossed the room to her computer, and hit a few keys. I walked up behind her and read the text that appeared on the screen. "'Zwerg Chemical and Industrial Supply Company. Ames, Iowa.' Oh my God! Is that her son? He owns a chemical company?"

Nana nodded. "I never would a checked if I didn't get that E-mail from Alice."

"But when would Bernice have slipped Andy the poison? I can't recall her ever being around Andy, and you said she never even spoke to Shirley."

"You must a forgot, dear. They sat beside each other on the plane comin' over."

A chill rattled my spine. *That's* the memory I'd been trying to recall—Bernice standing in the aisle, letting Andy out of his seat so he could use the lavatory. While he was gone, she could have poisoned his food, his coffee, his water.

"I guess I'm not such a good judge a character after all," Nana pined.

I circled a comforting arm around her shoulders. "I'm so sorry, Nana. I wish it had turned out some other way. I guess it's the people closest to us who sometimes surprise us the most. You realize we're going to have to notify the police."

"I know, dear. But if it's all the same to you, I'd like to make the call. She's my friend. I figure it's my responsibility."

"You stay here and wait for the police then." I gathered up another armful of shopping sacks. "I'll be back as soon as I can."

"You want me to help you deliver those, Emily?"

"I'll be fine. A few more trips, and I should have it taken care of."

An hour later, with all my parcels delivered, I returned to the room to find Nana still waiting for the police to arrive. "I think they slack off a little when there's no body involved," she reasoned. "You look tired, dear. You have a headache?"

"A headache. A toothache." The ugly truth was, I was a mess. Could I deal with stress or what?

"Maybe you should get more a that Motrin from Jane," Nana suggested.

"I think I'm going to have to." And I'd better hurry before she packed up all her pharmaceuticals.

A few minutes later I was knocking on Jane Hanson's door. "Do you have any more Motrin?" I asked when she answered. "My tooth is killing me."

She was wearing a terry bathrobe, and her hair was mussed, but she opened the door wide for me. "Sure I do. Come on in. But you'll have to wait a minute because I just packed all my meds and toiletries into my carry-on."

"I was afraid that would happen. I should have come sooner."

"If your tooth was hurting, why didn't you?" She disappeared into the bathroom.

"I had lots of errands to run." I was apparently interrupting her packing because her pullman was open on the bed, but there was nothing in it yet. I let my gaze roam idly about her room, the visual equivalent of counting sheep, until I spied something the size of a small perfume bottle lying beneath the desk where her computer sat. She'd kept her medications on that table. Had she dropped something when she'd packed them up? "Have you heard about tomorrow yet?" I asked as I scooched down to fish the thing out.

"I was in the shower when Wally called, but he left a message on voice mail."

I heard rattling and clinking from the bathroom as I studied the cobalt blue bottle in my hand. Not perfume. It was makeup remover. The expensive kind sold only in department stores. I frowned. What was Jane doing with makeup remover? She never *wore* makeup. Odd. I set the bottle on the desk so she'd be sure to pack it, but my eyes kept wandering back to the gold labeling on the front. What was wrong with this picture? "Too bad we have to leave, huh?" I called across the room.

"What's that? I can't hear you." I jumped when the phone rang. "Would you get that, Emily?" Jane's voice echoed off the tiles. "It's probably Wally with a change of plans."

I walked to the nightstand and picked up the phone. "Hello?"

A beat went by. "To whom am I speaking, please?"

It wasn't Wally. He had a German/French/Italian accent. It was Etienne! "Oh! I'm so glad you called. This is Emily. We—"

"Emily, say nothing. Just listen to me. Get out of that room. Do you hear me? Put the receiver down and walk out the door. I'm in a car heading toward the hotel. I'll be there in a few minutes. No heroics, darling. Just get out. Ms. Hanson has killed one person, perhaps two. I won't have you be number three."

Ms. Hanson? Jane was the killer? No-no. That couldn't be right. It had to be Bernice. Nana and I had worked it all out. I paused. "Are you sure?"

"We have the analysis from Shirley Angowski's camera bag. Jane Hanson's fingerprints are all over it."

"Really?" I could hardly wait to tell Nana! She'd be thrilled Bernice wasn't the killer. But I guess this meant the police were pretty sure Jane was. Unh-oh.

Jane walked out of the bathroom holding a tablet of Motrin and a glass of water. I smiled at her, hoping she wouldn't notice that my hands were suddenly trembling. She looked at me expectantly, as if presuming I'd hand her the phone, but when I didn't, she set the pill and water on a nearby table and eyed me curiously.

"Okay, Wally," I said, my tongue so dry it was sticking to the roof of my mouth. "Thanks for calling. I'll pass the message along." I put the receiver down. "That was Wally." My voice cracked midword. "He just wanted to double-check that you got the message about our leaving tomor-row."

"There's your pill." She gestured toward the tablet on the table. And then it hit me. Oh my God! Jane Hanson wasn't at all who she appeared to be. She wasn't a kindly pharmacist. She was a cold-blooded murderer! She'd killed Shirley. She'd probably killed Andy. And if she'd poisoned Andy, what would prevent her from poisoning me, too? The Motrin looked tempting, but if it was going to relieve my toothache by causing immediate death, forget it.

"You know something, Jane? The tooth actually feels much better, so I think I'll just tough it out. Sorry to have bothered you." I sidled toward the door, but she was three steps ahead of me, intercepting my exit. "I really need to get back to the room and pack. I haven't even started yet. And you need to pack, too. Look. You haven't thrown any-thing into your suitcase. And I should remind you that you need to have all your luggage outside your door by five, which means you'll have to save room in your carry-on for your nightgown because—"

"Shut up, Emily."

"Okay." I suspected the jig was up. I lunged for the door, but Jane was faster. She blocked the door with her body and locked it, then yanked the belt of her bathrobe out of its loops and slapped it against her palm. Unh-oh. I didn't like the looks of this.

"Why don't you tell me who was really on the phone," she hissed.

"It was Wally. Honest. He—"

She cracked the belt at me like a whip. "Ow!" It caught my forearm, stinging the flesh under my jersey. "Hey, cut that out."

"Try again, Emily. Who was on the phone? What did they tell you that made your face turn so white?"

"It's this new foundation of mine. I swear. Revlon Skinlights Face Illuminator. Haven't you seen it advertised? It's the new look. Makes your face radiantly white, or pink, or bronze. I bet you sell it at the pharmacy. You probably even know what aisle it's in."

She snapped the belt at me again, but I leaped out of the way. "Liar. I hate liars."

"Shirley Angowski never lied to you," I said, backing toward the bed. "Why did you kill her?"

"It was the police on the phone, wasn't it? They found the camera case. They discovered my fingerprints." She thwacked her forehead with the palm of her hand. "I should have worn gloves, but I forgot them on the bus. Damn. I didn't intend to kill her right then, but when I saw her perched on that ledge with no one around, I thought, why not?"

Hmm. The decision to kill someone was apparently no more momentous for Jane Hanson than someone else's decision to hit the snooze button on their alarm clock. "Why did you push her?" I shot back. "What did she ever do to you?"

"She was going to sleep with Andy! Do you think I could stand by and let that happen?"

"Why should you care?"

"Because he was supposed to be in love with *me!* He was *my* soul mate, not hers. He was supposed to be loyal to *me!* But how could he be loyal to me when he wasn't loyal to anyone? He tricked me. He hurt me. So I made him pay. Just like I'm going to make you pay."

"Me? What did *I* do?"

"Poor, Emily. Think of it as being in the wrong place at the wrong time."

I'd said those exact words to Shirley Angowski two days ago, and now she was dead. Not a good omen.

"You know far too much for me to allow you to live," said Jane. "So I'm going to have to deal with you the same way I dealt with Andy, and Shirley, and Lucille."

"Lucille?" Had I missed something? "Oh my God! What have you done to Lucille?"

She twisted her mouth to the side in what looked like acute exasperation. "Nothing, actually. Those morons screwed up my plan completely. Lucille was supposed to take the hit, but wouldn't you know. *She* didn't want the ice cream with the nuts, so it looks like Dick ended up eating it."

I let out a gasp. "Dick? You killed Dick?"

"Not on purpose. Weren't you listening? It was an accident."

I remembered the ice cream Dick had offered me earlier. Had that been the one laced with poison? I felt my throat close at the thought. "You poisoned Dick just like you did Andy. You put dimethyl sulfate in that ice cream today!"

Jane looked surprised. "Do you think I'm crazy? I never would have taken dimethyl sulfate into the country. That stuff is poison. You can die just by inhaling it. I used something quite benign. In fact, I take it myself. Synthroid."

"Oh yeah? If it's so benign, how come Dick is dead?"

"Because I gave him too much. I'd planned on giving

Lucille a series of overdoses to kill her, the little cheat. But with Dick's heart condition, one overdose was enough to kill him. An excess of thyroid hormone can wreak havoc on the body's metabolic system."

I was beginning to question the wisdom of her telling me all this. Throughout movie history, when the murderer starts spilling his guts, it usually spells curtains for anyone within earshot. Since I was within earshot, I suspected her confession meant curtains for me. Not exactly the way I'd planned to spend my last evening in Switzerland. But one thing was for sure. Jane Hanson was bonkers.

I slid my hand into the pocket of my slacks. "How did you kill Andy if you didn't bring the poison into the country with you?"

"That was easy. He bought new disposable contact lenses the day before we left, so I laced a free sample of his rewetting solution with the dimethyl sulfate. He must have used it right away because, as you know, he didn't last too long after we got here."

"That's so diabolical," I fired at her. "What was in the glass you just brought out of the bathroom and wanted me to drink?"

She looked confused. "Water. You needed something to wash down the Motrin."

"You didn't put any poison in it?"

"*Uff da,* Emily. I'm a druggist. I have ethics to uphold."

Like I believed that. "I should have known it was you," I accused as I wrapped my hand around my Swiss Army knife. "You had the easiest access to the poison. You probably keep it right in the pharmacy."

"We don't keep dimethyl sulfate anywhere near the pharmacy. I bought a liter of it at a chemical recycling website on-line. You can buy anything on-line these days, Emily. Groceries. Poison. Love. I should think you'd know that."

She wrapped the ends of her belt around her wrists and snapped it tight between her hands like a clothesline. Or a garrote. Unh-oh. Last time I checked, strangulation wasn't high on my list of favorite ways to die.

She took a step toward me.

I took a step back. "Okay," I said in desperation. "You guessed right about who was on the phone. It wasn't Wally. It was the police. They're on their way over here right now, so if I were you, I'd make a run for it before it's too late."

"I intend to make a run for it"—she took another step closer—"after I finish you off."

"Don't come any closer," I warned. I whipped my Swiss Army knife out of my pocket. "I'm armed and dangerous."

Jane laughed. "What's that? A pocketknife?"

"It's not just *any* pocketknife. It performs twenty-nine different functions." I plucked one of the gizmos out of the housing. A retractable ballpoint pen fell onto the floor.

"An inkpen? What are you going to do? Write me a letter?"

Considering the size of the pen and the probable ink supply, a letter was out of the question. A postcard, maybe. I popped out another gadget. Jane squinted at the thing. "Is that a can opener?"

"I don't think so." My can opener back home had an electrical cord and plugged into the wall. This thing was a flat piece of metal that was curved into a hook. "I think it's some kind of primitive cuticle remover."

"It's a can opener. But I don't understand why it's blunt on the end instead of pointed."

"Maybe *that's* the cuticle remover."

"You're so stupid, Emily. You don't even know how to use your knife."

"Me, stupid? I'm not the one who's killed three people! If you ask me, that's pretty stupid!"

She gave me an evil look and snapped the belt again. When she did, the front of her bathrobe parted to reveal a dark navy coatdress beneath. I sucked in my breath. "That was *you* on the stairs with the velvet heels and platinum hair! You were in disguise." I didn't know *why* she was in disguise, but the good news was, at least she'd finally bought herself a decent pair of shoes.

"You didn't recognize me in my wig," she said smugly. "I bought it at the same salon where Dick Stolee bought his, only I paid a lot more. It's made of real hair instead of that synthetic crap."

"You paid *more* than three thousand dollars for that wig?"

"Try twice as much."

"Six thousand dollars?" I hope she avoided the River Reuss on windy days. "Boy, am I in the wrong profession."

"I didn't know you had a profession."

"Well, I don't at the moment, but maybe it's my hair color that's holding me back. You look good as a blonde. Maybe I'd be more dynamic as a blonde, too. What do you think? Here's an idea! Maybe I could try on your wig."

She cocked her head and gave me an assessing look. "You might make it as a blonde. But if you want to try on my—" She narrowed her eyes suddenly. "Oh no. You're not going to divert my attention, and your flattery will get you nowhere."

"It's not flattery! Really. You're a knockout as a blonde. And with those shoes and the dress. I thought you were one of the natives." I could say something about her makeup job, but I wasn't completely stupid. No wonder she'd needed the remover, but I'm surprised one bottle had been enough.

Her eyes sparkled for a moment before they turned

dark again. "Good. I hope I look like a native, because I'm going to become one of the natives."

"What do you mean by that?"

"I'm staying in Switzerland, Emily. I moved the last of my belongings to another hotel tonight. I'm already checked in under my new name. I can't go back to Windsor City, can I? Too much suspicion. Too many arrows pointing in my direction. Jane Hanson will disappear tonight and never be seen again. And tomorrow, I'll start my new life as . . ." She looked suddenly petulant. "I'm not going to tell you what my new name is."

"How can you start a new life with a passport that says you're Jane Hanson?"

"My new passport has my new name, Emily. Like I told you, you can buy anything on-line these days. The technology is incredible. And now I suppose I should finish up matters here before the police arrive."

I snapped open another gadget on my knife. No guesswork here. Scissors. They were pointy and sharp, but they were about the size of toenail clippers. I squeezed the handle and scissored the little blades threateningly at Jane. "Stay right where you are. Don't make me use these."

"Are you planning to give me a manicure?"

"That's a nice dress you're wearing. It might not look so nice when I'm through with it." I jabbed the scissors into the air. Right and left. Up and down.

"Are you kidding? Those scissors aren't even big enough to poke my eye out."

I gave them another look. Hmm. Maybe she was right. I released another doohickey. Magnifying glass. Key ring. Screwdriver.

"Give it up, Emily," Jane advised as she walked menacingly toward me. "I'm afraid nothing can save you now."

I kept flipping open gadgets. A toothpick. Tweezers. WHERE WAS THE ROOM FRESHENER WHEN YOU NEEDED IT? A fingernail file. "Hey, I could give you that manicure now."

She was closing fast. I catapulted myself onto the bed and bounced around on the mattress. I unfolded another gadget and stopped bouncing as I regarded it. "Okay, smarty, you think *I'm* so stupid. What's this one?" I held it up for her to see. It was a small file with one straight edge and one slightly serrated edge.

Jane shook her head. "I don't know what that is. A ruler?"

"I was thinking more like a little saw." Though you wouldn't be able to cut down a very big tree with it. Maybe a dwarf cherry.

Jane shrugged. "Half the tools on those knives are useless anyway. But men think it's neat to have all those silly gadgets. They can't be happy with a pocketknife that has only one blade. Nooo. They have to have *lots* of doodads on their knives. Just like they can't be satisfied with only one woman. They need to have a whole string of them to be happy."

"Like Andy," I said.

"Yes," she agreed wistfully. "Like Andy." She angled her head toward her computer. A faraway look glazed her eyes. "He used to make me feel so special when he came into the drugstore. He paid so much attention to me. I could hardly wait for the days when he'd come in to pick up his prescriptions. And when I'd e-mail him to tell him about our upcoming sales, I'd always add a personal note, just so he'd know I thought he was special, too. And then I bought a personal computer, so I started e-mailing him from home. Of course, he couldn't tell from my screen name that it was me. He simply knew me as the secret e-mailer. But he liked the mystery. And he liked my messages. He sent me back long, intimate replies every day. We became soul mates. He said we'd continue to write to each other until we became one mind, one soul." She sighed. "I could have been content living out the rest of my days on nothing more than his words, but then he went and spoiled everything."

I'd seen this happen before. "He changed on-line servers?"

"He changed women! I went to see him in that Christmas play. I even brought him flowers. But when I went backstage to find him, he was kissing Helen Teig's niece! And I don't mean some friendly peck on the cheek. He had her backed against the wall with his hand up her dress. It was disgusting. I felt so crushed, so betrayed. And then his messages got shorter, and more infrequent. I went from hearing from him daily, to hearing from him once a week. He apparently didn't have time for E-mail with all the attention he was having to shower on his new lover. But I couldn't give him up. I couldn't live without his messages. I wrote to him and asked if there was any way we could salvage our relationship. I said he was still special to me, and I didn't want to lose him. He wrote back and said he wouldn't be writing to me anymore because there wasn't anything that needed to be said that was more important than what he was doing. The little bastard! How's that for letting someone know how valuable you are to them? He made me feel as inconsequential as something stuck on the bottom of his shoe! The self-important little runt."

Yeah. That had always been my opinion of Andy, too.

"What a crock he fed me!" she whined. " 'We'll write to each other until we become one mind.' I had the shelf life of one of his plays—a limited run of six weeks, then he struck the set and moved on to someone else."

"Good analogy," I commended her.

"Thanks. I thought so, too."

"So you decided to get even with him by killing him?"

"He ruined my life, Emily! I fell into a depression. I was put on Prozac. Do you know how expensive Prozac is if you're not on the right health plan? I spent weeks in intense therapy. I still can't retrieve my E-mail without suffering pangs of how things used to be. He cut me off without giving a minute's thought about how *I'd* cope or feel or react. We have AA to help people recover from alcoholism. We have the patch to help people recover from smoking. We have *nothing* to help people recover from failed E-mail romances."

She had a point there. The closest thing I could think of was the Gameshow Network.

"He deserved to die," she said viciously, "and so did Lucille, and Shirley, and all those other women who slept with him. But I couldn't get to them all. I made a list. There were just too many of them."

Okay, so if Jane was the lone killer, there'd been no death squad. But that still left a major question unanswered. "Not to change the subject or anything, but do you happen to know what Grace Stolee was talking about the other day when she said that she and the Teigs and the Rassmusons were planning the same thing for me that they'd planned for Andy?"

"She was probably talking about the surprise party. They'd planned one for Andy on our last day as a thank-you to him for being our escort, but since Andy wasn't available, they decided to throw it for you instead. They even bought little party hats."

"That's so sweet of them!" I cooed, instantly sorry for all my suspicions about them. "They were planning a party? For me?" But wait a minute. "I thought you said the Stolees and Andy weren't on good terms."

Jane rolled her eyes. "Grace attended some religious

retreat recently, and wouldn't you know, the theme was forgiveness. After all these years, she decided she should try to be civil to Andy again, so she agreed to go along with the party idea."

That still didn't wash. "So how come they all looked so sour last night at the Chateau? They sure weren't in party mode. They didn't crack a smile all night."

"You were wearing the same dress *Grace* bought at Spengler yesterday. Didn't you notice? But it looked much better on you. Grace has a roll of fat at her waist that she refuses to acknowledge. What was there to smile about?"

She had a point. "With everything that's happened, I don't imagine they're still planning to have the party, are they?"

"It doesn't matter. You won't be attending."

She rushed the bed. I chucked my twenty-nine-function Swiss Army knife at her. THUNK! It grazed the side of her head, stunning her momentarily. Twenty-nine functions? Hunh! By my count that would make it thirty.

"That hurt!" she wailed.

"Don't know how to use my knife, do I? Huh!" The fog started to clear from her eyes. I swooped her empty suitcase off the bed and hurled it at her.

BAM! She fell backward onto the floor with the suitcase on top of her. She struggled to get up. I grabbed a pillow.

WHUFF! It smacked her in the head. I grabbed another one and launched it. WHUFF! It smacked her in her midsection.

I seized the corner drapery on the bed's canopy, gave it a hard yank, and flung it in her direction. It landed on top of her like a fisherman's net. I heard footsteps in the hall. Running. I vaulted off the bed. Jane screamed epithets beneath the drapery, punching it wildly until she threw it off.

I ran for the door.

Jane ran for the window.

I threw open the door.

Jane bounded onto the windowsill.

"Stop right there!" Etienne ordered as he burst into the room.

Jane swung the window open. "I've already lived through one Hell! I'd rather *die* than live through another!"

"Don't do it!" I screamed.

Out the window she went, her cry echoing hideously in the cold night air.

"Oh my God!" I shrieked hysterically. "She jumped! She actually jumped!"

Etienne wrapped his arms around me as two officers raced toward the window. "It's over, Emily. Shhh. There was nothing you could do to prevent it."

"She didn't have to die! She was sick. She needed help. But she didn't have to die." My eyes welled with angry tears. "Don't you people believe in window screens?"

The two officers leaned over the sill and shined their flashlights into the courtyard. I felt my stomach churn at the grisly sight that would greet them on the pavement below. "I need to sit down," I choked.

"Phone an ambulance," one of the officers called out.

"An ambulance?" said Etienne. "Not the coroner?"

"Not for this one, Inspector. She landed in the Dumpster."

CHAPTER 14

"Last call for Swissair flight 328 with nonstop service to Chicago. All ticketed passengers should now be onboard. Last call, please, for Swissair flight 328."

"Are you sure you can't stay a few more days?" Etienne nuzzled the lobe of my ear. "A few more years?"

I was so tired from lack of sleep, I was afraid if I closed my eyes, I'd miss my plane. Between filing my statements at the police station and rushing back to the hotel to pack, I hadn't even had time for a catnap. I slid my arm around Etienne's waist and held him close, liking the way his body fit against mine. "I would give anything to stay. But I can't. I'm the escort."

"You could say you had to stay in Lucerne to make sure we treated Ms. Hanson properly."

"How long do you think she'll be in the hospital?"

"They performed surgery this morning with no complications. It could take her a while to figure out how to walk on two broken legs though. The doctor said she'll be good as new when she heals, but he wouldn't recommend jumping off the third floor of a building again anytime soon."

"What will happen next with her?"

"I'm not sure, darling."

I loved the way he called me "darling." It was such a German/French/Italian thing to do.

"We'll be working in close cooperation with American authorities on her case. She killed three people, Emily, so it's no small matter. I can't predict the outcome, but you can be sure we'll take into account her mental health at the time of the crimes. I seriously doubt she'll be walking the streets of Windsor City, Iowa, anytime soon, however."

"You could walk the streets of Windsor City," I invited seductively. "You could come visit me. My apartment's pretty small, but I have a really big bed."

He growled in my ear, his breath warm, his lips soft. "If your goal is to frustrate me with images of you lying in bed, wearing a smile and nothing else, you've succeeded. My sister says Chicago is lovely at Christmas. Perhaps I should take her up on her invitation."

"Really? You're not just pulling my leg?"

"I would love to pull your leg, but I fear I wouldn't stop there. And while we're on the subject of legs, we picked up your Mr. Nunzio last night in the lounge of the Hotel Alpha pro Filia."

Mr. Nunzio. I'd forgotten all about him. "Was he hitting on another woman?"

"I suppose you could call it that. Mr. Nunzio is a hair-stylist who specializes in hair care for the over-fifty set, so he drums up business by haunting the lounges of all the local hotels, giving his pitch in rather broken pidgin English/Italian to potential customers."

"What kind of pitch?"

"A somewhat original one. For an additional fee, he'll come to your room and cut your hair in the nude."

"Last call for Swissair flight 328," announced the voice over the loudspeaker.

"This isn't fair," I complained. "We're not supposed to leave for another half hour. Why do we have to board so soon?"

"What time is it?" Etienne asked against the corner of my mouth.

I plucked my Swiss Army knife out of my raincoat pocket. "It's—" I regarded the clock face, then pinched my eyes shut in hopeless resignation.

"What's wrong?"

I held the knife up for his perusal.

"Ah, yes. It's something of a problem to quote the correct time when your clock has no hands."

I slid the knife back into my pocket. "If I'd known Jane's head was that hard, I wouldn't have thrown it. But it's not a total loss. It performs twenty-nine other functions."

"Last call, please," the agent blared over the loudspeaker.

"I gave you my phone number," I said desperately. "You'll call me?"

"I'll do one better," Etienne said as he lifted me against him for a final farewell kiss. "I just bought a new home computer. Do you have an E-mail address?"

At eleven o'clock in the morning three days later, I was sitting in the office of Mr. Ollie Erickson, president of the Windsor City Bank. I'd returned the envelope of medical forms to him and was waiting with bated breath to see if he'd make good his promise to reimburse my expenses for the trip. Considering what a fiasco the Golden Swiss Triangle Tour had turned out to be, I wasn't getting my hopes up.

"Too bad about Andy and Dick," Ollie remarked as he sat behind his big walnut desk. "It was nice of the Teigs and Stolees to stay with Lucille over there in Lucerne until they could make arrangements to fly Dick's body home. Helen called this morning to tell me they'd be on a flight back tomorrow."

"The five of them must be prostrate with grief," I said.

"Actually, Helen said they'd been trying to stay occupied. They've visited a Swiss castle, taken a cheese tour, and today they drove down to Lugano, where Switzerland meets Italy. She said the weather is spectacular. Eighty degrees and sunny. They even had to use sunblock."

I wrestled with my tongue, trying not to bite through it. "How nice for them."

"Now, what are we going to do about you, Emily?"

I could hear it in his voice. I was going to have to pay extra for screwing up. Dick Stolee had decided to sue me for assault. The Swiss police had discovered that Dick Rassmuson had actually died on German soil rather than in Switzerland, and I was wanted for questioning. Bernice was blaming me for damaging her hearing aid and I'd have to buy her a new one. And that was just the obvious stuff. To borrow a phrase, *Uff da*.

"Will a check for five thousand dollars cover it?" he asked.

Eh! It was worse than I'd imagined. "Five thousand dollars? I don't *have* five thousand dollars! At least, I don't have it right now. But when I find a job, maybe we could set up some kind of payment plan where I send in small amounts of money every month. It might take me a few years to pay it back, but if you give me a favorable interest rate, maybe—"

"I don't think we're communicating very well, Emily." He slid a piece of paper across the desk. "I want to give *you* five thousand dollars. Considering all you had to put up with on the trip, I figure it's the least I could do. That should cover all your trip expenses plus provide you a little extra for pain and suffering."

My mouth fell open, but I remained speechless. As my mother would tell you, a rare occurrence indeed.

"George Farkas just dropped off the evaluation forms that everyone filled out on the plane, and I must tell you, I've never seen anything like them."

Euw boy. I wondered if he'd notice if I ran out the door about now.

"Other than one mark of poor, which we eliminated because it was from Bernice, you received no mark below outstanding, Emily."

"I didn't?"

"Everyone loved you."

"They did?" I suspected George had somehow mixed up my evaluation forms with Wally's, but discretion being the better part of valor, I didn't mention the possibility.

"As you know, since Andy's untimely death, we're minus one tour escort. What would I have to do to interest you in filling the position, Emily? Now that you're on the payroll, I'd hate to lose such a conscientious, hardworking, efficient employee. The job pays an annual salary of forty-five thousand dollars, and you get to travel on the bank's dime. We're planning trips to Australia, England, and Italy, but our next scheduled trip will be a ten-day tour of Ireland. What do you say?"

Was he nuts? Did he think I was crazy enough to take another trip with these people? Did he think I could continue saving them from themselves? Did he think I enjoyed bad food and lousy weather? Did he think I wouldn't go insane dealing with the lost luggage, dead bodies, unscheduled dental work, and broken watches? Did he think I had no pride? No self-respect? No—

"Did you say Italy?" I'd always wanted to visit Italy. To ride in a gondola on Venice's Grand Canal. To toss a coin into the Trevi Fountain. To eat spaghetti prepared by someone other than Chef Boyardee. Italy wasn't so far away from Switzerland. And Etienne was in Switzerland. Hmm.

"Okay." After my Golden Swiss holiday, I could use a vacation.

Pocket Books
Proudly Presents

Top O' the Mournin'
A Passport to Peril Mystery

Maddy Hunter

Now available in paperback
from Pocket Books

Turn the page for a preview of
Top O' the Mournin'. . . .

CHAPTER 1

The guidebook says the weather in Ireland is normally wet, except when it isn't, which can be often, or not often at all. The sun *can* shine, mostly when it's not raining, but it rains most of the time, except when it doesn't.

In other words, the weather in Ireland is a metaphor for my life.

I'm Emily Andrew, twenty-nine-year-old once-married working girl with a degree in theater arts, currently employed as escort for a bank-sponsored group of Iowa senior citizens on a ten-day tour of the Emerald Isles.

Going back to my weather metaphor, my life had been sunny when I'd moved to New York City after receiving my BA, married fellow actor, Jack Potter, and landed a part in a Broadway play. The rain started when Jack began wearing my underwear. The deluge hit when he left me a note one night telling me he was running off with his leading man's understudy.

When the shock wore off, I did what any native Midwesterner with no money to pay Big Apple apartment rent would do. I moved back to my hometown of Windsor City, Iowa, had the marriage annulled, and found a job where I could use my acting skills. Phone solicitations.

For three years I was the premier fund-raiser for Playgrounds for Tots, until the president of the organization was arrested for fraud because there WAS no organization.

He went to jail. I went to Europe. *Not* as a fugitive from justice. I had a long-standing commitment to be my grandmother's companion on a seniors' tour of Switzerland, so off I went, hoping to ease my jobless woes by experiencing the vacation of a lifetime.

It turned out to be an experience all right. We were promised temperatures in the seventies. Spectacular views of the Alps. Gourmet cuisine. What we got was bone-chilling cold. Dense fog. A steady diet of cornflakes. And three dead guests.

The one ray of sunshine on the trip was that I met the man of my dreams. Etienne Miceli, the police inspector who investigated the three deaths. He's everything my first husband wasn't. Forthright. Dependable. Heterosexual. We've been communicating by phone and E-mail for eight months now, and you might say our relationship is at a crossroads. It's too intense not to be together. But he lives in Switzerland. I live in Iowa. See what I mean about my life? Rain. Sun. Rain. Sun. Not unlike the weather in Ireland.

"Dublin's nothin' like I imagined," said my grandmother. Her voice vibrated as we jounced down one of Dublin's most traveled thoroughfares in the back of a horse-drawn carriage. Nana was known as "a sport" in her retirement village back in Iowa. She'd won millions in the Minnesota lottery the day my grampa passed away, so in her golden years, she had the means to go anywhere and do anything, and she was taking full advantage of the opportunity. "Is it like you imagined, Emily?"

"I imagined rain." I peered skyward in search of storm clouds, but found only a brilliant wash of blue. Windex blue. Like Etienne's eyes. I sighed with the thought. In Dublin for five hours and already I was suffering the first pangs of loneliness. I needed to snap out of it, else it would be a very long ten days.

Our hackney driver tipped his head to the right. "Saint Shtephen's Green," he said in a lilting brogue. "Firsht enclosed in 1664. Twenty-two acres of manicured lawn, ponds, and quiet in the middle of Ireland's busiest shity."

Cute accent, but he could use some speech therapy for the lisp.

"Remember that statue a Molly Malone?" Nana whispered, referring to the shapely bronze sculpture we'd seen on an earlier walk down Grafton Street. "Why do you s'pose they made her so bosomy? Did you see the cleavage? I bet she was wearin' one of them push-up brassieres. Probably where she got that nickname, 'Tart with a Cart.'"

"Wait a minute. *I* wear a push-up bra, and *I'm* not a tart."

Nana patted my knee. "Of course you're not, dear. You marry the men you sleep with. I think that's very commendable. Oh look! A double-decker bus. I've always wanted to ride in one of those. Haven't you?"

I'd never given public transportation much thought. What I *really* wanted was to be one of the great stage actresses of the century. Windsor City boasted only a small community theater, so the odds were against me, but I remained optimistic. Entering a new century had given me an extra hundred years to make a success of myself.

"Easy, Nell." Our driver steadied his horse as she chafed against her traces. "She's frishky today. To your left is the

Shelbourne Hotel." He guided us past the elegant, redbrick building where our tour group was scheduled to spend our first night in Ireland. "Built in 1824. They sherve a brilliant afternoon tea in the Lord Mayor's Lounge at half-three."

The wrought iron railings and flower-glutted window boxes reminded me of the quaint little hotel where Jack and I had honeymooned so many years ago, and, recalling our wedding night, I smiled. Poor Jack. He'd possessed the extraordinary good looks of a Greek god but the brain chemistry of a Greek goddess. And it had only taken me two years to figure it out. Am I a quick study or what? I hope he'd found happiness with his partner, living in upstate New York, laying kitchen tile, but that didn't seem the kind of existence that would make him happy. Jack was happiest when he was onstage, sporting layers of pancake makeup and eyeliner. But he was probably happier now than when he'd been married to me. And so was I. Mostly because I didn't have to share my underwear anymore.

As we rounded the north corner of St. Stephen's Green, I sat back in my seat, soaking up the Dublin atmosphere. The hordes of people. The crush of traffic. The blare of horns. The stench of diesel fumes.

"Do you smell that?" Nana asked suddenly.

"Diesel. Must be the fuel of choice over here."

"That's not it. Smells more like"—she inhaled deeply— "alcohol." She plucked her guidebook out of her Golden Irish Vacations Tour bag and flipped through the pages. "I remember readin' there's a Guinness brewery nearby, and they give away free samples at the Hopstore."

"But Guinness is dark beer. You don't like dark beer. You don't like beer, period."

"I know, dear, but I like free samples. Look here, the Guinness brewery is number seventeen on the map. Maybe our driver could drop us off if we pass by. Should we ask?"

I gave her one of my patented "It can't hurt" shrugs and leaned forward, tapping the driver on his back. "Excuse me. If we pass the Guinness brewery, could you—"

In the next instant he slumped forward and landed on the floor of the carriage with a thump.

Nana gasped. "You didn't need to push him, Emily. A polite tap would a worked."

"I didn't push him! Oh my God. What's wrong with him? Is he dead? He *can't* be dead. This *can't* be happening again!" I'd discovered three dead bodies on the *last* tour we'd taken. If it happened on this trip, too, I'd be labeled a jinx and could probably kiss my tour escort job good-bye.

We popped out of our seats for a better look. "Does he look dead to you?" I asked.

"All's I can tell from this angle is that he's bald."

"I'll check his pulse."

"No!" yelled Nana. "Grab the reins!"

My gaze fell on the leather straps that were slithering out of the driver's hand. I lunged across the back of the seat, arm extended, but they disappeared over the dashboard before I could seize them. I looked at Nana. Nana looked at me.

"Unh-oh," I said. The carriage swayed suddenly, then lurched forward as Nell discovered her head. With no driver to guide her, she broke away from her traditional route, jumped the curb, and shot down the sidewalk at a full gallop. BUMPITY-BUMP. BUMPITY-BUMP. Nana tumbled back into her seat. I clutched the driver's seat for support. Pedestrians leaped out of the way at our approach. Into bushes. Onto the hoods of parked cars. People gawked. People pointed. I saw a group of Japanese tourists crowding the sidewalk ahead of us. "Get out of the way!" I screamed, flailing my arms. "Move!"

I heard excited chatter and a symphonic click of camera shutters as we screeched around them on two wheels and swerved onto the main walkway of Saint Stephen's Green.

"Do somethin'!" Nana bellowed at me.

"Like what?"

"Make the horse stop!"

"That wasn't part of my training!" On the other hand, if the horse were choking, drowning, or needed CPR, I was your girl.

"Cowboys did it in the old movies all the time!" Nana yelled. "Jump on her back and grab her reins. I'd do it myself if I wasn't wearin' my good panty hose."

I knew nothing about horses. I was from Iowa. I knew about seed corn, which wasn't really helpful in this situation. I did have an idea though. "HELP!" I cried. "Somebody help us!"

The park became a blur of trees, shrubs, and flower beds as Nell raced across a lush stretch of lawn that looked like the course at Pebble Beach, only without the ocean view. Fat clods of grass flew left and right beneath her hooves. Divots here. Divots there. BUMPITY-BUMP. BUMPITY-BUMP. Unh-oh. This wasn't good. Parents grabbed their children and ran for cover. Oh my God. What if we plowed into someone and killed them?

I craned my neck to peek at our driver again. The violent jostling was causing his body to skid toward the open end of the carriage. One major dip in the terrain, and he'd shoot out of the vehicle like a log out of a flume.

I needed to do something.

"Look at that pretty circle a red flowers up ahead," Nana said in a high vibrato, as we approached a major intersection of pathways. "Be nice to stop for a picture."

We were beyond them before I had time to blink.

"I don't mean to complain, dear, but we're missin' all the good photo opportunities."

I scrambled over the backrest of the driver's seat, crouching precariously on the cushion. "Whoa, Nellie!" I yelled.

THUMP-THUMP. The carriage pitched sharply to the right, bouncing the driver across the floor. I grabbed a fistful of his jacket to keep him from falling out. I looked up.

Dead ahead was a stand of trees, and Nell was racing straight toward them.

"Hold on tight!" I yelled to Nana.

I ducked low on the seat. WHUP-WHUP! WHUP-WHUP! Foliage thrashed the sides of the carriage as we whipped between two trees. I heard an ominous creak. I opened one eye to see what was ahead.

Oh no.

We hit the pond at breakneck speed and hurdled the concrete lip like one of the losing drivers in the chariot race in *Ben Hur*. Off flew a front wheel. Off flew a back wheel. *Creeeeek!* KABOOM! The sudden stop catapulted me off the seat and into the air. I landed on my back in a foot of water that shot up my nose all the way to my brain. Snorting, sputtering, and blinded by streams of nonwaterproof mascara, I jackknifed upward to hear a man shout, "You there! There's no swimming allowed in the pond!"

I let out a startled yelp as our driver's body sluiced out of the carriage and landed eyeball-to-eyeball on top of me.

"That goes for him, too!" the man added.

Most single women who visit Ireland probably dream of having their bones jumped by an Irishman as witty as Oscar Wilde, as inspiring as William Butler Yeats, and as handsome as Pierce Brosnan. That my bones were being jumped by a short, bald guy who didn't appear to be breathing was fairly typical of the direction in which my life was headed. All that was missing was the freelance photographer who would snap my picture and sell it to a tabloid newspaper. I could see the headlines now: TOUR ESCORT HAS SEX WITH DEAD MAN IN POND! That would go over really well in Windsor City.

It was at that moment that I heard the unmistakable whirr of Nana's new Polaroid Insty-Print camera. "Smile, dear!"

"Here's one of the pond in Saint Stephen's Green." Nana handed Tilly Hovick a photograph as we stood at the front desk of the Shelbourne Hotel, waiting for our room keys. Tilly was a retired professor of anthropology at Iowa State University, and was slated to be Nana's roommate for the duration of the tour.

"Interesting composition," Tilly said as she inspected the Polaroid through the magnifying glass that hung around her neck. "Who is that man lying on top of Emily?"

"Our driver. He passed out and crashed us into the pond. Then he fell on top of her. We thought for sure he was dead. Then his cell phone rang, and he answered it. He would've laid right there talkin', too, if Emily hadn't done somethin'." Nana handed Tilly a second photograph. "This one's of Emily kneein' the driver in his privates." And a third. "This is the driver curled up in pain after Emily kneed 'im. And you can see there, he's still talkin' on his cell phone. That was pretty impressive."

"What caused him to pass out?" asked Tilly. "Seizure?"

"Sloshed," said Nana. She handed Tilly a final photo. "This is the policeman who dragged Emily outta the pond and gave her a written warnin' for swimmin' in an unauthorized area."

Tilly, who made ordinary mortals quake with her legendary bluntness and direct stares, stabbed a long finger at the policeman's photo. "Did you get his name? We should march right down to the Garda Station and file a complaint. This situation was *not* Emily's fault. She was treated unfairly." She turned to me. "And if I were you, I'd sue the carriage company for damages. Look at you. You look like one of the contestants on *Survivor*."

I caught a glimpse of myself in the gilt-framed mirror decorating the lobby wall. *Ehhh*. My dark brown hair was a wild, dripping mop of corkscrew curls. Mascara circled my eyes. My new rayon blouse and skirt clung to my five-foot-five-inch frame in a series of wet, misshapen folds. I didn't look as good as a *Survivor* contestant. I looked more like Alice Cooper meets Xena, Warrior Princess.

Nana regarded Tilly with a twinkle in her eye. "You watch *Survivor*?"

"Reality television, Marion. Anthropology for the masses. I think of it as a modern version of Margaret Mead's *Coming of Age in Samoa* without the monographic analysis."

"I think of it as *Days of Our Lives* without the script."

Tilly looked pensive. "I hadn't thought of it that way, but in a sense, you're perfectly right. That's a very astute observation. Do you have a favorite contestant?"

I'd been concerned that Tilly and Nana wouldn't be compatible as roommates. Tilly had a Ph.D. Nana had an eighth-grade education. Tilly was five-foot-eleven, built like a beanpole, and carried a fancy walking stick. Nana was four-foot-ten, built like a fire hydrant, and carried a really big handbag. Tilly had never married. Nana had been married to the same man for over fifty years. *Survivor* was the only thing they had in common, but, come to think of it, that was probably a lot more than most *married* couples had in common. Heck, they'd probably become fast friends.

I waved my arm to catch the notice of a desk clerk. My appearance was making me nervous. I needed to change my clothes before someone issued me a written warning for shedding water in an unauthorized area. "The key to room 410, please? And I'm in something of a hurry."

Bernice Zwerg shuffled up to us at the front desk and looked me up and down. "Is this a new look for you, or did you find another body of water to fall into?" Bernice had the body of a rubber chicken, a dowager's hump that made her clothes hang funny, and a voice that screamed of eight packs of Marlboros a day before she finally kicked the habit. She'd accompanied us on our earlier tour to Switzerland, so we had history.

I narrowed my eyes at her. "I was a victim of circumstance."

She flashed me a tight little smile that said she'd heard that one before. "I thought you'd want to know that the other bus just arrived from the airport."

Since our flight from Des Moines had arrived so early, the tour company had bused us the short distance to our hotel rather than make us wait at the airport for the other flights to arrive. We were expecting a contingent of people from the East Coast and a few stragglers from the Continent to add their numbers to the twenty Iowans I was escorting.

"I heard a bunch of people from New York will be joining us," Bernice continued with a sour look. "They'll probably be loud. And pushy."

Which meant Bernice would fit in with them just fine.

"What have you got there?" Bernice asked, snatching the photos from Tilly's hands. She flipped through them quickly. "Looks like Emily having sex with a dead guy in some pond."

"He wasn't dead," Nana objected. "Emily would never engage in necrophilia, would you, dear?"

I shook my head, remembering those occasions when making love to Jack had been like having sex with a corpse. But we'd been married, so in my case, the necrophilia was legitimate.

"How come you don't have a digital camera?" Bernice asked Nana, handing the photos back. "Polaroids are old technology."

"I'm waitin' for the price to come down," Nana said in a no-nonsense tone. She might be a millionaire, but her Midwestern frugality still reared its ugly head from time to time.

"Room 410," the desk clerk said, handing me my key.

"I'm going up to change, so I'll see you later," I said to Nana.

Bernice gave us a squinty look. "What? You two aren't rooming together?"

"Escorts get rooms by themselves," said Nana, "so I'm roomin' with Tilly."

"Tilly?" Bernice sucked in her cheeks. "When I asked you to room with me, you said you already had a roommate, so I assumed it was Emily. You never said you were rooming with Tilly. *I'm* supposed to be your best friend, Marion. What's the matter? I'm not good enough for you anymore?"

"Tilly asked me first."

"Oh, I get it. It's on account of the mashed peas, isn't it?"

Back in December, Nana had slipped on some mashed peas on the floor of the senior center and bruised her tailbone. She'd had to sit on an inflatable doughnut during the entire holiday season, which didn't work out too well during Midnight Mass, when my nephew punched a hole in it with his Moses action figure with authentic scale-model staff. All Nana could say was that we were lucky David hadn't brought his GI Joe. Joe carried his own grenade launcher.

"I don't blame you for that at all, Bernice, but you *were* the person in charge a cleanin' the floor after the Christmas luncheon. And you didn't do it."

"Couldn't be helped. I had to leave early to catch the bus to the casino. But you know about the pea situation. Every time we have a luncheon for the Lo-vision people, they leave mashed peas all over the place. How come you don't serve a vegetable they can *see?* You're on the food committee. You ever think about serving broccoli spears?"

Hmm. My guess was, Bernice was going to be the first one voted off the island.

Thinking it might be best if the ladies mediated this themselves, I waved to Nana and slipped away. As I headed to the elevator, I looked toward the lobby, to find a troupe of people muscling their way through the front door behind a willowy blonde who was all legs and teeth. Ashley Overlock. Our tour guide. She'd introduced herself to us at the airport in a voice that dripped Southern charm, then sent us on our way, but the men were still suffering palpitations from the initial meeting.

I shook my head. Men were so blind. Couldn't they see all her phony reconstruction? I ticked off the list. Bleached blond hair. Collagen-injected lips. Capped teeth. Silicone-enhanced breasts. Acrylic nails, or maybe they were silk wraps. I couldn't tell from this distance. Her legs started at her neck and were definitely her own, but wearing those spike heels was bound to give her varicose veins. In a few years she'd be forced to wear support hose under that six-inch miniskirt of hers, then we'd see how many heads she turned. Of course, there was one benefit to the support hose. She wouldn't have to shave her legs so often.

The commotion in the lobby continued as every male with traceable testosterone found an excuse to mill around Ashley. Scarlett O'Hara at the barbecue. Geesch. The scene made me grateful I wasn't one of the beautiful people. The ogling. The gawking. The fawning. How did she stand it?

"Y'all need to proceed to the front desk to pick up your room keys," I heard her call out. "No, I don't need assistance. Y'all just take care of yourselves. Yes, I already have plans for dinner. No, you don't need to know my room number. The front desk is right through there. Just keep moving."

I pressed the elevator button again and sidled up to a plant, hoping to camouflage myself as a potted palm while the tour guests swarmed the front desk area. A full five minutes later, the door opened and I scooted inside the car, followed by a woman who announced, "Fourth floor," as if I were the elevator operator. And she didn't say please. She obviously wasn't from the Midwest. My guess was . . . New Jersey.

The doors glided shut. The elevator hummed to life. "Are you on your way to a costume party?" she asked as she lounged against the handrail. It didn't help my mood any that she was a gorgeous brunette with the most exquisitely applied makeup I'd ever seen. Razor-thin eyeliner above and below the eyes. Lips perfectly outlined and stained. Foundation and blush that made her complexion appear luminous. I knew only two groups of people with the expertise to apply makeup so precisely: makeup artists and Texans. I revised my first opinion. Okay, she was from New Jersey by way of Dallas.

"I don't always look like this," I said. "My mascara ran."

"It's a shade too dark for you anyway. Brown would be better. Have you ever had your colors done? My guess is, you're an autumn."

This was handy. Take an elevator ride. Get an instant color analysis. I wondered if this was part of the tour package.

She smiled. I smiled. I lowered my gaze to the floor. Whoa! She had the biggest feet I'd ever seen, but great shoes. She must have to order out of the catalog.

"Emily?" she said suddenly.

I checked to see if I was wearing a name tag. Nope. How did she know my name? I exchanged glances with her, thinking she looked vaguely familiar, but unable to identify her. "I'm Emily, but I'm afraid I don't know who you are."

"Emily!" She rushed at me, smothering my face with kisses and enveloping me in her arms. "It's me! You don't recognize me, do you. It's Jack! Well, Jackie now."

I tried not to look as confused as I felt.

"Jack Potter!" the woman burbled. "Remember? Your ex-husband."

**Visit the Simon & Schuster
romance Web site:**

www.SimonSaysLove.com

**and sign up for our
romance e-mail updates!**

Keep up on the latest
new romance releases,
author appearances, news, chats,
special offers, and more!
We'll deliver the information
right to your inbox—if it's new,
you'll know about it.

2800.02